SAVAGE MARRIAGE

MURPHY'S MAFIA MADE MEN

VI CARTER

ALSO BY

Other Books by VI CARTER

<u>WILD IRISH SERIES</u>

FATHER (NOVELLA)

RECKLESS # 0.5

VICIOUS #1

RUTHLESS #2

FEARLESS #3

HEARTLESS #4

<u>THE BOYNE CLUB</u>

DARK #1

DARKER # 2

DARKEST #3

PITCH BLACK #4

<u>THE OBSESSED DUET</u>

A DEADLY OBSESSION #1

A CRUEL CONFESSION #2

<u>YOUNG IRISH REBELS</u>

MAFIA PRINCE #1

MAFIA KING #2

MAFIA GAMES #3

MAFIA BOSS #4

MURPHY'S MAFIA MADE MEN

SINNER'S VOW #1

SAVAGE MARRIAGE #2

SCANDALOUS PLEDGE #3

CONTENTS

CHAPTER ONE

JASON

SIX MONTHS AGO, MY father opted out of life—for good. The blow of his death almost shattered our family. When I say we're barely hanging on by a thread, I mean it. Each of us carries the sorrow like a torch, burning us up from the inside out.

William, my baby brother, glances over his shoulder. He's keeping a very close eye on the long alleyway behind us. His jaw is set, his shoulders stiff. I want to tell him to relax, but I'm sure I'm as tightly wound as he is. I return my focus to the job at hand and snap the lock on the coroner's office door. The moment I push the heavy wooden frame open, the lock clinks onto the brown tiled flooring. The noise is sharp and loud as the sound bounces back.

I step into the hallway, and William follows me as he holds his gun with both hands.

"Are you expecting trouble?" I ask my brother while glancing at the 9mm in his hands.

He fires a quick peek my way as he passes me and takes the lead down the hallway. Like he should be protecting me and not the other way around.

"Hello," I call out, and as I expected, I get no response. I open the top button of my gray suit jacket while I shoulder past William.

He tuts. "Can't you just wait until I check the place out?"

"I called ahead. No one is here." I turn into the large, open waiting room, and there's nothing appealing about it. A small reception desk is tucked away in the corner of the room. The bamboo wood on the front of the desk is cheerful, along with the Hawaiian poster that's pinned to the back wall. The whole assembly makes me think of a beach, not a place of death.

The other furniture in the room is a small black two-person couch. It sits low to the ground.

William slides his gun back into its holster, close to his hip. "You could have told me you called ahead and got no answer."

I move around the desk and shuffle the Post-its and random paperwork. "I'm telling you now," I reply as I pick up a piece of paper.

William's jaw clenches, and I fight a grin as he walks to the small table that holds some glossy magazines. I return to the piles in front of me: invoices, quotes, and reordering of stock are all I see. I glance up as William steps up to the desk. There are those moments when I see him. He's not my baby brother anymore. At twenty-seven and over six feet tall, he's very much a man. A man with so much anger in his eyes that he's fucking drowning in his sorrow.

"Anything?" he asks, looking across the desk.

I shake my head in answer, and he walks away, pushing his hands into his navy trouser pockets. He's grown stocky from all the time he spends in the gym. It's his new coping mechanism. It's better than his old one, which involved so much drinking and drugs that I'm surprised he was able to kick the habit.

He's the one who found our father hanging in his office.

He's the one who helped take the old man down from the rafters. He's the one who wouldn't leave our father's side as the Gardaí removed the rope from around our father's neck.

I witnessed none of the destruction, but my mind sure as fuck filled in every little detail with its own vicious black paint, making sleeping an unpleasant ordeal.

I step out from behind the desk and take a final look around the room. A dying plant in the window is the only other decoration. My hands itch to get the plant some water. Our father loved plants and nurtured them. He would restore this plant to life if he had the opportunity. Too bad he doesn't.

"You spent last night with Matty?" I ask, with my back turned to William. Matty is the second youngest and more fragile than the rest of us. He's also a topic no one wants to discuss except for me. I'm close to Matty, and I hate how lonely he always seems. But being around him is taxing on a good day; on a bad one, I want to shoot myself or him.

"Yeah, we just chilled. Watched some TV."

A smile grips my lips, and I glance back at William and allow him to join me. He's already smiling. Some of the anger has left his eyes. "Fuck you" is his reply.

I laugh. "I said nothing." We enter the main office. I don't like how closed up the room smells or how much dust I spot as I get closer to the desk and the long row of filing cabinets. I count six large silver ones.

"You didn't have to say anything. We sound like two old fuckers waiting to be returned to the soil." He sniggers as he speaks. "You know he had a pack of those mints. When he offered me one, I thought to myself, 'This can't be my fucking life.'"

I laugh again at the image of them sharing a pack of mints. But the truth is, William being clean for six months makes me so fucking proud. "I'm proud of you, William. I really am."

He shrugs off my praise and starts looking at the medical examiner's desk. Yeah, he's not good at taking praise. I suppose none of us are.

Praising us isn't something our father did. We thrived on the negative and spent too much time trying to fix what our father saw as weaknesses. Alex and I took the brunt of his criticism; being the two oldest sons, most of the responsibility fell on our already burdened shoulders.

I pull open the filing cabinet drawer with the letter *M* on the front. It doesn't take long before I find our father's name, Edward Murphy. I stand there holding the file, unable to open it. This is the moment of truth.

William is looking over my shoulder. "Open it." His voice is low, but I hear the fear and anticipation. Sliding the drawer closed with my knee, I open the file.

My gaze darts to the cause of death. This is the moment I want to prove William wrong. He convinced Aidan, the middle brother of us five, that father hadn't hung himself. That someone had staged it that way. His whole theory was built on the knots in the rope that our father couldn't make. It made sense, but it also sounded too much like hope to me.

"I fucking told you." William smacks the file with two fingers, nearly knocking it out of my hand. I reread the cause of death again:

Blunt force head trauma. Blood Loss.

I'm unsteady as I read over the words once, twice, three times.

"I told you. I told you," William keeps repeating, but I honestly think he's as shocked as I am.

"You did." I turn to William and close the file, gripping the paper in my hand. "Someone murdered our father." I'm holding the evidence. "Why weren't we told?"

"Where is the pathologist?" William asks the same question I've been thinking.

This is huge. This is so fucking huge that it's bound to rip a hole in the Irish Mafia. The murder of a leader. It's the cover-up of the fucking century.

A hand lands on my shoulder and drags me out of my thoughts.

"We will get the motherfucker." William raises both brows as he dips his head with a feral look in his dark eyes.

I nod.

William releases me. "I'll check out the rest of the place."

I reopen the file and reread the cause of death. Why? Our old man didn't deserve this kind of death. If he had been murdered, he would have gone down as a fucking hero. Whoever did this made sure the world saw our father as weak.

Guilt gurgles and spits in the pit of my gut. I'm one of those people who saw his actions that day as a weakness. Shame of what he had done forced me to not shed a single tear. Not as the news was told to me during a meeting. Not as Alex and I organized the funeral. Not as I found out that everything was in our Uncle Frank's name, leaving us Murphy brothers with nothing. I didn't cry as they lowered my father into the ground and covered his coffin with soil and holy water.

I place the file onto the desk like the weight of the truth is too much for me and power up the laptop. My brain is on repeat. Someone murdered our father.

The icon spins on the screen as I wait for the pop-up box that requests a password. There isn't one. I'm straight into the desktop. For me, that's odd. But it could be my family's paranoia. Everything with us was under lock and key. Yet someone got to our father and killed him.

My suspicions are justified as I click from one empty folder to another. I open up Google and am surprised to see some search history. A shoe store, some porn, a handle for a grill, and flights to Spain. I check the dates. Five days after my father died. If this had been me, and I had killed a leader, and if I had made the death appear as a suicide, I wouldn't leave any evidence around like the actual pathologist did. I'm already sure he's dead. Rotting at the bottom of some green river. Someone wiped the computer and did random searches to leave something on the laptop. So why leave the file? The drawers were unlocked. My mind spins. Did someone want me to find the file?

I open the three drawers one at a time but find nothing. The dust on the desk has been disturbed in certain areas. We could get forensics down here, and it would be worth a shot. The red light on the voicemail flashes. I hit the button and let the recordings play over the room as I take another look around.

The voice recordings are mostly people waiting on reports. One message catches my attention.

"Dad. It's your weekend to have me. I'm still waiting for you. If you don't come in the next twenty minutes, I'm staying with Mum." The young voice of what I assume is a teenager sounds bored.

So, the pathologist had a son. The son isn't a strong line of inquiry, but I file that snippet of knowledge away. The floor has been cleaned, and it makes me wonder if the pathologist died here. I don't smell bleach, but there isn't anything on the brown tiles. A dark shadow under one of the filing cabinets grabs my attention. I bend my neck to try to see, but it doesn't help to enhance the view of whatever is there.

Getting down on my knees, I get a better look at the small black device that must have slid under the filing cabinets. Maybe during a struggle? It could lead me to something. The recordings continue to play as I lift the cabinet, and my fingers graze a cell phone. I squat as low to the floor as possible and try to grab the phone. My fingers tighten around the device just as a bag is pulled down over my face.

My vision is unclear, and my air is restricted instantly. I drop the cabinet, and it nearly crushes my fingers as I fight to get the plastic bag off my head to see who the fuck is trying to kill me.

CHAPTER TWO

KIRA

I FOLLOW MY BROTHER down the long hallway. I sense that the click of his cane on the tiles is an intentional action. A reminder of what we survived together. A reminder of what we lost together.

"Nicco. Is everything okay?" I ask as a last ploy to understand what might be happening this morning. His mood is darker than most mornings, and I wonder what I've done.

Nicco doesn't answer me, but when he pushes open the double doors that lead out to the patio, I tighten the belt of my cream silk robe like I can keep myself together, because I'm so close to falling apart.

Too much races through my mind. Like, will he kill me? What would he tell people? Would he pretend some intruder murdered me? Would he vow that he would turn over every stone on the planet and wouldn't rest until he found my killer, just like he had sworn in front of the Bratva about our father?

The air grows tight, and instead of letting the turmoil pour out, I focus on the two glasses of orange juice that wait for us on the small round table. The air is crisper this morning, and I inhale the sweet oxygen to try to release the anxiety that promises to crush me. I'm waiting for the blow as my brother sits down and rests his cane against the table.

"It's a beautiful day." Nicco smiles. The curl of his lips pulls his scar tighter. I remind myself that he's my brother, so he may show me mercy.

He once was a boy who played with me and watched the road runner under the cover of night. We kept each other's secrets from our parents and shared in the grief of losing our mother. We placed a gold coin each on an eye so she would have the fee for safe passage to the next life. I wonder who will pay the ferryman's fee for me.

Pain and loss have me looking out on the pristine lawns. A few years ago, I yearned to see my own children play here. That dream would be a nightmare. It's one promise I've made. I will never bring children into this world.

Nicco watches me, and I realize I haven't said anything. I pick up the glass of orange juice. "The day is nice and warm," I say before taking a sip. The acidic taste sours my stomach, just like it does every morning.

"You are getting married," Nicco declares. He hasn't touched his orange juice. He joins his hands together as he watches me carefully.

I place the glass back on the small table and trace the surface with my finger. The watercolors that decorate the top reflect my emotions—a mesh of everything. I have dreaded this moment my entire life. An arranged marriage was something I knew I would have to enter into, and that time has arrived.

But there is a bubble of excitement.

A ray of light.

Hope.

I feel hope for the first time in a long time.

I could be free of Nicco. He's still watching me. The black grandfather shirt is tight against his neck, and the dark color makes his pale skin stark in the morning light. My body overheats as I struggle to sort through my emotions quickly. "When?" I ask.

He exhales and touches his scar. "Too soon." His voice sounds distant.

I'm ready to slump into the chair, but I remember how closely Nicco observes me.

"Before father's time, marriages only happened between purebloods."

My fingers pause in their unfocused circles along the top of the table. Everything in me freezes. I had known this and heard the jokes of how we Tarasova were inbreds, and the soiled bloodline caused madness in the family. I'm glad our great-grandfather abolished the disgusting rule. But here is Nicco, with insanity in his eyes and words.

"I would gladly have that rule back," Nicco continues.

The impact of his words takes the air from my lungs. I can't hold his stare. Repugnance has me tightening my hands. God, I hope the arranged marriage is soon, as in today, so I can get away from Nicco. He's lost his mind.

"If you and your future husband object to this arranged marriage, I do have the power to take it higher."

I'm careful as I slowly make eye contact with Nicco. If he had the power to do anything about the arranged marriage, he would have already; that shines clearly in his gaze. Nicco studies me.

"Has my future husband given his objection about the marriage?"

"No." The agony in Nicco's gaze is ungrounded.

"It's my duty, Nicco." This is our path. We have known this our whole lives. If this was before, I would gladly object, but getting away from Nicco takes precedence.

His lip curls up, his blue eyes turning frosty. There is a flair of cruelty in how he tilts his head. He's getting ready to strike; I'm waiting for him to insist I object to the arranged marriage.

I can't.

I won't.

"You must also produce an heir."

I'm shaking my head before I can think better of letting him see my horror at what he is saying. My cheeks heat. There is so much loaded into that statement. To bring a child into this world is cruel. To bring a child into an arranged marriage seems crueler. To have an uncle like Nicco, I'm sure, will be a nightmare. If he's as overprotective of his niece or nephew as he is of me, they will suffocate.

"I know. It's revolting." My brother shows his disgust by snarling. "I have requested you be placed in a separate wing with your own staff."

"You did?" Surprise filters through me. Why would he do me such a kindness?

"I don't want him touching you," my brother admits.

Abhorrence swirls and spirals until I'm looking away again. My brother hasn't been right since our father's death, but this new way of looking at me is lunacy.

"Kira." My brother says my name softly, and the tenderness of his voice heightens the unease that dominates everything else that spins through my mind.

"We should have been a king and queen." He smiles so fondly at me. Would he smile if he knew how much I detested him? Would he smile if he knew the revulsion I felt at even having him look at me?

"I don't think I would be strong enough to be a queen," I answer honestly. Queens rule. My whole life, I have obeyed and followed others, not given them.

"You would have me by your side." My brother's response is fleeting, as his attention gets soaked up by one of his men who waits by the patio doors. Our morning time is up.

"We will discuss this later."

I pick up the orange juice even as the smell has me holding my nose. I smile up at him before taking a sip and letting the liquid flow down my throat without tasting it.

He watches me for a moment before leaving, and I am finally free of him for the rest of the day.

The arranged marriage takes center stage in my mind as I get up and take the glass of orange juice with me. I water the grass with the offending substance. Once, I enjoyed a glass, but it will forever be a reminder of Nicco.

"He's gone." Angel speaks from behind me. Her playful tone is low. She's not stupid, but we have learned over time when we can jest without getting into trouble.

I tighten my hold on the glass as I turn to Angel. "For now."

She holds her hand out to me, and when I reach her, she links her arm with mine. "So, what shall it be today, Princess Kira? A stroll through the city? Shopping on the strip? Or a long swim at the beach?"

I smile at Angel and pretend to think, even as my mind stays latched onto every detail of my conversation with my brother, but I try to allow myself to slip away for a few short minutes. "A stroll through the city."

"We could people watch." Angel squeezes her hold on my arm.

I leave the empty glass on the table, and we walk to my bedroom. I like to play this game with Angel. Imagining what that would feel like to sit somewhere and watch others while no one watched me. A stroll through a city like that would compare to a jog through a minefield to my brother. And the beach? I may as well ask to swim with sharks. Everything is off limits. So I learned to live my life through others. Angel being one of the others.

"And what do we see when we people watch?" I ask.

Angel moves briskly around my room, pausing every few seconds as she delivers her analysis. "A woman all dressed in red. She wears a hat with a long black point. I think she's on some sort of mission."

I strip out of my robe. "What mission?" I ask. My mind takes an unwanted yet inevitable detour away from Angel and to the arranged marriage. Angel continues to tell me her tall tales as she moves around the room while cleaning.

"Are you even listening to me?" Angel says.

"I'm sorry. My mind is somewhere else." I'm ready to turn away from Angel as the force of what I have to do rains down on me.

Angel's steps are quick as she glides in before I can turn away. She takes my hands, pulling me down onto the end-of-bed bench. "What happened? Did he do something?" She doesn't have to tell me who *he* is. She's as afraid of Nicco as every other member of our household staff is.

I shake my head.

Her fingers tighten around mine. "Kira?"

"I have to get married. It's an arranged marriage," I admit.

Angel's soft brown eyes spark, and her large red lips rise. "You are leaving. I mean, I don't want you to leave me, but Kira"—she squeezes our joined hands—"you get to leave him." Her eyes glisten, and I'm in her arms. She's hugging me so tightly that it forces my emotions to the top.

"You don't have to be controlled by him." Her voice wobbles, and her hand moves up and down my back.

I would be controlled by another. I break the hug. "I have to produce an heir."

The horror I feel is reflected in Angel's features.

Before she can ask questions or tell me how barbaric that is, I take her hands in mine this time. I've already been thinking about how to resolve this issue, temporarily anyway.

Time isn't a luxury I have. "I need you to do something for me," I say immediately. "I need you to tell Nicco I have a bad headache and that you're taking me to the doctor."

I don't like dragging Angel into this, but she's already nodding in agreement. "Anything, Kira." She's smiling again, her white teeth on full display. She's so pretty and such a good friend.

I already feel the loss of our friendship, and I can't let her see the pain, so I pull her back into a hug. "Thank you." I press a kiss on her cheek.

She doesn't ask why I want to go to a doctor but leaves my room to make the request. If I spoke to Nicco, he would ask too many questions, and I didn't want him to hear the lie in my voice. With Angel, he would take her word for it. Considering her name, he does see her as a very truthful and kind Angel.

My fingers drum along my thighs, and I close my eyes, wondering what my mother would say to me if she were still here. Would she hold me and tell me Father would not allow this to happen? I squeeze my eyes tight against the fairy tale. Women had no say in our world.

"You're my eensy weensy spider…" The song comes out of my mouth on broken strings of pain and panic. A song that once soothed me as a child now makes the tide of pain rise so high inside me that I stand when Angel returns. The sense that I can outrun my pain evaporates when I see Angel's face. Things didn't go well.

CHAPTER THREE

JASON

I THROW MY WEIGHT backward, hoping to connect with the fucker who's trying to suffocate me, but I meet air as he jerks to the side and manages to dodge my attempt at hurting him. A weight slams down on the back of my knee, and a scream sucks the remaining air out of the bag. I crumble to the floor. My vision wavers, black dots dance and float, and I'm clawing at the plastic in a last attempt to stay alive.

They say your life flashes before your eyes when you die. That's not what happens to me. My head hits the ground, and all I can think is, am I really going to be murdered, just like my father?

Me: Jason Murphy.

I stop clawing as my body twitches involuntarily. Ice-cold air hits my face before a hand connects with my cheek.

"Breathe, you bastard." William's roar and the impact of the slap has me sucking in a lungful of air. It's not enough, and I gasp a second, third, and fourth time. My vision starts to clear. William raises his hand to hit me again.

"I'm breathing," I gasp. I can't get off the floor yet, but I tilt my head to the left. The body of my killer lies motionless. I try to turn in an attempt to get up, but my body burns everywhere. I groan.

"Just stay still, Jason." William runs his hands down his face.

"You called me a bastard," I manage to croak.

William's laughter is unexpected, but it filters through the room before he lowers himself to his haunches. "You are a bastard for almost dying." His laughter dwindles. "How did he creep up on you?"

I manage to sit up. "I was busy." I glance at the filing cabinet the phone is still under. I'll get the phone, but first, I need to find out who just tried to kill me.

The blood that pools from the man's head is visible as I rise up on my knees. My hands still shake, but I force myself to ignore the tremble.

"Did you have to kill him?" I bark at William as I pull the mask off the man's face. The blond stubble makes him appear young. I pull down the collar of his black shirt, but there are no tats.

"I didn't have much time to think. But maybe I should have waited." William kneels down on the opposite side of me and pats down the man's black combats and jacket.

"You don't have to get smart. Just, we could have questioned him." I push up the sleeve of his jacket and spot an array of star tattoos on his wrist. I glance up at William. "He's Bratva."

William tilts his head so he can get a better view of the tattoos. "I thought they wore them on their shoulders."

I drop the man's wrists and open his shirt. "They used to, but since every Tom, Dick, and Harry in prison was doing it, they started tattooing their wrists." The man's chest is clean, but I've seen enough. I get up. "But most Bratva members don't tattoo to show their rank anymore. They prefer to look like businessmen."

We both stand up and glance down at the body at our feet. "You shouldn't have killed him," I repeat. We could have questioned him. He was a potential lead to finding out about our father. Why else was a Bratva member here?

William shakes his head. "I just saved your fucking life."

"He could have had information about our father's killer." I glance back down at the young man.

"Fuck you, Jason. I'm always a fuckup in your eyes." William turns away from me and starts to leave the room.

"What are you talking about? I never see you like that."

He flips me the bird before disappearing.

Shit.

I take my phone out and ring for a cleanup crew. I wonder if marrying Kira has got anything to do with all of this. A Bratva member arrives here and tries to kill me while I find out my father didn't take his own life. Frank got us involved with the Bratva. Did he have the Bratva kill our father? My bones shudder with anger.

This new wife of mine is one of those people who may have killed my father. I'm sure she would have been delighted to hear the news of my death.

I grit my teeth and turn away from the body and my thoughts. I take a final glance at the door and consider going after William, but I need the phone. I'm more aware of the sounds in the room as I bend down and lift the cabinet. The phone comes out easily, and I release the cabinet and let it settle back down before I rise. I press the power button on the device, but nothing happens. The screen remains blank. Pushing the phone into my pocket, I grab the file off the desk and leave the pathologist's office.

Outside, a slight drizzle rains down from the sky. I loosen my tie, still not feeling like my body is getting enough air. That fucker almost killed me. I keep rubbing my throat like I can wipe away the pain in my esophagus. The alleyway is empty, apart from a stack of boxes along the wall. A black lump comes into focus, and I slow my footing as the lump takes form, and I recognize the shape of a man's body.

Too much registers at once. I also recognize the wide shoulders, the hands, and the side of William's head. A gash oozes blood, and I withdraw my weapon as I move closer to my brother. I scan every spot of the alleyway as I lower myself to crouch beside him. Without taking my eyes off the alleyway, I search along his neck for a pulse. At first, I don't find one. I drop my guard and my gun and turn to William. The file flutters to the ground as I pull the neck of his shirt aside. I force myself to stay calm as I check for a pulse. Closing my eyes, I focus on what my fingers can sense; there, it's so slight, but I manage to find a flicker of life.

I snap open my eyes and take out my phone while also picking up my gun.

"William's in bad shape. We are at the pathologist's office. Be careful." I fire off to Alex. He doesn't ask questions.

"I'm on the road, so hold tight for five."

I hang up and push the phone into my pocket. I take a peek at William. "Stay with me, brother." I plead to him, I plead to the alleyway, and to any God that may be listening. I wasn't exactly a spiritual man, but we were brought up in a Catholic home.

I raise my neck like I'm drowning but hold still while William's life slips away beside me. Two men appear at the bottom of the alleyway, and I stand, holding my gun high. They both stop and raise their hands.

"It's us, Jason. Edmond and Jake."

I lower the gun, my heart thrashing in my chest. "Come on," I shout as they lower their arms and walk toward me.

"We were attacked," I say. They're ready to ask questions, when Alex comes dashing down the alleyway.

His appearance gives me strength.

"The man is in the office." I point at the building behind us, and they know better than to question me. I scoop up the file as Alex reaches me.

"Grab an arm and a leg. I've got this side." Alex is calm as he reaches for William. William's head wound is bad, and we both lift him off the ground.

"What happened?" Alex asks as we move William slowly to the end of the alleyway, where Alex's Jaguar hums.

"I was attacked in the medical examiner's office. Some fucker tried to suffocate me, but William killed him." I shift slightly, moving William's weight. He's been hitting the gym hard. I can't ever recall him being this heavy, even when he was drunk and we had to get him into bed.

"William got testy with me and stormed off." We reach the car and lower him into the back. "I told him he shouldn't have killed the guy, that we could have questioned him."

Alex closes the back door and gets into the driver's seat as I slide into the passenger seat. I pivot so I can watch William. He looks like death warmed up.

"That would piss off anyone," Alex says.

"When I left, I found him outside like this." I can't look away from William's lips, which are slowly turning blue.

"Did you find anything?" Alex asks.

I turn to my brother, but I'm staring at his profile. "Father was murdered."

A muscle tics away in his jaw. His knuckles turn white as he grips the steering wheel.

"He took a hit to the back of his head." I return my focus to William. "Whoever killed him hit him from behind. Just like William. We need to check the area for cameras." I start my brain, racing through our protocol.

"I've already got men on it. I made the call while driving here." Alex is always calm and collected.

"It's the Bratva."

William's lips look bluer, and I stretch back and check his neck for a pulse. I have a moment of pure fear before I find a slight heartbeat. "Are we nearly there?" I ask. William doesn't have much time.

"Yeah. Why do you think it's the Bratva?" Alex asks before adding, "Hang on."

I grip the seat as he takes a hard left. My other hand springs out and keeps William in place. When the car resettles, I release William.

"The guy who tried to kill me had stars on his wrists." The hospital appears on my right, and I sit back in my seat as Alex pulls up to the main hospital doors.

It takes two of us to get him inside. A team is waiting, and I don't ask Alex how they know. He must have made several phone calls on his way to William and me. The doors behind us open again, and Aidan rushes in just as the doctors take William out of our arms. He's placed onto a gurney and rushed toward a set of red double doors.

"What happened?" Aidan stares after William.

"He was attacked. We don't know by who yet," Alex answers Aidan.

"When?" Aidan glances from me to Alex, and I see the accusation in his eyes. He's wondering who allowed this to happen. William and Matty should always be protected, especially by myself and Alex, as we are the eldest.

"He was with me at the pathologist's office," I start.

"I'll go find out what's happening." Alex walks off, leaving me with Aidan, who wants answers quicker than I can give them to him.

"So how come you're fine?" Aidan fires.

"It happened after he left me," I grind out and try to hold onto my control. My fucking throat aches, but I'm not going to start complaining.

"You aren't even fazed, are you?" Aidan questions, and before I can answer him, he follows Alex over to the reception desk.

I'm too exhausted to fight, so I sit down on one of the blue waiting room chairs and take out the black phone I found in the pathologist's office. I'm staring at it like it might power up.

The ringing of my own phone has me putting the device away and taking out mine. The name that flashes on the screen gives me pause. What are the chances William is attacked, and after weeks of silence, Frank rings me? I take a peek at Alex and Aidan before I slip out of the hospital.

CHAPTER FOUR

KIRA

I'M STUCK IN REVERSE. That's what it feels like as I stare at Angel. She's chewing her lip. A thin layer of skin breaks free.

"It's okay," I say. It's not okay. I can assume Nicco didn't agree to me going to the doctor. My stomach balls painfully. Did he know she had lied?

"What did he say? Did he believe you?" I'm whispering from the fear that courses through my system. I squeeze my eyes tight before opening them.

"It's okay," I reinforce with more strength than I feel.

Angel releases her damaged lip from between white teeth. "He believed me. But we have to take Lev with us."

Lev is my personal bodyguard and also my cousin, so that's not the worst news, but Angel doesn't seem to agree as she narrows her eyes. "I don't like him."

"He's the best out of a bad bunch. And you know he's my personal bodyguard," I say as I gather my purse while my body breathes a sigh of relief. For just a moment, I thought that he had known we were lying. For a moment, I thought the worst.

"I'm sorry. I know he's a relative." Angel looks sheepish as she takes my silence and internal struggle for something else.

"Not by choice." I stop in front of Angel. "If I had a choice, you would be my sister."

Her smile is instant, and she bounces on her feet. "Let's go, sister."

Her joking nature ends the moment we leave my room. Lev greets me with a nod of his head.

"Hi, Lev." I try to keep my voice low and my gaze guarded.

"Kira." Lev isn't much of a talker, but he's been around me forever. He looks very much like his father—a big blond brute. He's a giant and not the friendly kind. But I like that I'm safe with Lev. No one would dare look at me wrong. In our world of hungry men, I need someone to look out for me. I take another peek at my cousin. What will it be like when he's no longer by my side? When there is no barrier between other people and me?

I feel a mixture of emotions as I leave my home. My driver, Fedor, opens the back door of the SUV, and I climb in with Angel beside me.

Lev sits in the front passenger seat, and once everyone is settled, Fedor pulls away from the house, and we make our way to the doctor's office.

The private health service is gated, and we go through our normal paperwork before we are granted access to the grounds.

I tighten my hand on my purse until my fingers ache. Angel subtly brushes against me. I relax my fingers, and when I glance at her, she's not focused on me; instead, she's looking straight ahead. I take a peek at Lev and notice he is watching me. Angel was warning me.

"My head is throbbing," I declare and turn my focus out the window. The SUV pulls up outside the building. The courtyard is pristine, and I often admire all the colorful flowers when I'm here for my monthly checkup. But today is different.

Once the SUV comes to a complete standstill, Fedor gets out and opens my door. The sound of running water and the heat on the back of my neck makes me think of somewhere that might offer me freedom, like a beach or some undiscovered waterfall hidden in the hills of Donegal or Clarney.

I pass the water feature. I don't have to look behind me to know that Lev and Angel are following me into the building and into the waiting room.

The room isn't conventional. This has a touch of class and a surprising amount of Irish culture hangs on the walls. The bodhran, with its intricate Celtic knots, always makes me reach out and touch the soft wood.

"Kira." Doctor O'Connell greets me with an outstretched hand. I take her fingers and accept the tight handshake. She's also businesslike in her white suit and large black glasses.

"I hope you weren't waiting?" she asks.

She knows I wasn't. My brother wouldn't allow such an inconvenience. "No, we just arrived."

Lev leaves and enters the doctor's office. This is routine. He's checking the room for intruders, bugs, and who knows what exactly. But this is a standard procedure. Doctor O'Connell and I talk briefly like we aren't standing out here because we have no choice about the matter.

Lev arrives back into the waiting room and gives a nod of approval, letting us know we can go in. I take my purse with me and enter the doctor's office. Once I'm seated, she closes the door.

"What can I do for you today, Miss Tarasova?"

I wait until she sits.

"It's a private matter. One I want to keep between the two of us."

She leans back in her chair. "Of course."

I'm already shaking my head. "You can't tell Nicco."

She swallows and props herself a bit straighter in the chair. "It's my duty to inform Mr. Tarasova of all visits."

"Your duty is to me. Of course you can tell him of my visit, just not the nature of it." I hold my head high and try to force an authoritative tone into my voice.

She's watching me and finally she nods in agreement. "What has brought you in today?" She grips an arm of her glasses and fixes them back up on her nose.

"I need contraceptives."

Relief widens her gaze. "Oh, that's normal for a girl your age."

I'm over twenty-one. A twenty-one-year-old virgin; I'd hardly call that normal. "I just don't want to have this conversation with my brother."

"I understand." She smiles before she writes out the prescription.

I can make this work. I will accept the arranged marriage, but I'll take the pill so I didn't have to bring a child into this world until I've figured out a way to break free from it all.

Hope blooms and flourishes in my chest. "I will need a prescription for my headache, too, please," I inform Doctor O'Connell as she hands me the first prescription for the contraceptive pills. I fold the piece of paper and put it in my purse.

When she hands me the second one for pain tablets, I hold that prescription and stand. "Thank you for your discretion."

Doctor O'Connell rises as well. "I actually might have some of the pain tablets here." She withdraws the prescription from my fingers. It isn't unusual for her to have some of the tablets on hand. It's just a pity she didn't have the contraceptives. But I'd have to figure out a way to get to a drugstore.

"Brilliant." I smile.

"If you want to give me a moment, you can retake your seat in the waiting room."

Angel rises once I step into the room. Her gaze slides to me, and I give her a nod.

"Doctor O'Connell is just getting me my tablets."

Lev doesn't say anything, but I know he heard me. Angel's gaze burns the side of my face as I retake my seat and wait for the doctor to return. Her constant watching me has an uneasy sense skittering along my spine.

I take a peek at Lev, who's glancing around him, before my gaze settles on Angel. I widen my eyes, wondering what is wrong with her.

She shakes her head and looks away, but trouble is brewing in her gaze. I keep glancing at the door, wondering what's taking the doctor so long. Panic escalates like a sneeze through my system. My knee jangles, and I clamp down on it to stop the trembling.

"Here you go, Kira." Doctor O'Connell arrives with a small plastic bag that holds a few tablets. I take the package, and I want to run out the door.

"Thank you."

She readjusts her glasses but doesn't move.

There is an uncomfortable silence. "Anything else for me, Doctor?" I ask.

She seems to snap out of her reprieve and steps aside. "Take care, Ms. Tarasova. I hope your headache clears up."

I force a smile and tighten my hold on my purse and tablets.

As I leave the doctor's office, I have a feeling of success at achieving what I came here to do. Having contraceptives may not stop things completely, but it will definitely give me time until I find a way out of this mess.

Outside, I let my fingers trail through the water fountain as I pass. Fedor holds open the door for me. As I approach with Angel at my back, he steps away from the SUV.

"Angel, just a moment," Fedor says.

I have a second of confusion before I see the cane my brother holds tightly. The sight of the hook of his fingers around the silver lion's head sends fire across my chest. Nicco's fingers loosen before they grip the cane again.

I hesitate. I don't want to get into the SUV.

"Kira." Nicco's voice is low. He's struggling for control. I glance over my shoulder and take one final look at Angel. I can see the fear reflected in my friend's eyes.

Getting in, I don't have a moment before Nicco rips the purse and tablets from between my whitening fingers. I open my mouth to speak, but he holds up a raised hand for me not to interrupt him.

"Do you remember when Mother died? How I held you every night?"

"Nicco," I plead, but he cuts me with a stare.

"Do you remember, Kira?"

Of course I remember. I could never forget those horrible nights. "Yes."

"Was there anyone else that held you when you cried?"

"No." Not even Father. There was only Nicco.

He looks down at the tablets and opens the plastic pouch. He removes two tablets and holds them out to me. "Take them."

Is this what took Doctor O'Connell so long? Was she ringing Nicco? Delighting in telling him how I had lied?

"Nicco," I plead again.

My lids snap closed as he throws the tablets in my face. My heart jumps, and when his fingers tighten around my jaw, I open my eyes and look at my brother.

"You lied to me." His gaze wavers with unshed tears. "You betrayed me." He releases my jaw roughly.

When he sits back, he fixes his vest before running his hands through his hair.

"I won't bring a baby into this world." My pulse pounds and thrashes.

Nicco leans closer, and his lips curl up into a snarl. "Yes, you will."

I bite my cheek until my mouth fills with blood.

"But not by him," Nicco adds.

Bile rises hard and fast. "No." It's a whisper, but I can see in his eyes what he's implying.

I'm waiting for his anger, but Nicco looks away from me. "We will place a pureblood on the throne." He holds his head high before he turns back to me. "I already told you that you'd be in your own part of his home. I have secured your safety. So lying to me or having Angel lie..." He shakes his head, his gaze glazing over.

Nicco glances out the window, and I follow his stare. Outside, Lev stands behind Angel. Even through the tinted window, she looks sickly. Nicco shifts closer to the door and raises his hand. He stares at me with a cruelty that makes each knock of his knuckles on the glass feel like the drums of doom. Fedor opens the door.

"Angel, get in," Nicco commands. "We're ready to go."

Angel steps toward the SUV, and seeing her makes everything in me scream. Her movements are jerky as she slides in. I sit back and look out the opposite window. Nicco stays in the rear of the SUV with us. Lev gets in, and Fedor starts the vehicle. As we drive away from the doctor's and to our sentencing, I don't just fear for my own safety. I fear for my friend's. My brother's cruelty has no bounds.

CHAPTER FIVE

KIRA

I PUSH ALL MY emotions down, so far down that I become numb. Numb to the trepidation that threatens to choke me, numb to the pain that wants to drown my every logical thought. I push it all down as we drive back home. Nicco doesn't speak, and neither does Angel. The SUV becomes a steel coffin. From the outside, I'm sure I appear bored, dormant, controlled, and unaffected.

If I show an ounce of fear for Angel, Nicco will use that against me. So, as we pull up to the house and climb out, I don't give Angel a second glance, not even as we enter the hallway, where I'm ready to get away from Nicco and escape to my bedroom.

"Kira."

My footfalls stall as he says my name. I turn but don't find him looking at me; Nicco is already walking away, so I'm facing Angel. Terror is etched into her features, draining her big brown eyes of life, and she's a mass of fear. I want to say I'm so sorry for dragging her into this mess, but I don't dare speak to her right now. I gather my courage and relish the idea that she won't be punished for my stupidity. Why did I think for one second that Fedor, Lev, and the doctor wouldn't betray me? I know better than that. A moment of panic led me on this path, and if I walk away from this unscratched, it's a mistake I will never make again. I take a step toward Nicco when he speaks again.

"Angel," he calls over his shoulder.

Angel obediently follows my brother. Her shoulders curl forward, and I want to reach out and touch her shoulder to make her relax. Why couldn't he leave her alone? I'm looking left and right, for what, I'm not sure. For someone to intervene. For my father to reappear and ask Nicco what exactly he's doing. I can hear my father's voice right now and how he always sounded so disappointed when he spoke to Nicco. That disappointed tone didn't go unnoticed. Nicco always grew agitated around Father. It had been a vicious circle, yet Father had kept Nicco in line.

Nicco's cane clicks loudly with each step he takes, pulling me away from my thoughts of Father and the fantasy of someone helping.

Nicco takes us into one of the many living spaces. It's one I haven't been to in a while, and I'm glancing at Nicco, wondering why he picked this room. We shared so much time here as kids—watching TV, playing Snap, and frightening each other with stories of the dead. The large wide-back TV is still present in the room. The old red rose wallpaper has never been stripped. I wonder why no one ever redid this room.

Nicco stops in the center of the space and spins like a play director getting ready to coach his actors. I place my hands behind my back.

Nicco holds out his hand to Angel. I'm screaming in my head, praying she doesn't take his hand, but in reality, she has no choice. Like she could decline him in any shape or form.

Angel takes two tentative steps toward my brother. He smiles softly at her, and dread grips me by the throat. I want to get her out of the room.

When Angel's hand is firmly in Nicco's, his gaze swings to me, and his smile disappears swiftly off his face.

"You told Angel to lie." It's not a question but a statement.

"No, I lied to Angel."

Nicco doesn't look away from me. My heart beats uncontrollably in my chest. I keep my hands clasped behind my back.

"I would hardly tell her the truth," I say as Nicco continues to observe me. "She would have told you." I give Angel a cutting look, as if she has no loyalty to me and that knowledge displeases me. In my head, I repeat the mantra, *Please don't hurt her. Please don't hurt her.* I ask my mother and father to help me.

Nicco releases Angel's hand, and the relief I feel is so crushing that it threatens to buckle my knees and destroy my composure.

"On your knees, Angel." The sharpness of Nicco's words confuses me.

I foolishly take a step toward Angel. "What are you doing? I just told you..." I stop talking when his hand connects with Angel's face. Angel's startled cry makes me flinch.

Flesh meets flesh again, and the sound is brash in the wide room.

"She is your servant?" Nicco asks.

I'm struggling to hide my alarm for Angel, but if I intervene, I will make this worse. "Yes," I answer.

"Then she shall be punished for your crimes." Nicco smiles again, but as he lands an open-handed slap on Angel's face, his grin evaporates, and I want to disappear.

He hits Angel harder, and she sobs, but Nicco keeps watching me, waiting for a reaction. *Bruises will fade*, I tell myself. He will make it worse if I try to stop him, so I push it all back down and become numb.

Nicco strikes her two more times before he stops. Hitting Angel is feeding his hunger for pain, but I can see it in my brother's gaze—it's not enough, not even close. I should have known he wouldn't stop; imagining Angel would walk out of this room was wishful thinking. Nicco keeps eye contact with me as he brings the cane up into the air, and with all the hate he can muster, he snarls, distorting his features until he appears grotesque as he brings the cane down onto Angel's back. Her sobs become screams as she hits the ground. Her pain infiltrates the room and finds its way into my bloodstream.

"You will give me an heir," Nicco says as he raises the cane again. He gives pause, and when I don't respond, he draws the cane down onto Angel's back once more. This time, the fabric of her top splits, and the blood rises and pours out of her broken flesh.

Angel lies flat on the floor. Her cries are agony, and I want to help her as she grips the floorboards to drag herself away from Nicco and toward me.

He smiles when he sees what Angel is doing. "Do you think she'll save you?" he asks Angel while pushing his foot down on her buttocks, keeping her in place. "If I want you dead, you will die." He removes his foot and steps across Angel to get to me.

I blink, unable to stop the tears that spill down my face.

"When someone lies to me once, it makes me wonder what else they've lied about." His hand springs out and grabs my face. When I don't respond, Nicco's gaze darts to my mouth. I try to pull out of his hold, but his grip grows tighter, and he inches me closer.

"In three weeks' time, I will come for you. You will sign the paperwork that will free you from this marriage to Jason Murphy."

I want to ask why three weeks, but I don't breathe a word.

"But right now, you have other paperwork to sign." Nicco releases me roughly, and I roll my jaw as he turns his back on me. Angel isn't moving, and I take a terrified step toward her.

"You touch her, Kira, and I will put a bullet in her head."

I'm frozen as I wait for Nicco to return with the documents. I can't even see the words as my gaze swims with unfallen tears.

A pen is pushed into my hand. "Sign here." Nicco taps the bottom of the page.

"What is it?" I murmur and blink as tears fall down my face.

"Sign it," Nicco barks.

The pen glides hurriedly across the line, and Nicco smiles. I'd do anything to get away from him. The papers are removed before I can even read what I just signed.

Salty liquid enters my mouth, and I swallow my tears.

Nicco breezes past me, and my focus is drawn to Angel, who's still unmoving on the floor. Blood soaks through her frayed top, and I have the first drop of real fear that she might be dead hit me.

The screech of the door behind me and the roar of my heart are the only sounds that filter into my brain. That is, until two security men approach Angel.

"No." Their presence snaps me out of my stupor. I dash forward and whirl, blocking their path.

Everything in me stills as I look up to find Nicco watching me.

"Your transport is ready to take you to the Murphy residence." Nicco slams his cane twice into the wooden floor; the two loud knocks make me jolt. The security men circle around me and pick Angel up off the floor. Her sobs tear flesh from my soul.

"What will you do with her?" I ask.

Nicco doesn't smile like I expect. "She is no longer welcome in my home. She will go with you."

Surprise surges from the pit of my stomach, making my chest tighten. Already, I want to know what the catch is, but I don't get to ask as Nicco spins and leaves the room. The men lift Angel past me, and she whimpers.

"Go easy with her," I demand and sure enough, they carry her slower and with gentler hands. She's alive—that's all I can think about as the front double doors are opened and, like Nicco had promised, an SUV is idle in front of the house.

Fedor opens the back door. I can't even look at him as I climb into the SUV. Lev is in the passenger seat, and he is another I avoid eye contact with. I turn so I can help Angel into the back of the car.

"Lie her down gently," I say. They do, but it doesn't stop the pain that causes Angel to cry out. The door closes, and in the privacy of the back of the SUV, I allow the horror of what just happened to spur me on.

"Fedor, we need to take Angel to a hospital, now." I want to touch her back, but I don't want to hurt her. So I reposition my best friend until her head is in my lap. I could help her. Once I get Angel to a hospital, I would somehow get her enough money so she could flee and start a life somewhere else. I run my hand across her hair as the SUV pulls away from the house.

"Orders are to take Kira to Jason Murphy's." Lev's icy words have my fingers stilling in Angel's hair.

"Fedor is my driver." My voice swells with emotions. "Fedor, you will take me to a hospital."

Lev turns in his seat and glares at me. He has a look in his eye that causes my stomach to squirm. "He was given a direct order from Nicco."

I'm ready to protest. When Lev peeks down at Angel's damaged back, he asks me, "Don't you think having one person hurt is enough?"

His words are like a slap in the face. Some dark part of me doesn't care what happens to Fedor or Lev. All I care about is Angel. She trembles on my knee. A cold sweat soaks her forehead.

"I don't give a shit. Take me to the hospital now." My voice is sharp, but the reality is that it doesn't matter how much I shout and scream; my words make no difference. Fedor disregards my order and takes me to Jason Murphy's home, with my dying friend trembling on my knee.

CHAPTER SIX

JASON

"WHAT DO YOU WANT?" I say into the phone before I take another look at my brothers, who are still at the front desk. I seize the opportunity to slip out of the hospital while their backs are turned t o me.

"I heard you got attacked." Frank doesn't sound upset or gleeful. He's just stating a fact.

A car pulls up outside the hospital. The driver races around to the passenger door. The woman he helps out is sweating and breathing heavily. Her swollen stomach looks ready to blow.

"Did you orchestrate the attack?" I ask.

The man helps the woman, and even through the pain of her nascent labor, she glances at him and smiles before they disappear into the hospital.

"Don't be so foolish," Frank answers, his words sharp like I've just insulted him.

"Did you kill my father?" I hurl out another question before transferring the phone to my other ear. I glance back at the hospital to make sure my brothers are still inside. They are.

"No. I would never harm my brother. I was looking into his death."

"And..." A traffic cop takes out his small black machine as he walks up to the car that the pregnant woman just came from. I take a step toward him but pause as Frank speaks.

"And I think you have come to the same conclusion I have. My brother was murdered."

"My condolences," I say dryly.

"You shot me," Frank growls, and I smirk, taking satisfaction in what I got the chance to do, and clearly how much it pissed him off.

"It was a flesh wound. You were lucky it was me pulling that trigger and not Aidan or you would be dead, Frank."

Silence stretches out and as I look up, the traffic cop is gone, and a ticket flaps on the car windshield. I wanted to tell the traffic warden that the woman was pregnant. Anyone parked outside the hospital is here because they need help. Not a fucking fine when they return to their vehicles.

I turn back to the hospital.

"Aidan killed Gilbert," Frank finally says.

My gut squirms. "Gilbert should have kept his mouth shut." Instead, he had gloated about the fact that he had abused Raven. Gilbert could have walked away, but he believed he was invincible, and now he's six feet under.

"How are you so cold?" Frank snarls.

I smile with no sympathy.

"You made me that way, Frank." I hang up as one of my early memories of Frank shaping me into the man I am today springs to mind.

"If you can control pain, you can control the world." Frank glances at me from across the car. I'm waiting for the punch he normally delivers into my side. I'm clenched and ready for the blow. The only rule is I can't react. Sometimes I impress him, but most times, I fail. After several broken ribs, I'm getting better.

I brace, waiting, and when nothing happens, I take a peek at Frank.

He pushes the cigarette lighter in. "The pain is all in your head."

The pop of the cigarette lighter makes me clench my fists.

Frank slows the car and pulls over into the gateway of a field.

"Take off your shirt," he orders.

I do as he says. "Frank." I'm ready to ask him not to do this. I'll take a punch instead.

He pushes on the smoke lighter again and faces me. "Men can walk on hot coals. They can defy what we believe is undefiable. Do you want to know how?"

My gut is clenched so hard I feel bones crunch.

The pop of the cigarette lighter has both of us looking at it. Frank takes it out; the top glows, and the redness is eerie in the late afternoon light. Frank leans close to me, and I lean back. He's so much larger than me, so when he clamps his hand on my fourteen-year-old shoulder to keep me in place, I have nowhere to go.

"It's all in your head," he tells me before he sinks the cigarette lighter onto my shoulder.

I roll my shoulders like they can still remember the level of pain Frank had inflicted on me over and over again. Pain melted into pain until it all stopped, and he made me what he wanted—someone who would be unstoppable.

I reenter the hospital. Alex watches me, and when I join him and a frazzled Aidan, he glances at the pocket where I've placed my phone.

"Who was that?"

"Just a meeting I needed to cancel."

Alex doesn't look away. "It looked tense."

He sounds almost suspicious of me, and I seek the control that I use to control pain. "It was," I answer. "Any word on William?"

"He's in surgery," Aidan answers before sitting down in one of the chairs. He runs his hands through his dark hair. "How did someone get the jump on him?" Aidan springs to his feet like a jack-in-the-box. "Why was he on his own after everything with Frank?"

"He left the building on his own accord," I answer. "He's a full-grown man."

Aidan snarls. "Why are you so calm?"

Alex steps toward Aidan and places his hand on Aidan's shoulder. "No one is calm right now, Aidan."

Aidan's gaze softens, and he nods at Alex. Alex removes his hand and turns to me. "You need to follow protocol and take security with you at all times. Going to that office with no one was stupid." Alex is our leader, a decision made by the Bratva and not us. If we had to go by rank, then Alex would take the place after his father, but Frank had been our leader, so his son would have led us instead.

"I wasn't alone. I had William. Taking a team of security would have attracted too much attention."

"I don't care, Jason. It's an order. You must have two men with you at all times."

I want to ask him where his or Aidan's men are. Maybe Aidan can see the question in my gaze.

"One of my men is outside, the other in the car."

"My men are outside, too," Alex answers.

My phone rings, but Alex hasn't released me from his stare. "I'll follow protocol," I finally give in.

He nods. "Good."

I turn away and take the call.

"Master Jason, Miss Tarasova has arrived. I know you wanted to be informed of her arrival."

"Thank you Al. I will be home shortly."

"You are welcome, Master Jason."

I end the call, but I can't stop the anger that pulses through my arm and tighten my fingers around my phone. She was Bratva, the man that tried to kill me was Bratva, and most likely the one that hurt William is Bratva too. What are the odds?

Alex and Aidan are both sitting.

"I have to go home," I say.

"I will ring you when we hear something," Alex tells me.

"How can you leave right now?" Aidan rises. I've always had his back, even when he killed Gilly. Too many times I had to talk Frank down from killing Aidan for his disobedience.

"Aidan, ease off," Alex says.

But Aidan, being Aidan, squares up to me. "What aren't you telling us?"

"I don't know what you are talking about."

"How could you not have seen something? It doesn't make sense."

My temper sparks. "I don't have X-ray vision to see through the fucking walls."

Aidan takes a step back. Losing my temper isn't something my brothers would see of me.

"It's just not adding up." Aidan frowns, and I see something in his eyes I've never seen before. Distrust. Can I blame him? Not really.

I leave before I say something I regret.

"I'll give you a lift," Alex calls after me.

I don't look back. "I'll grab a cab." It's not something I've ever done before. Public transport has just never been necessary. We were brought up in a world of drivers and pilots.

I leave the grounds of the hospital and wave down the first cab I spot. I give him the address, and he drives me home.

I slide the phone that I had found out of my pocket before I take out my own.

I call Zach. "Can you get me a Samsung charger? It looks like a flat, wide head."

"I mean, I have fuck all to do."

I grin at Zach's biting words. A loud splash sounds in the background, and the closer I listen, I can hear the squeak of seagulls.

"What are you doing?" I ask, but I don't really want to know.

"Dumping a body. I'll swing by the electrical store once this fucker sinks."

The docks are only five minutes away from my home. He might get there before me. I glance at the driver, who's focused on the road. I don't think he would be able to hear Zach, anyway. "I'll see you soon."

Zach is trigger-happy, but it's a plus in our line of work. He's loyal to only me, and that's worth its weight in gold.

I slide each phone into separate pockets and loosen my tie. I run my hands along my neck; the memory of not having enough air has me jerking my chin out and pushing my head back as if I'm searching for air. My throat still aches from the earlier abuse it took.

Closing my eyes, I picture William's skull cracked and bleeding. The image flickers to bloody messes, distorted bodies, arms bent back too far, and legs removed. I push the heels of my palms into my eyes like I can wash my sins away.

The drive home takes longer than I want, and I keep returning to the car where Frank held the cigarette lighter to my shoulders until the heat got soaked up by my skin. I reach up and touch my left shoulder but drop my hand as the lights of the front of my home have me sitting forward.

The taxi pulls up at the front gate. "Thanks." I push a fifty into his hand. "Keep the change," I say as I climb out. The two large gates open, and I nod up at the cameras, knowing Al must have been watching out for me. I step off the main road that leads up to the house and enter the dense woodlands. I'm not ready to go back home.

I'm replaying the scene in my head of finding William. I stop at a tree and lean against it, just wanting five minutes.

"That bad, boss?"

There go my five minutes, pulverized to five seconds. I shove off the tree. "William is in surgery," I tell Noah.

He pushes the dark glasses up on his forehead. "We will get them, boss."

Of course we will, but in the meantime, we have no idea if William will be okay. I nod.

"Do you need a minute?" Noah asks as he pulls the sunglasses back into place.

"No." I walk around the tree and make my way in the direction of the house. I spot three more security men within the dense woodlands. Each greets me with a nod. None are as forthcoming as Noah, but that's because Noah has been with me for years.

I break through the tree line. Both security men who are posted outside the main door stand a little straighter. A string of "boss" follows me as I make my way to my office. Maybe here I'll find the silence I'm seeking. I take the phone out of my pocket and place the device onto the desk. Now that I'm alone with my thoughts, I don't want to be. Powering up my computer, I log into the security cameras. She's in the west wing, and I'm about to bring up the footage, but I close the screen as a knock sounds on the door. I don't get to speak as Zach enters the room. He holds up a hard plastic package. Inside, a charger is visible.

"Am I your fairy fucking godmother or what?" he asks while handing me the package and sinking into the chair. He runs his hands along his red beard, which covers most of his face.

I rip open the package. "Who were you making disappear?" I ask as I plug the charger into the wall and then connect it to the phone.

"Some junkie who was dipping into the cookie jar." He wiggles his fingers, coated in rings.

I place the phone onto the desk and hate the fact that I have to give it a few seconds to power up. "All the lads dip their fingers into the cookie jar,"

I state. We factor that percentage in. Not one of the mules or drug runners are a hundred percent honest. We know that.

"He was sticking two fucking hands in."

I nod, understanding.

Zach leans forward. "How's William?"

"News travels fast."

Zach shakes his head slightly. "Nah, I just know shit."

"He's in surgery. Alex is going to keep me informed."

Zach isn't a fan of Alex's, and his silence is like a huge fuck you.

The light on the phone turns from red to green as I power it up.

"I found this phone at the pathologist's office. It was stuck under a filing cabinet. It might give me an answer," I explain as I wait for the Samsung logo to disappear. Once the phone has a network signal, I glance up at Zach. He nods and splays both hands on the desk. I open the call log and take down a few numbers that have been saved without names. Instead, they're objects.

"Hammer." Zach reads one. "A bad porn name."

I finish writing down the numbers.

"I can look into these for you." Zach takes the piece of paper.

"Thanks." I return to the phone and open the images. I scroll quickly through random ones of his days in his home. Him sitting on a couch with a cat on his chest. The images give me nothing until I stop at one where he's fishing. A man stands right beside him. I zoom in on Alex's smiling face.

What is Alex doing with the pathologist?

CHAPTER SEVEN

KIRA

"**S**HE'S STILL BLEEDING." THE blood continues to ooze from the gash on Angel's back, and I've never felt so helpless in my entire life, not even when Nicco killed my kitten because he was jealous of the small ball of fur. How easily he had walloped the defenseless animal across the head with the garden shovel. Or when he had whispered cruel words to Mother as she slowly lost her mind to depression.

I run the back of my hand across my forehead, trying to mop up some of the sweat that's soaked into my hairline.

"We are nearly there." Lev's words sound like they've been chewed or placed in a blender.

"She needs a doctor." I take in a deep, shaky breath. My frustration burns my eyes and throat.

I keep my focus on Angel until the vehicle stops. Lev is already out of the SUV and bolts around to open Angel's door.

"Be careful," I say automatically.

Lev picks Angel up with care, and she groans in pain. Fedor says something to me, but I ignore him as we approach an arched wooden door you might see on a side entrance of a castle.

A man in his late fifties bows his head. "Welcome, Miss Tarasova."

"I want to see Mr. Murphy," I say.

"Where can I lie her down?" Lev asks, and the man responds by opening the door. "This way."

We enter the building. The click of my small heels on the old slate flooring bounces around the wide walkway that has arches on the right. They open up into a huge living space. Columns divide the zone, and the natural light pours in from the skylights.

"You can use this room." The man opens a door to our left, and we enter a modest room that holds a queen-size bed. Lev lies Angel down, and once again, her cries have me turning to the man.

"I want to see Mr. Murphy now." I hold my head high.

"I will let Master Jason know of your request." He dips his head and departs.

Lev is removing his suit jacket and rolls up the sleeves of his white shirt. "Get me some damp cloths." He doesn't look at me as he speaks. Lev removes the earpiece, and it dangles down to his shoulder. When his sharp gaze swings to me, I move. Not because I fear him, but because he's helping Angel.

The beige flooring and white walls in the bathroom are soothing for all of a few seconds. I don't meet my gaze in the mirror as I run two cloths and a small hand towel under the tap. I wring them out before returning to Lev.

He takes them, but before he presses anything to Angel's back, he pushes her hair away from her face. His gentleness surprises me.

"This is going to hurt," he warns her. Lev doesn't hesitate, but his jaw tightens as he presses the cloth to the damage my brother inflicted. Her cries send the hairs rising along my bare arms. I'm looking at the open doorway, and I make a decision.

"Stay with her. I'll be back." Lev doesn't acknowledge my words, but I know he heard me. I leave the house and circle back around to the front. The gravel under my feet crunches loudly, and I approach the main doors.

Two security men glance at me. I gather my skirt as I climb the three wide steps. One of the men opens the front door for me.

"Thank you." I enter the main part of the house, and as impressive as the west wing is, it's a miniature version of the grand hallway I enter.

He has another security man inside the door, who doesn't seem startled to see me. I walk quickly across the open entrance, and like the west wing, a large living space to my left runs the length of the hallway. The space darkens, and I stop walking as the man who greeted me steps out of a room with an empty silver tray in his hand. He closes the door gently, but when he straightens and sees me, his face pales.

"Miss Tarasova."

"Where is he?" I take a step forward, my gaze darting to the room he just appeared from. "Is he in there?" I point at the door.

"Master Jason is in a meeting."

I gather every fiber of strength I have and march toward the room.

"Please, Miss Tarasova, just let me inform him that..." He doesn't get to finish as I push open the door.

My hand tightens further on the handle as two men stare at me. The one who sits behind the desk raises a dark brow. My heart jumps in my chest. There's an anger in his gaze that makes me think twice about entering his office unannounced.

"Master Jason, I do apologize. Miss Tarasova was settled in her quarters." The man clutches the tray. His fear should be my warning, but right now, I have a friend who might be dying.

"That's okay, Al. You can leave."

I release the door handle. Master Jason. So this is my future husband—or was meant to be. Nicco said he would return for me in three weeks. And after that, I can't bear to think of what comes next. All I can focus on is the here and now.

"Did you want something?" Jason's voice holds a depth of anger that makes me pause once again.

"I need a doctor," I request, and I'm surprised to hear the strength and stability in my voice. I feel neither.

The second man rises. "I'll give you some space," he says to Jason. He shoulders past me with a hard look in his eyes, like I did something to him. Unless disturbing his meeting warrants that kind of hostility, I've never met the man before in my life.

"Unfortunately, all our doctors are occupied." He folds his hands on the desk, and the red ruby ring on his pinky finger should make him appear feminine, but it has the opposite effect. His masculinity roars like a wild lion.

"My brother has sustained some serious injuries, but I'm sure you already knew that." He stands up and looms across the desk.

"No, I didn't know that. I'm sorry about your brother, but I need a doctor for one of my staff."

His lip curls into a sneer, and when he steps from behind the desk, my stomach squirms. But I hold still even as he approaches me. He towers a head above me, and when he leans in close, his cologne sends my head spinning. "Get the fuck out of my office." His whispered words are filled with rage that, once again, I have no understanding of.

I swallow my trepidation. "I wouldn't ask if it weren't important." My own frustration breaks through the curtain of terror that has slowly started to weave around me. I'm caught like a fly in his web.

His laughter sends waves of uncertainty down my spine.

"I said leave." His jaw is clenched so tightly that the strain is clear on his features.

I hate turning my back on a man. I have no idea of his capabilities. Being in the Mafia should make me wary, but for a moment, I had thrown caution to the wind. It didn't pay off. Asking again wouldn't work. That much is clear on Jason's face. I take one final look at the man as I open the door, his green eyes blazing. He's gripping the ring on his pinky finger as he glares at me, and I remember I have to birth an heir for this man. That thought has me racing from the office. The thought should revolt me, but to my own shock, it doesn't.

I pass the man who had been in Jason's office. He narrows his gaze with hate. I won't let these people affect me. Three weeks and I will be gone, but for now, we need to help Angel. Outside, rain has started to fall, and it turns into a torrential downpour. By the time I reach the west wing, my clothes are soaked through. I slam the door behind me, and shame at failing has me leaning against the door. What do I do now? Leaving the property wouldn't be allowed. Not even Lev would let me take her to a hospital. He has to let me. I push off the door, and I'm half running down to the room I left Angel and Lev in.

The moment I enter in a flurry of panic and dread, I expect Lev to look at me, but he's still pressing a cloth to Angel's back.

"He said no." I hate how broken my voice sounds.

"Did you hear me?" I walk toward Lev when he doesn't respond.

"Yes."

"Lev, we need to take her to a hospital."

This time, he looks at me. I flinch at the level of anger and pain I see in his eyes. My confusion grows at his reaction, and I wonder if he cares for Angel.

"Your brother has forbidden it."

I take a look at Angel. Her eyes are closed, and a sob breaks free from my lips, remembering the viciousness in which my brother beat her. "I didn't think he would hurt her," I admit, while the guilt is churning and growing as time passes. "He enjoyed it so much," I whisper. I have to turn away from Angel.

"Get changed, Kira. You'll get a cold." Lev stands and gathers all the bloody clothes. He looks at me when I don't move, but his gaze doesn't hold as much hate. "I found some painkillers, so she should sleep for a while."

I can't even speak. I just nod as Lev goes into the bathroom with the stained clothes.

I hate how hard it is to step closer to Angel, but it takes a lot for me to stand over my friend. "I'm sorry," I tell her. "I'm so sorry."

I know my words have no power here. My mother often said there was something wrong with my brother, even when he was young. I would hear her say it to Father, who would brush it off as him being a boy. But sometimes, I could see fear in my mother's eyes as she looked at Nicco. How right she was. We had everything to fear from him.

When Lev returns with fresh clothes, I step away from the bed and find a chair to sit in. Lev leaves the clothes on a bedside table before reentering the bathroom. He returns with a large towel, which he hands to me. Without a word, I take it, and he returns to nursing Angel. I watch how gentle he is with her and realize he cares deeply for her. I wonder if she knows how he feels.

"Does she know how you feel?" I ask.

He pauses briefly. "No."

His answer makes me smile sadly. "You should tell her."

Lev doesn't speak, and I use the towel he gave me to dry my hair. I release the long strands from the ponytail and let it fall across my shoulders.

"I would take her to a hospital even if it meant him killing me, but he wouldn't stop there. He'd kill her too."

Embarrassment at the level of my brother's cruelty has me curling up in the chair like I can escape it.

I don't hear anything, but Lev stands and withdraws a gun from the band of his trousers.

Al, Jason's butler, stalls at the doorway. "Master Jason wishes to see you."

Lev lowers his gun, and I see it in his eyes—hope. But I don't hold any. The last time I spoke to Jason, he clearly wasn't giving in.

CHAPTER EIGHT

JASON

"WELL, THAT WAS INTEREST-ING."

Zach scratches his brow and sinks back into the chair before dragging a leg up on top of the other. He grips his heel as he waits a little longer for me to explain who I was just speaking to. Today has been full of surprises.

"That was the Negotiator."

Zach raises both brows. "You sure had a lot to talk about."

I glance at the clock on my phone. Nearly ten minutes of a conversation, according to my clock. "He's Kira's brother." That news floored me. He had informed me with a warning in his tone.

Zach shrugs, disbelief in his gaze.. "You're telling me you didn't know that before? You didn't look into the girl you were marrying, the one who's wandering around your home?"

I couldn't blame him. Kira wandering around my home wasn't something I had expected. I truly thought she would keep to her side of the house and out of my way. Clearly, that isn't her intention, and I know why.

"I knew she had a brother, but as the Negotiator's identity was never revealed to us before, I had no clue. The Bratva kept the information hidden from non-Bratva members. That is, until Frank dragged us into this mess." I glance down at the phone, the image of Alex with the medical examiner not sitting right with me. Why didn't Alex mention that he knew the medical examiner? On a personal level, no less. They both look pretty happy and comfortable in the picture. Alex is holding up a fish he caught. The medical examiner is gripping his fishing pole.

"So what did he want? Just a chin wag?" Zach asks, pulling me away from one problem and into another. "Seems unlikely."

"He only wants Kira here for three weeks, and then she's returning to her home. Our marriage won't proceed." I let the phone in front of me go blank, and the image of Alex disappears. "He wants her kept in separate sleeping quarters, and in three weeks, I sign a release form, and he takes her."

"That's it?" Zach drops his leg back onto the floor and pulls himself closer to the desk. "Why is she here?"

"To spy on me, I would think," I answer.

Zach juts out his chin. "Keep her in her own fucking corner, and don't let her out until she's gone."

"On the contrary, I'm going to move her into my room." I pick up the phone and dial the main service room. Al answers on the second ring.

"Bring Miss Tarasova to me."

"Of course, Master Jason," Al responds.

I hang up, and Zach glares at me like I've lost my mind.

Maybe I have. But this is an opportunity I can use to my advantage. "The Negotiator thought telling me who he is would scare me into compliance. But, knowing I have his sister under my roof... That's something I can't not use."

"Use how?" Zach isn't buying my plan.

I exhale slowly. "That part, I don't know yet. But like they say, keep your friends close and your enemies closer."

Zach snorts. "I don't think they mean in your fucking bed."

I grin at Zach. "The secrets she must know."

"And you think she will just tell you? What are you going to do, threaten her? Tie her up and beat the information out of her?"

I smirk again. "No, I'm going to charm her."

Zach's laughter would be insulting if it was anyone else. It's loud and harsh, like the idea of me charming anyone is ludicrous. I'm not known for my charm, but that doesn't stop women from wanting me, and I've never been without.

"Good luck with that," Zach says as a knock on the door has him standing. "You will need it." He finishes just as he opens the door.

I'm expecting to see Miss Tarasova with Al, but he's alone. "I'm sorry, Master Jason, but Miss Taraosava is refusing to leave her quarters."

Zach takes a cigarette out of a pack and shoves it behind his ear. The grin he wears has me rising.

"Thank you, Al." If she won't come to me, I'll go to her.

Al leaves, and Zach folds his arms. "What's next, Romeo?" He's really finding this amusing.

"I'll keep you posted." I pat my friend on the back and make my way to the west wing of my home.

I have no idea what I'll find, but I expect Kira to be alone. She isn't. I enter from the rear part of the house, so it takes them a few moments to become aware of my presence. The man who's pointing a gun at me is the first to notice me. I grin and step into the room.

"You're going to shoot your host?" I ask.

His gaze dances to Kira, and he speaks in Russian. He must be asking her a question. She nods, and he lowers his gun. When my life is no longer being threatened, I step closer to the bed. A girl lies still, and cloths coat her back.

"I had requested your presence," I speak to Kira, who hasn't acknowledged me. Her hair is loose, and the blonde strands trail down her back. She appears like she's showered, but on closer inspection, I notice wet patches on her beige top and floral skirt.

"I was busy." She holds her head high as she speaks, folds her hands in front of her, and takes a tentative step toward me. "I do apologize, but I hope it was nothing important."

She should have been a politician. She has a presence about her that, even in her circumstances, doesn't weaken her. She is the sister of the Negotiator. She is bound to be strong in a world like theirs. I don't think I would allow a sister of mine, if I had any, to take part in this world, especially if they looked like Kira.

I glance at the man who's still watching me with suspicion. "Who are you?" I hadn't been told that Kira would be coming with an entourage, and now I wonder what happened here. Is this why she wanted a doctor? The girl on the bed must be hurt.

"I'm Lev, Miss Tarasova's personal security."

"We have our own security here." Did the Negotiator think I couldn't protect Kira? Or was it to have more than one spy in my home? Either way, it's insulting.

"Miss Tarasova requested my presence," he answers quickly.

She nods in agreement.

"And the girl?" I ask Kira.

"My maid."

"She doesn't look like she's up to much cleaning."

"That's why I requested a doctor." Kira's words are biting, and she shifts to the left, blocking my view of her maid.

"I'll get you a doctor."

Her brown eyes widen before she nods several times. "Thank you."

"Pack a few belongings. You're coming with me."

Confusion fills her features, and I take a step closer to her. "We are leaving now."

"I was told I would have the west wing to myself."

"I've changed my mind." I turn, expecting her to follow.

"No," she fires out.

I glance at her over my shoulder. "Fine. I won't send for a doctor, then." I make it to the living room, where all her bags are stacked, before she stops me.

"Okay, get the doctor for her, and then I'll leave."

I push my hands into my pockets. I can't let her think she can control the situation. "Wrong answer, Miss Tarasova. This is your last chance. Pack a few things and we leave. Then I will ring the doctor, and only then."

Anger curls her hands into fists. She's glaring at me, but I flash her a warning, and she moves to the stack of suitcases. She grabs one off the top and pulls it away from the rest. "I'm ready." I thought she might at least go through her luggage to decide what to take, but she really wants the doctor for the maid. Now, I think of her sweaty and disheveled presence earlier in my office and wonder what exactly had happened before she got here.

I nod and lead her back the way we came. I fire a text to the house doctor to get herself to the west wing. When I pocket my phone, I glance at Kira. She's glaring at me with hate in her dark eyes. She doesn't speak as I take her into the main part of the house.

"The doctor?" she prods.

"Has been contacted. I messaged her," I add, seeing as she's ready to open her mouth again.

"How long must I stay here for?" She's clutching her bag with both hands.

I take my time and really assess her. She's different now that I know who she is. The Negotiator's sister is standing in my hallway. She keeps her mouth relaxed and allows me to look at her, but her nostrils flare as I walk closer and circle her. "As long as I want," I answer. Three weeks and her brother is coming for her. I wonder why three weeks. Why does he want her back? Does it matter? The real question is, why is she here?

I walk in a full circle until I'm standing in front of her again. I'm a head taller, but there is nothing small about Kira. Her brown eyes are fired up with fear but also strength. Some people take pain and become victims; others take the pain and spin it into power. Kira is the latter. I can see it clearly in her eyes. Standing this close, I'm aware of how transparent her beige top is around the bustline, and she has a full chest. "Why are you wet?" I ask and step closer until she has to crane her neck back to look me in the eye.

"I got caught in the rain," she says.

"Let's get you changed."

Her eyes flash with fear before her dark lashes flutter closed. I don't remove her fear. I could tell her I won't touch her, but I don't. I reach out and take her bag from her hands. Our fingers brush lightly, and she quickly pushes her hands behind her back. The contact was brief, but I liked the softness of her fingers. As I grip her bag, I can't help but imagine what her hands on my body would feel like. My cock starts to grow hard, and when I stand far too long, she peeks up at me from under her lashes.

Now I know why I didn't promise her I wouldn't touch her, because it's not a promise I can keep. On some subconscious level, I was already aware of that.

CHAPTER NINE

KIRA

I'M STANDING HALF AN inch from the foot of his bed. Our bed. The dark bedding is an abyss that's sucking the hope out of my fragile system. The moment I stepped into the room and my high heels sunk into the gold and beige carpet, I sensed doom.

How quickly this situation has flipped on its head. Only this morning, Nicco informed me of this arrangement, and now here I am. My gaze dances across the wardrobe doors on either side of the bed. The large dark oak doors make me take a step away from the bed; they dominate the room. I don't know why the wardrobes seem so frightening. This room would be a nightmare to a child. What boogeymen hide in those wardrobes? What secrets would pour out if I pulled a door open? Logically, I would be faced with Jason's clothing, but my frazzled mind is conjuring childlike nightmares. I spin away from the bed, and the idea of monsters in wait gives me pause.

Jason has a look in his eye I can't decipher. He blinks and enters my personal space while slowly taking off his black suit jacket.

"Tell me about yourself."

What a loaded question. Isn't this part of getting to know each other? That question should be a normal part of this arrangement. Only Jason has broken our previous arrangement. What would stop him from breaking more rules? I fold my arms across my chest as I think of giving him an heir and how much that excites me. I push my mind past that fact and go back to my childhood.

"When I was five, my parents took me out of Russia, and we settled in Ireland. I've been here ever since." Jason shoves his hands into his black trouser pockets. He hasn't stepped away from me, and I hate that the bed is at my back. I'm boxed in, and everything is making me think of being physical with this man when I should be thinking of how to get away from him.

"That must have been a hard transition," Jason says.

"I was homeschooled in Russia and also here, so not much changed for me. As I said, I was five, so I knew no different," I answer quickly. In truth, I hated Ireland. As I grew, I wanted more from life, but each time I sought anything that would give me experience, I was told no. That my safety was paramount.

"Hmm," Jason says before he grips the green tie's knot and pulls it harshly. Once the loop is wide enough, he pulls the tie over his head and drops it on the bed. The color is almost the same as his eyes.

Once again, I'm very aware of how close we're standing. My gaze diverts to the circular Persian rug I'm standing on. I'm not one to hide from people. I've always thought I should never show fear. I raise my head, refusing to show any weakness. If a man sees a weakness in a woman, they will use it and twist it until she's a shell of her former self. Anger tightens my jaw.

Jason removes the gold cufflinks from his shirt sleeves. His closeness, I sense, is an intimidation tactic, one that I refuse to allow to affect me.

"Who is the security you brought with you?" Jason rolls the cufflinks from one hand to the other. His gaze keeps dipping to my chest. I tighten my arms, and his eyes spark with a hidden grin.

"Lev. He's my personal bodyguard and also my cousin."

Jason stops rolling the cufflinks and raises a brow. "How interesting."

"Is it?" I ask quickly, wondering what part of that is interesting. I'm also wondering why he's asking me so many questions. In three weeks, I will have left this place and him behind. Maybe he doesn't know that yet. Maybe he's trying to get to know me. That thought frightens me more than it should.

His hidden grin comes out of hiding and lifts his lip. "What happened to your maid?"

I let my hands drop to my side, and I'm unsure of how to proceed. "She was punished." I frown. For something she didn't do. For something I did. For not wanting to give you a child. What would he do if he knew?

Jason finally steps away but doesn't go far. He's still at arm's length from me. He drops the cufflinks onto the bed alongside the tie before he starts to unbutton his white shirt. My stomach quivers with unease, and it takes all my strength to hold his stare. His green eyes blaze as they dip to my chest. I want to tighten my arms over myself, but I remain still.

Jason shrugs out of his shirt, and I try not to take in his wide, tanned chest or six-pack. The *V* dips below his trousers, a small line of hair disappears, and my heart jumps too many times. He takes a step back toward me. "Who punished her?"

He's too close. The scent of his cologne tantalizes my senses, and once again, I'm thrown into the knowledge that I'm supposed to produce an heir for this man. My mind flashes to an image of Jason on top of me, and I quickly look away from all that tanned flesh. He shouldn't affect me like this. No one ever has. I've been around men my whole life, men who were built like soldiers, men who towered over me, but none of them interested me. So why is my body responding so quickly to Jason? Is it because he was meant to be my husband?

My chest tightens. My brother will return for me in three weeks, and then what will happen? I'm tempted to reach up and rub the ache between my breasts. "Why am I here?" I ask.

"Did they not tell you? We are going to marry." Jason's tone drops a few degrees, and the cold snakes around my spine and travels up until the hairs rise on the nape of my neck.

"I mean, in your room? I was promised privacy."

"I changed my mind." His answer terrifies me. It means his word has no value. He could continue to change his mind about anything or everything. Where does that leave me?

He turns his back on me, and all my thoughts scatter as I take in his damaged back. Scars have twisted the skin across his shoulders. It looks like it was burnt severely. My gaze travels down and stops at a large white scar that disappears around his side. Lots of small scars crisscross his back.

"What happened to you?" I ask.

"My father taught me life lessons." His words carry no emotion as he gathers up his cufflinks and tie from the bed. His emerald green eyes are devoid of emotion, too. "I'm going to shower."

I'm frozen as my mind conjures images of water cascading down Jason's perfect body; even the imperfect part of him is perfect. I squeeze my eyes closed the minute he leaves, trying to gather my wits. His own father did that to his back, yet Jason doesn't seem to care. Is hurting one another standard practice here? My heart starts to hammer like it's just realized that this situation isn't good.

The black teardrop chandelier that's lit above my head has me looking up. A slight breeze coming from an open window makes the chandelier shift slightly, and the lights dance around the space. I glance around the room and pause before taking a quick peek at the bathroom door. It's shut and I use the moment and walk to the mahogany writing desk, where a stack of mail sits, along with a silver letter opener. I pick up the sharp object that could be used as a weapon. If he's used to violence, he might be violent with me. I have to find a way to protect myself. My brain begs me to put it back, but I quickly go to the bed and stuff it under the pillow. I hope I've picked the right side of the bed.

A shiver flashes across my flesh, reminding me that I'm still standing in wet clothes. My top has patches that are transparent, showing off my black bra and chest. That's what he kept looking at. I grab the bag I brought with me and open it on the bed. I keep looking at the bathroom door, expecting him to be standing there in a towel. My face burns, and my hands shake. I focus on getting clothes out of the bag, only to curse myself for not looking through the other bags. This one is filled with my bedtime clothes. I take out a pair of black silk shorts and a matching tank top. These are better than all the knee-length nightgowns. My fingers stall on a fresh bra, but I wouldn't dare chance removing the wet one in case he returns.

I don't look away from the door as I strip quickly and pull on the dry clothes. I catch a glimpse of myself in the free-standing mirror and consider putting the wet clothes back on. So much of my skin is on display. My fist tightens around the wet top, and my mother's soothing song wafts through my mind. Instead of calming me, all I can think about is Angel and if Jason really sent for a doctor. Or if my friend is still lying in pain with Lev tending to her. That's the only consolation: Lev cares for Angel, so he won't leave my friend on her own.

The handle of the bathroom door rattles, and I brace myself as Jason steps out. Relief that he's clothed lasts all of two seconds. He's drying his dark hair but stops when he sees me. He slowly takes the white towel away from his head, and his gaze drags across my flesh. He raises a brow.

"I need my other bags. I brought the wrong clothes with me."

He continues to pour his attention over my flesh, and I hate how he makes me feel like a woman. Like someone who should be desired.

"No. I already gave you a chance, and you didn't take it." His offhand comment has him returning to drying his hair. He continues to walk toward me until we're toe to toe.

"What am I supposed to do? Wear my pajamas day and night?"

"That's not a bad idea." His words startle me because they're low, and I hear the desire in them. I inhale his freshly washed body and some undercurrent of cologne. When he licks his bottom lip, fear has me taking several steps away from him. Before he can react to me retreating from him, his phone rings from one of the many dressers around his suite.

He walks to the device and turns so he can observe me even as he takes the call. "Yes." His green eyes darken along with his features, and I have this primal urge to run. Run to the bed, run to the letter opener I can use to defend myself. Something is very wrong. Something is making Jason give me a murderous stare.

When he gets off the phone, I'm moving to the pillow. I'm moving toward the makeshift weapon.

CHAPTER TEN

JASON

WILLIAM IS OUT OF surgery and awake, but he has no memory of what happened. We have no idea if this is permanent or temporary memory loss. He knew who Aidan was, but he didn't recognize Alex. I slip the phone into my pocket, and it's like the universe has placed a solution in front of me.

Kira.

She knows more. She's trying to distract me with her body. Why would she pick such flimsy clothing? Her brown eyes widen, and she spins.

My instincts kick in. She's running, so I give chase and spring for her. It's an automatic reaction. I don't expect her to dodge my arm or dive for the bed. Did she really think she could get away from me by climbing onto the bed? Her hand slips under the pillow, and instead of getting up on the duvet, she pivots; the light catches the silver letter opener she holds steadily between her pretty fingers.

"None of this was part of the agreement. I was meant to stay in my own quarters." Her chin juts out, and I take a step toward her. I'm expecting her fingers to tremble, her gaze to grow unsteady, but neither happens.

"One more step, and I'll stab you."

I laugh at her fiery words. She's brave, I'll give her that. But she needs to learn I'm not one of her brother's foot soldiers. I clear the distance. She reacts. I sense the slice more than feel it. All the training with Frank didn't make me immune to pain; it just gave me a far higher tolerance. But I know she's stabbed me from the look of shock on her face, how her mouth forms a small *O*. A vein on her forehead becomes more prominent. Yet she still doesn't drop the bloody blade. Her fingers tighten around the letter opener, and I'm over my shock that she stabbed me and starting to see Kira for what she is.

I reach out. She jerks the knife, but I twist sideways, and the blade strikes the air. I don't allow her to recover but smoothly grip her wrists, applying pressure to the bone. She screams and her fingers unlock. The letter opener clatters to the floor, and I drag her into me.

"You stabbed me." It's not a question.

"Take your hands off me." She's afraid now and she should be.

I grin and pretend to think about it. "Okay." I release her and before she has a moment to even think of her next move, I push her small frame until she lands heavily onto the bed.

Her bewilderment turns to panic as I climb on top of her. She tries to spin under me, but I squeeze my thighs on either side of her waist and grip her arms. It's easy to pin her to the bed. She's still struggling, and I watch her as she tries to bite my wrists while she wriggles savagely under me. Her movements have my cock growing, and I don't know when she feels my erection, but she stops abruptly. Her focus is solely on me, but I can't see her face clearly through the long blonde strands that coat her cheeks.

She tries to blow the hair off her face; the strands lift before falling back into place.

"Do you make a habit of stabbing people?" I ask.

Kira continues to try to blow the hair out of her face.

I grip both her wrists with one hand and push the hair off her face. Her cheeks are flushed, her eyes wild, and I grin down at her.

"I was protecting myself." Her gaze shoots around the room before returning to me. She struggles to get her breathing under control.

"Protecting yourself?" I hadn't done anything to warrant her to protect herself. The warm wetness has me glancing down at my white shirt, which is soaking up the blood. When I look back at Kira, she's staring wide-eyed at the blood.

"I thought you were going to hurt me."

"Why would you think that?"

She swallows before licking her lips. The action isn't meant to be sexual, but with the sheen of her lips, my cock throbs. My reaction to Kira has me releasing her wrists and climbing off her. When I get to the end of the bed, she still lies where I left her, staring up at the ceiling.

"It was the look in your eyes," she answers as I clear the doorway and enter the bathroom. I keep a stash of bandages and sterile wipes under the sink. Peeling off my shirt, I take a look at her handiwork in the mirror. She put a lot of force behind the letter opener. The cut is more than a flesh wound; the amount of blood that oozes is a testament to that. Running the tap, I wash as much blood off as I can before ripping open a pack of sterile wipes. My actions are quick and precise, and suddenly I'm back in the basement, staring at my seventeen-year-old self in the broken mirror.

The cut on my face continues to bleed, and for the first time, I don't clean the wound immediately. I'm assessing everything. I don't want to clean the wound in case it takes the memory of Frank inflicting the pain on me away. This is the first time he has marked my face. I don't know why. I lean closer to the mirror. The cut is under my left eye. It's not deep, but it's long. It will take time to heal. My body heals at a quick rate, but the softness of the skin under the eye tells me this will be my longest recovery. So why place a mark where everyone can see it?

The creak above me has me wiping the blood away just as the basement door opens. Each step tells me how much weight presses down on the steps. The wood groans under Frank's heavy boots. When he clears the last step, he walks up to me. A part of me wants to turn around so my back isn't to him. My brain is screaming that he's a threat, but I push past that barrier of fear and continue cleaning my face.

"Did it hurt?" Frank asks, and his fingers tap the buckle of the belt he used to hit me with.

I honestly would have expected far more damage. "No," I answer. I'm aware I've been hurt. My brain fired the warning, but once I moved past that initial spark, I could dampen my emotions.

"Good. You're getting stronger."

I don't bandage the wound. It's in an awkward place. "What do I tell people?" I ask, facing Frank.

His smile is slow and deliberate. "Phase two of your training. How good of a liar are you?"

I don't think it's a question. "I had a run-in with a boy at school." I shrug. That shouldn't be hard.

"You aren't trying to convince me. Convince your family."

I blink at myself in the mirror before turning away and reentering the bedroom. Kira is no longer where I left her. She's standing closer to the window. I walk around the bed and notice the letter opener is missing.

I hold out my hand. "Give it to me."

Kira folds her arms. I could take the letter opener easily. I can't see it, but I could spend some time searching her for the weapon. "Tell me about your brother."

That's what's most important here—finding out everything I can about the Negotiator to see if I can save my family from the clutches of the Bratva.

Kira doesn't answer.

I take a step toward her. Her gaze travels across my bare chest and down to my bandaged torso. My scars are on full display, but I've never hidden them. My brothers think it was in the line of duty that I received each one. Women are either horrified or find them sexy. Either way, I don't give a shit. I've never cared about anyone but my family.

"Did your brother hurt your maid?" I ask, going down a different path, one where I can show her compassion.

"Yes." Kira unfolds her arms.

I take another step toward her. "Why?"

"She broke the rules," Kira answers, but there is depth to her words.

An urge to hurt him has me stopping, and I suppress that feeling the same way I do pain. She is the enemy. Protecting her isn't necessary. I glance down at my bandage.

"What rule did she break?" I ask.

She's thinking about her answer and that urge to protect her comes back stronger, and I don't like it at all.

"Whatever she did, she must have deserved it," I say, before turning my back on Kira. I don't look at her to gauge her reaction. I'm sure she's sharpening her letter opener with outrage. I would never harm a woman, but Kira doesn't know that.

I retrieve a fresh white shirt and re-dress. I take my time placing my cufflinks on my shirt. Only when I finish with my tie, do I look at Kira. She has her back to me. Her arms are folded again, and I allow myself a moment to appreciate her long creamy legs and round ass. Her hair spills down her back, and when she senses me watching her, she glances over her shoulder. She holds my stare, and I'm the one to look away.

I leave the room and make my way to my office. The Negotiator sent over documents for me to sign that allow Kira out of this marriage. I, of course, had agreed. Her being here for three weeks is politics. A time period I will surely use to my advantage.

I'm not off to a great start. I'm sure Zach would piss himself laughing at the idea of Kira stabbing me. She's brave—that much I'll give her.

I enter the office, and true to his word, a stack of papers sits on the tray of the fax machine. The light beeps rapidly, telling me I have a new fax.

I reach for the documents, which are thicker than I thought they would be. I flick through them and see the line for me to sign Kira back over to her brother. A set of new documents starts halfway through the pile. He hadn't mentioned a second contract, and I flick through it only to see Kira's signature at the end. I assume it's for the same thing, to end our arrangement. I take a quick glance at the lines above her signature, and my gut curls.

This is a petition to the Bratva to bring back an old law of allowing siblings to have pure-blooded children. I'm staring at the large section of writing, trying to take in what I'm reading. Kira wants to fuck her brother. I keep rereading the section. The girl upstairs in my room doesn't seem touched in any way. I'm sickened.

I have an urge to get her out of my home, but I can't do that. Instead, I take that need to remove the filth from my home by making my way to the west wing. The maid is still in the bed, the bodyguard still seated beside her. The moment I enter, he reaches for his jacket, which sits on top of a bedside table. I have no doubt his gun sits under his jacket.

"Is she awake?" I ask.

He shakes his head. "No, the doctor sedated her."

"Leave my home," I order.

He stands, his gaze darting to the maid. "Who will take care of Angel?"

"Since when do I have to answer the question of a lowlife like you?" I take a step closer. I want him to react. I need to release the disgust at the thought of Kira sleeping with her brother out of my system.

He picks up his jacket, revealing his gun. Once his jacket is on, he places the gun in the band of his trousers.

He pauses a foot from me, his jaw clenched. I want him to say something, but he shoulders past me. The minute the front door closes, I take out my phone and make a call.

"I have a guest in the west wing I want removed," I order without saying anything else. I end the call and glare down at the dead weight that will soon be taken care of.

The only good that has come out of this is the knowledge that Kira is far closer to her brother than anyone could ever have imagined.

I have to push past my disgust and use this to my advantage.

CHAPTER ELEVEN

KIRA

"*Y*ou know, we have *a thing called a hairbrush. You might try using it." Nicco laughs. Tears run from my mother's eyes. I don't know why I don't intervene. Maybe I hate the tears as much as I hate Nicco's taunting.*

I try to protect myself from Nicco by remaining silent. Loading my plate with vegetables and small salad potatoes is what I focus on.

"Or why don't you try a shower?" he continues, his voice tinged with anger and laughter. I'm not sure which one wins out. "Or just a quick wash."

My hand stalls in midair, and I can't help but look at her.

I wonder if Nicco ever really loved our mother. Could you love someone and threaten them with such cruelty? She's like a damaged porcelain doll. Her beauty has always been remarked on, but the cracks that race across my mother's gaze, and deeper, are unfixable.

"Stop it," I grind out.

Nicco turns to me, a laugh seeping from his lips. "Come now, sister, can't you see our mother needs a shower?"

Tears spill down my mother's cheeks. Her gaze is downcast, her hands folded on the table. The dirt under her nails makes the food on my plate undesirable. She always painted her nails a deep red, but not anymore.

"Can't you see you're hurting her?" I bite back.

Nicco wipes the corner of his mouth with a napkin, his smile evaporating. The atmosphere grows so heavy it's almost choking me.

"Can't you see she's gone?" His roar lifts me from my seat. Hairs rise along my arms when Nicco's fist crashes down on his plate, sending food across the table. His face grows red. "Can't you see we don't have a mother? She's useless, docile. She's better off dead."

I suck in a lungful of air and shake my head. "Don't say that."

Nicco's smile twists his lips. "I know deep down you want her to die too." He blinks and tears spill down his face before he wipes them away roughly and faces Mother. "We all wish you had died." He says it so offhandedly that something cracks and twists inside me.

Maybe it's because he's right. There have been times I've thought her death would be easier to handle than this. Guilt restricts my throat.

My mother glares at Nicco, and it's the most life I've ever seen in her eyes. Did Nicco break through some barrier? I'm gripping the edge of the table in anticipation.

My mother blinks, reaches for the bowl of potatoes, picks one up, and throws it at Nicco, clobbering him in the eye.

His shout of anger and how he launches out of his chair should have her running, but she sits smiling at my brother like a demented woman.

Nicco picks up his napkin and wipes the broken spud from his face. I'm waiting for the blowback of her actions. Instead, the napkin flutters to the table. Nicco straightens his gold and black jacket and marches from the dining room. I'm staring at my mother, waiting for her to say something. She starts to fill her plate with a disturbing smile on her face.

I'm so beat down when she starts singing "Eensy Weensy Spider." The song she had made up for Nicco and me, which once brought us comfort and joy, only left pain and a longing for a mother who would never return.

I'm pulled from the vicious memory and the reminder of how Nicco uses his words as weapons, along with his fists, when Jason lugs in my suitcases, practically dropping them at my feet before he straightens.

"Get dressed. We're going out."

I'm still all twisted and emotional from the memory of my mother. I don't move, and Jason doesn't like that. I'm not dancing to his tune.

"If you don't start getting dressed, I'll dress you, Kira. Don't think I won't."

Somehow, I believe him. But I also have to make my mark here too. "Do you think that's wise?" I ask.

He towers over me, folds his large arms, and dips his head. Everything about him is designed to be intimidating. I want to tell him too bad. I've been around intimidating men my whole life. I've had to learn how to navigate my way around them.

He's waiting for me to explain, so I do. "Since your brother was attacked?" Wasn't he all worked up about his brother all day? Going out for dinner is hardly appropriate.

"That's exactly why we are going out. Now get dressed." He dismisses me, and I can't figure him out. I stabbed him, and he hasn't hurt me? Why not? I remind myself there's more than one way to hurt someone, and I haven't even been here twenty-four hours.

Give him time, Kira. The thought has me kneeling down and opening a suitcase to distract myself from my thoughts.

The second suitcase holds my dresses and high heels. I remove the high-neck red dress, which was made for me by some famous Italian designer. They all seem to be famous nowadays. Jason disappears into the bathroom, and I can sense his impatience to get going. I draw the red dress up my body before pulling the short sleeves on, I remove my pajama top. Once the dress is in place, I shimmy out of my shorts. The dress is fitted and stops just below the knee. I pull up the zipper as far as I can, but this requires help. Angel would normally help me with getting ready. My chest tightens when I think of my friend.

I inhale a quick breath and exhale, getting ready to ask Jason to zip me up the rest of the way, but I don't have it in me to ask for help, especially not from him. So I put on the red high-heeled shoes that strap at the ankle. Running my fingers through my hair is tough with all the tangles. That's how Jason finds me: wrestling with my hair. He's freshly shaven, and I hate how my body reacts to him. I stop fighting with my hair and try to stem the panic that rises inside me. I turn my back on Jason to give myself a moment.

"Could you zip me up?" My voice is strong, but that's not how I feel. Around Jason, I've never felt so weak. Even weaker than when I'm around Nicco. It's like Jason melts something inside me. With Nicco, I must remain quiet, obedient, but inside I'm seething.

I hold the air in my lungs as his knuckles graze my bare skin. Time drags and when his hands rest on my shoulders, I try not to tense.

His hands tighten for a brief moment before he removes them. I think he's gone when he grabs my hair from my shoulder and places it down my back.

"Let's go." I turn just as he walks to the door, and I follow him out of the room and all the way outside without a word.

I have no idea what to make of this dinner. We don't have a driver or any security with us, and that in itself is foreign to me. I'm reaching for the back door of the car when Jason stops me. "You're sitting up front."

I'm still gripping the handle of the back door.

"Unless I scare you?" He grins at me from across the hood of the car. I release the handle and reach for the passenger door as Jason disappears inside.

"What a perfect gentleman," I say once I'm seated up front.

His jaw tenses. "I'd hardly call you a lady." He looks me dead in the eye as he insults me. "I've never met one who would stab me."

Embarrassment scorches my cheeks. He's right. I've never harmed anyone in my life, but I had really thought he was going to hurt me. There was a look of madness in his eyes that set off every alarm in my body.

I secure my seat belt as Jason starts to drive. "Why have you no security?" I don't ask for Lev, as I don't want him to be taken away from Angel.

"You don't think I can protect you?" he fires back.

I do. I don't doubt he can protect me. Jason seems very much in control of everything. "I've never been anywhere without security. It's just odd," I answer.

Jason doesn't respond; instead, he turns up the radio. Some pop singer sings about a party she woke up from. Another thing I can add to the long list of things I was never allowed. Pop music was banned in our home. My father believed it was a bad influence on me. I'm sure Nicco could listen to whatever he wanted to, but not me.

The hotel we stop at is buzzing with people coming and going. It almost appears as if the restaurant has poured out into the street. "Is there something going on?" I ask.

"They know we're coming," Jason answers when we pull up at the front of the hotel, blocking the row of cars that quickly gather behind us. "Stay where you are," Jason says without looking at me. He gets out and cameras flash. He doesn't smile but buttons up his suit jacket as he makes his way around to my side of the car.

He opens the door for me like the gentleman that he wasn't when no one was watching. If I could, I'd stay in the car. But the honking of the horns and the darkness in Jason's gaze have me taking his hand and allowing him to help me out of the car.

"All of a sudden, you're a gentleman?" I say with a smile.

"All of a sudden, you'll be looked at as a lady."

I want to pull my hand out of his, but his fingers tighten painfully, and I have no choice but to allow Jason to hold my hand as we make it to the sidewalk. The car is driven away, the traffic freed up as we step onto the red carpet. I have no makeup on, but I smile like I've just been pampered by a team of hair stylists and makeup artists.

We pass the cameras, and I'm assuming he rang to let them know we were coming. He really wants everyone to know he's out and about. We're greeted the moment we arrive, and under any other circumstance, I'd drink up every single sip of this experience, but fear and uncertainty have me frazzled. We are seated at a large round table in the center of the room. The table is large enough for ten people, so with just Jason and me, I feel very much on display. Once again, that's exactly what he must want. Jason finally lets my fingers go and pulls out my chair for me. I mumble a thank-you and sit down. Jason removes his suit jacket, and I'm aware how he doesn't show any signs of his injury. My stabbing him must have hurt, but he didn't react. I'm staring at him far so long that when his lip drags up, I realize my mistake.

"I didn't know you were the sister of the Negotiator," Jason says while he smiles at a man and woman across the room who haven't taken their eyes off us. A waiter arrives and places a bottle of wine onto the table. Jason nods and our glasses are filled. The waiter leaves.

"I am." Not many people know who the Negotiator is, not until you meet him. But his actual name isn't public knowledge.

"Is he negotiating for another suitor for you?" he asks, and I sense my answer means something.

I glance at Jason. He waves at a group of businessmen who raise their glasses in his direction.

"I'm not sure," I answer as my stomach curls with the reality of Nicco's plans. I can't allow my mind to go there. Right now, I don't have a solution. I already have a problem in front of me, and I need to get out of this as quickly as possible.

"I got my papers to sign." Jason faces me for the first time.

I pick up my glass and take a sip.

Jason leans closer, and the scent of his cologne has me gripping the glass a bit tighter between my fingers.

"Just to let you know, I signed them, so, in three weeks, you're free."

I still don't know why it's three weeks, but maybe it takes that long for them to look over the paperwork. I have no idea what reaction he's expecting from me, but I don't get to respond, thankfully, as a lady in a navy floral dress and three young men stop at our table. All siblings. The curly red hair is a dead giveaway.

"My boys are obsessed with you. Could we"—the woman glances at me apologetically—"just get a quick picture?"

The three boys in question look starstruck. They haven't taken their eyes off Jason. Another man approaches our table. He doesn't appear happy.

"I do apologize, Mr. Murphy. I'll deal with this."

Jason rises. "It's fine." He waves off the man, who must be the restaurant manager.

"Which one of you is a wing forward?" Jason asks the three boys, and the manger takes his leave.

Before they answer, the one in the center smiles with pride. His face heats, and he puffs out his chest. "Me, sir."

Jason smiles at the boy.

"Just like you." The boy wrestles with his smile, but it's no use. He's too starstruck.

I had no idea what sport they're referring to. I assume football. But all of this is like a whirlwind as Jason smiles with the boys and signs one of their arms. The mother thanks Jason before thanking me, too. I have no idea what to say, so I smile. Jason sits back down, and I realize something that nearly chokes me up.

He signed me back to Nicco.

It shouldn't matter. I don't know him. But once again, I'm disposable.

It shouldn't hurt this much, so why does it?

CHAPTER TWELVE

JASON

K IRA'S GAZE HOLDS so much pain, and I want to know why. What has made her look at me like something has scorched her skin? I know all about flesh being heated so much that it melts and disfigures. I shrug my shoulders like I can banish the memory. Frank didn't just use the cigarette lighter from the car. As I aged, he grew more creative using live electrical wires down in the basement. That was a new kind of pain.

My appetite disappears. Each serving is cleared away with barely any food touched.

"Let's go." I wipe my mouth with a napkin and rise. Kira hesitates, with a question in her gaze. I'm sure she's wondering why I want to leave now. I hate the look in her eyes, and most of all, I detest how it makes me feel. Like I want to chase all the darkness away. I've known her less than twenty-four hours, but I recognize the haunted look in her eyes all too well.

She gets up, and I make my way to the back of the restaurant. I glance over my shoulder to make sure Kira is following me. We slip through the kitchen, and no one remarks on our presence. The steam, heat, and noise soon grow distant as we enter a small hallway before I pull open a large metal door that leads down into the basement, where my car will be waiting. I like to be seen arriving but not leaving.

I've taken three steps when I pause and notice that Kira isn't moving. "What's the problem?" I ask.

She's holding the door open with her foot while she folds her arms. "What's down there?" She looks over my shoulder.

I should tell her it's my car, but instead, I climb the three steps back to Kira. "Don't you trust me?" I ask with a grin.

Of course she doesn't trust me; I don't trust her. She unfolds her arms and releases the door with her foot, almost plunging us into darkness. The faint wall lights illuminate her face, and I don't think she expected how intimate she's made the space around us. Her lids flutter closed, and she takes the one step she can until I block her. When I don't move, she looks up at me. "Excuse me."

I've heard of people disliking someone just by the look of them. I've killed people at our first meeting. I've loathed people just from hearing a sentence from their mouths. But I've never liked anyone instantly. I can't put my finger on what it is about Kira that draws me in. I keep thinking it's the despair I see at times in her gaze, but it's deeper, and superficial too. She's stunning, though it shouldn't affect my judgment.

She hasn't so much as blinked as she gazes up at me. I'm not sure what she's waiting for, for me to move or say something. I do neither. Instead, I reach out and take her face in my hands. Her eyes widen, her mouth opens slightly, and I press my lips against hers. She forces her lips together like that could deter me. I'd laugh, only my cock demands to be buried inside her. I'm overcome with a need for Kira, and when I grip the back of her head and press firmly against her, she relents and her lips part. Her mouth is warm and sweet, and the aftertaste of wine fills my mouth as I run my tongue along hers. When she groans, I spin us so she's against the wall.

My body covers her small frame, and I think about how I had zipped up her dress before dinner and how easily I could zip it down. My fingers find the zipper, and she groans as I grip it. The moment I pull it down, she freezes under my mouth.

"Stop." Her one word has me instantly stepping away from her. I can't really go far, but I leave the width of the step between us.

"Why? Because you want to fuck your brother?" I've said it. The truth is that I can't wrap my head around the idea. I should be constantly disgusted by Kira, but the thought of anyone else touching her has me craving to kill them.

"Excuse me?" She hasn't moved from the wall. Under the light, she's a fucking picture. One I'm tempted to tear down; I remove the distance between us.

"Don't insult me, Kira. Your brother was kind enough to send me the petition to bring back the old law to allow siblings to marry, and your signature is on the bottom, so don't deny it."

She's shaking her head when she suddenly stops. Her fingers touch her lips, and I want to kiss her again.

"He had me sign a document after he beat Angel. I was so focused on her that I didn't even read what I signed." She looks at me with horror in her gaze. She folds her arms and turns to the side so I can't see her clearly.

"You expect me to believe that?" I ask, wanting to force her to look at me.

"I don't care what you believe." She sounds distant, and I don't block her this time as she hurries down the steps. Either she's an exceptional actress or her brother really had tricked her. I clear the steps and catch up with Kira quickly. I unlock the car. The lights flash and Kira doesn't slow her pace but gets in. She closes the door and focuses on putting on her seat belt. The moment I slide into the driver's seat, she looks at me.

"I want to see Angel."

I press the button to start the car. "No." I start to drive.

"Is she okay?"

I take the bend out of the underground parking garage before emerging onto the road. "Why don't you answer my question first?" The road has barely any traffic, and I slip in behind a silver Mercedes. "Tell me something about your brother."

"Like what?" she grits out.

"Just tell me something, and I'll let you know if it's worth me giving you information about Angel."

"You are a bastard."

I laugh at her anger. "That's about me, not your brother." I've begun to think she won't talk, as we've made it halfway back to the house before she finally speaks.

"Nicco is very sensitive about our mother." The words come in jagged pieces, like she can't bear to say them.

I laugh again. "Aren't we all? That means fuck all to me, Kira."

"What do you want to know?"

"Something important. Something maybe others wouldn't know." I slow down and turn on my turn signal, waiting for a gap in the traffic. It doesn't take long before I turn onto the secondary road that leads to my home.

She's breathing heavily beside me. "Did you take a look at Angel's back?"

"No," I answer before peeking at Kira. She's facing me, her features tight with anger, fear clouding her gaze.

"He beat her with his cane. He tore into her flesh like she was nothing. So, what do you think he will do to me?"

A buzzing starts along my arms and spreads across my chest at the idea of Nicco hurting her. I press the handbrake, and the car jackknifes in the middle of the road as I spin the steering wheel. Kira screams as I bring the car to a grinding halt. I was once the driver for the lads, so my control over a vehicle is next to none.

Once the car has settled, I unbuckle my belt and lean into Kira so she can really hear me. "I don't give a fuck what he does to you, even if he fucks you." The moment the words leave my lips, I feel like the bastard she's accusing me of being.

But I need something to save my family. I can see it clearly now that Kira is as much of a victim of her brother's brutality as my family is. But since when did she become *my* fucking problem?

"You want to know how your friend is, you tell me something right now."

Her chest rises and falls rapidly. She knows something. Her gaze shoots to the left, and she shakes her head like she's fighting with herself.

"Now, Kira," I say.

She refocuses, and I want this so badly. I need something about that son of a bitch.

Her brows drag close together, and I know the moment she's about to tell me something; I can see the defeat in her gaze. "He has a son," she whispers, and I sit back, allowing that knowledge to sink in.

It's something I wasn't aware of. Now I know who the Negotiator is, and I also know he has a son.

"Does he live with him?" I ask.

Kira's gaze sharpens. "Where is Angel?" She's firm now, her barriers rising again. But I'm willing to work with what I have.

"I need to make a call." I slip my phone out of my pocket. I need some distance from Kira, so I get out of the car and close the door to make the call.

"Zach, the girl who was removed from my home—where was she taken?" I ask. I just hope they haven't dumped her at the bottom of a lake.

"I told Noah to get rid of her."

Shit.

"Hold on, speak of the devil," Zach says before he calls Noah.

I glance in at Kira to find her glaring at me.

Zach turns our call into a three way call with Noah and relays the question.

"I left her at Columbus Hospital. She was in a bad way, and I wasn't sure what else to do with her."

Noah and his soft heart. For once, I'm happy with the decision he made. "Columbus Hospital, is that close to the old convent?" I ask.

"Yes, about one hundred meters away."

I turn back to the car. "Thanks, Noah." I end the call.

Kira's looking at me, and there's something strange in her gaze. I reach for the door handle, but as I do, she hits the lock, stopping me from getting into the car.

CHAPTER THIRTEEN

KIRA

S HOCK SHAKES THE BARRIERS that are holding me together. I'm not much of a liar, but I just lied about my brother. He doesn't have a son. Jason paces, pauses, glances in at me before he turns away. Everything in me quivers. When he finds out I lied, what will he do? It was a desperate moment. I needed to know where Angel was. I should have never left her, though rationally, I know staying wasn't an option. Pride swells once more at how easily Jason bought my lie. For a man who sees through so much, how did he not see through that? I take another look at him before I open the glove compartment of the car. I shove the manual aside, searching for a weapon, but come up empty. I'm ready to close the compartment when I hear Jason mention Columbus Hospital.

I know that hospital. My knee connects with the glove compartment door, flipping it closed. I lean over and hit the locks just as Jason reaches to open the door. His brows drag down for a split second before his eyes widen.

"Open the door." His warning is low and skitters fear across my flesh. It's a warning I should heed. Getting a chance like this again isn't likely. Women who are part of the Bratva aren't allowed to drive; no one ever taught us. I slip into the driver's seat and try to ignore the big, overbearing, angry man who's knocking on the window. His knuckles bang along the glass, and I finally glance at him.

"Open the door," he warns again.

I was one of the lucky ones. My mother took me out at night and taught me how to drive, just like her mother had taught her. I push my foot down on the accelerator while pressing the start button, and the engine purrs to life.

I want to smile at Jason in victory like they do in the movies, but this isn't a movie, and there is nothing to smile about as he gives me a murderous glare.

It takes all my strength to look away and shift the car into gear. Jason doesn't try to stop me, not that he could. As I pull away with a pounding heart and trembling hands, I glance in the rearview mirror to see him watching me. His large hand curls around the phone pressed to his ear. My time is limited. I push down on the accelerator and tear toward Columbus Hospital.

My mother told me a few things in her time of sanity. One, she always said to never tell a man everything. I remember how she had leaned in and whispered, "That includes your father, brother, uncles, and even your husband."

She had advised me to always have a backup plan—a secure amount of money and a getaway car in a location that only we knew. She told me where the location was, and at night, she would teach me to drive. I never thought too deeply about what she was sharing with me. I was more thrilled that my mother was spending time with me.

I never thanked her.

The sign posted for the hospital has both dread and excitement fluttering and battling in the pit of my stomach. I reluctantly slow the vehicle and look in the rearview mirror. There are many cars behind me, but I'm searching for a black SUV. That's what most of the security drive. I don't spot any men in black suits. But I'm also aware of how limited my time is. I park in the first spot I see and get out of the car. I take another glance around me before I cross the parking lot and make my way into the hospital. The lady behind the reception desk gives me a warm smile. I slow my steps and relax my shoulders.

"I'm here to see a friend who was brought in a few hours ago," I say. I'm tempted to peek behind me as the cold air brushes along my neck from the breeze the automatic doors allow in. I focus on the lady no matter how much my instincts beg me to check behind me.

"What's your friend's name, sweetheart?" the lady asks, her fingers poised over a slim silver keyboard.

"Angel, Angel Zolin." The breeze brushes the back of my neck again, and this time I look as the receptionist searches for Angel's name.

An elderly man wearing a large brown knit cardigan walks painfully slow toward us.

"Room number thirty-four on the third floor." She delivers her words with a smile.

"Thank you." I walk around the desk.

"How can I help you?" The receptionist's voice follows me as I push the door open and enter a busy corridor. People mill about, all with a purpose. I stop at a row of elevators and wait for the doors to open. I end up riding to the third floor with a woman and her crying newborn.

The lady cradles the child so carefully to her chest. She glances at me with tired eyes and a hopeful smile. "We just found out she's lactose intolerant. The poor thing is in pain."

I nod. "I'm sorry."

The lady coos at the crying baby. "No, it's good. At least I know what's wrong with her."

The doors open, and I get out of the elevator quickly. The woman and crying baby stay in the elevator. Room number thirty-four is close, and I pause outside the door. I want my friend to be okay, but if she's not... I can't finish that thought.

I open the door and enter a half-lit room; the soft beeping of the machines attached to Angel make me step gently on the floor. It's like being in a church. You don't want to make a sound and fracture the silence. I swallow as I take in Angel. Her lids are closed. She looks peaceful. The drip into her arm, I'm sure, is supplying her pain relief.

I walk to her bed and slip into the chair beside her. "Angel." I say her name softly at first. But as silhouettes move behind the white blinds that cover the large window, I speak louder, knowing any one of those silhouettes could be Jason or his guards.

"Angel."

She blinks.

"I don't have much time." I take her hand, and her eyes widen.

"Kira." She sounds panicked, and I shake my head.

"I'm fine, but you're not. I just need you to listen." I speak firmly.

Angel nods.

"I'm going to give you a location where there is a car and enough money to start over. I want you to go there now." I release her hand and walk around to the IV in her arm. Pulling out the line causes Angel to hiss, but I know how short we are on time. "Can you walk?" Can she even sit up?

Angel pushes herself up in the bed; sweat instantly bubbles on her forehead. As she struggles to get out of the bed, I grab a napkin from her food tray and a pen from the file that hangs on the end of her bed frame. I scribble down the address. "You go straight here."

As she stands, I turn and make my way to her. Pushing the napkin into her hand, I want to say something that will cover everything I'm feeling. Like she's my best friend in the world. I'm sorry I got her into this mess. I hope she gets to the location safely. Will I ever see her again? Every question and emotion they evoke wells and pushes to the surface.

A silhouette moves across the blinds. Only, this one seems bigger, darker, even as the person pauses at the door. I know. My time is up.

"I'm sorry" is all I get to say. Angel's large brown eyes waver as the door opens, and I turn to protect her from Jason's hardened gaze.

"I needed to make sure she was okay." I hold my head high like that might stop the anger pouring off Jason. I take a step away from Angel and toward Jason, letting him see that I've surrendered.

He juts his chin in Angel's direction. "Don't you move," he warns her.

Without looking at me, he takes my wrist and spins me so I'm facing Angel. I'm moving past her and toward a brown door. Jason opens the door and doesn't release my arm until we're standing in a tiny bathroom. The space is swallowed up by his sheer size.

"I would have told you where she was." His calm feeds my calm.

"I needed to see her." I don't tell him I gave her my only hope of ever having a life away from him or Nicco. I regret not leaving sooner, but I couldn't run from my home. I couldn't run with the knowledge I had about Nicco.

"You stole my car." Jason takes a step toward me. "You left me in the middle of the road." He ticks off his fingers. "You parked in a handicap spot, and now my car is clamped."

When Jason reaches me, the hairs rise along my arms. What will he do? Whatever he does, I know it's not a fraction of what Angel suffered because of me, so now she will have a second chance. I'm waiting for a slap, a roar.

Warm lips press against mine, large hands touch my shoulders, and it feels like Jason's scent and heat is everywhere, surrounding me, cushioning me, coaxing me into the kiss I lean into and part my lips for. His fingers tighten on my shoulders when I give in.

The screech of an alarm breaks us apart, and I'm left feeling out of sorts, like I'm trying to remember why I'm standing in a bathroom with Jason. Why do my lips buzz from his kiss?

"Stay here," he orders and leaves the bathroom. I lick my lips. My mind is still fuzzy. When I meet my gaze in the bathroom mirror, it breaks the spell that Jason's kiss had cast on me. I walk to the door and nearly slam into Jason.

"She's gone," he says and takes my hand, pulling me gently from the bathroom. I take a glance at the bed Angel had stood beside, and hope surges in my chest.

Out in the hallway is chaos as the alarm continues to wail. I'm sure that is exactly what Angel wanted to cause—confusion and panic as she slipped out of the hospital.

Pain twists in my chest at the idea of losing my friend. Jason continues to walk to the stairwell. He doesn't release my hand as we move with everyone else down the three flights of stairs. Once we're on the ground floor, the staff directs everyone out calmly. There's order to the chaos before us, and when we reach outside, I'm looking for Angel. I'm both happy and sad when I don't see her. Jason doesn't pause; we walk directly to an SUV. The moment we approach, a security man jumps out of the front and opens the door for us to get in. Jason doesn't release my hand, and it forces me to look at him.

He's watching me, inspecting me. I'm waiting for him to ask something, but instead, he releases my hand, and I get into the SUV. Jason slides in beside me, and the door is closed, cutting off the world. It makes the back of the vehicle feel more private and intimate. Jason's thigh brushes mine, and I have no doubt the move is intentional.

"What did you say to Angel?" Jason asks.

"That I was sorry I got her in trouble with my brother." I speak and stare out the window as we pull away from the hospital.

The security in the front passenger seat takes a call, and that cuts Jason off from asking me any more questions. That won't last, but for now, I take the small reprieve.

"What is it, Zach?" Jason speaks to the man in the passenger seat.

Zach turns, and I remember him from Jason's house. He doesn't acknowledge me but exhales loudly. "Frank is at your house."

The look on Jason's face tells me whoever Frank is, this isn't good.

CHAPTER FOURTEEN

JASON

I SHOULDN'T HAVE TO focus on chasing Kira across town or wondering what she told Angel. Why the girl fled when she wasn't in harm's way while staying at the hospital makes no sense to me. So what did Kira tell her?

I'm looking at the woman who has already managed to stab me, steal my car, and take pieces of my control from me in a mere twenty-four hours.

Zach runs his fingers along the side of the seat as he waits for me to react. "Let's see what Frank wants," I say.

But I'm pissed. Pissed that he had the nerve to show up at my home. If anyone sees him, what would they think?

When we reach the house and leave the vehicle, Kira is ready to run, but I grab her wrist, liking the feel of her skin. "We'll talk later."

She nods, and I can't help but admire the look of defiance that shines in her gaze. Fear also dances along the edges, but she's brave. So brave. I release her and watch as she marches up the stairs. She's aware I'm watching her. Her shoulders are hunched, her steps fast, and I like that I have that kind of impact on a woman like Kira.

"You want me to come in?" Zach asks.

I shake my head. "I'm okay. I can handle Frank."

Zach snorts a laugh. "You did shoot him, so I believe you."

I'm not in a laughing mood, so I reach out and pat Zach on the shoulder before making my way inside to the kitchen, where Frank is waiting for me. When I enter, my anger rises. He has his white shirt sleeves rolled up to his elbows. The coffee machine gurgles as he makes himself a coffee. Bewley's biscuits are stacked on a plate. I continued to buy them even after he ran.

"What do you want, Frank?" I ask and try to hide the fact that him being in my kitchen bothers me.

Frank doesn't answer or flinch at my arrival but finishes making his coffee, takes a sip, and exhales loudly in satisfaction.

I unbutton my suit jacket. "I'm tired, so make this quick," I say and press both my palms down on the island. That's what divides Frank and me. One black marble slab.

"Tired? Is the guilt of shooting me keeping you awake?" he teases.

"I'm more worried about my brother."

Frank's fingers tighten on the porcelain mug. He relaxes his hold, smiles, and takes another sip. "Cousin," he reminds me. He likes to remind me of my true place.

"Cousin, brother—it's hard to know what the truth is, Frank." My control is slipping, and Frank isn't enjoying seeing me falter. The corner of his gaze tightens.

"Have I taught you nothing?" He empties his cup before placing it onto the island.

Pain, pain, and more pain. "What do you want?" I ask again.

"I'm sorry about William. I really am, Jason. I know Edward's death affected you boys."

I have no idea if Frank is being sincere or not. He's always been a mind-fuck. "Did you know he was murdered?" I ask.

"Yes. I was looking into his death."

I take my hands off the Island. "You could have told us. It would have made us stronger, more united, if we had searched for Edward's killer together." The boys would have gotten behind Frank. I wouldn't have had to drag them all each step of the way.

"You think the knowledge that their father was murdered, and I got one hundred percent of the company wouldn't have all of them looking at me?" Frank picks up a biscuit and bites half of it.

He's right, everyone would have accused him, and rightfully so. "Did you kill him?" I ask.

Frank smiles, and I have to wait as he finishes the biscuit. "No. I didn't kill my brother."

I hate that I believe him. "So you came here to tell me what?"

Frank rolls down the sleeves of his shirt. "The O'Reagans are out for blood over Warren being shot."

I fold my arms across my chest. "The Bratva did it, so what does it matter?"

Frank stops fixing his shirt, and the boy in me flinches when he narrows his gaze. It's a look he has given me many times before a beating.

I'm not a boy anymore. I hold his stare, and the wolf inside him backs down. "It matters because we need the O'Reagans on our side. As you know, I'm the one that wanted them destroyed. It's not as easy as I thought it would be, and the Bratva has doubled-crossed me." The last part of the sentence is said in a lower tone.

I hold my hand to my ear. "What's that, Frank?" I bark. "I told you this would go wrong."

"I know you did, and now I need your help." Frank asking for help. This is a first.

"I'm meeting with the O'Reagans to see if they will form an alliance. But I can't go alone. They already think I'm in hiding," Frank says.

"Which you are," I remind him.

He dismisses my remark. "They also think Alex leads now."

"Which he does." I run my hand along my jaw.

"They think you shot me," he finishes.

Which I did. I don't say the words out loud.

"If you arrive at the meeting, the rumors will soon disappear."

I laugh. "You really are delusional."

Frank shrugs. "You also need to convince Alex to come with us."

"You can leave now." I've had enough of Frank's bullshit.

"You want your brothers to know that all you have done is lie to them?" Frank asks.

He can't use what he did against me. Yet he does. I'm gripping the collar of his suit jacket. "I never lied," I roar.

Frank smiles, like being in my hands doesn't worry him. "Yes, you did. Does Aidan know he's not your brother?"

Frank says the truth out loud, and it's too much, and I release him. But he's not done.

"Do William and Matty know you aren't their brother?"

I can't speak.

"How about Alex?" Frank tilts his head.

"I never asked for this," I say uselessly.

Frank straightens his jacket. "If you don't help me get the O'Reagan's on our side, the Bratva will fuck us so hard we won't be fit to walk another step." Frank pats my arm.

Through my anger and resentment, I know he's right. We won't get out of this mess alone. But how do I convince Alex to join us? To join Frank.

"The Negotiator has a son." I hand over the only bit of useful information I have.

"No, he doesn't," Frank corrects me straight away, and I'm tempted to grab him again and tell him to stop being such a jackass.

"My source is solid. He has a son."

Frank stares at me for a moment. "I've looked into the Negotiator, and I'm telling you, son, he has no boy."

"Don't call me that." I sound weak.

"You need to check your source." Frank's departing words make me go through the conversation I had with Kira in the car. Could she have lied? I could detect a lie, and she had sounded flustered, truthful, and the look of regret in her eyes after telling me that convinced me she was telling the truth.

Zach is waiting for me in the hall with a question on his lips. "We'll talk later. Go home," I tell him. He's my friend, but right now, I need to know if Kira lied to me. I'm not sure if I'm stunned with surprise or outraged that she deceived me.

I take the stairs two at a time, and when I enter my bedroom, she isn't there. The bathroom door is closed, and I march across the room, only to stop as the bathroom door opens.

For a moment, all is forgotten as Kira steps out. She's wearing tiny shorts and a black tank top. Her wet hair is brushed off her face, and my cock grows hard instantly.

"I'm going to ask you a question, and you can't lie to me." I take a controlled step toward her.

She doesn't agree or disagree. Kira is frozen to the spot.

"Does Nicco have a son?"

She nods, but I see her lie now. Her gaze flickers to the left before she refocuses on my face. Her fingers flex, and she juts out her chin.

Fuck.

Her lying to me isn't what has me shaking my head. It's the fact that I couldn't see through it.

"You lied to me."

"I panicked," she admits.

I take a step toward her. The smell of her freshly washed body wafts around me. Brown eyes track me and widen as I step right up to her. She's so much smaller than I am, and I use that to my advantage as I lean in; our cheeks touch, and her breath brushes against my face. "Are you panicking now, Kira?"

"You wanted information I don't have."

I detect the lie straight away, but I don't show her that I know she just lied to me. A pity I didn't pay more attention before. I push her hair across her shoulder and run the tips of my fingers along her flesh. The strap of her top falls away, and I move my head closer, wanting to press a kiss against her creamy skin.

"For lying to me, I have to punish you." I take the black strap and place it back on her shoulder before stepping away from Kira.

She nods. "I know."

She's so ready to accept her punishment, just like I was all ready to accept the torture that Frank inflicted on me. "You aren't going to fight me?" I ask and grin.

Her brown eyes darken. "I don't think I'd win," she answers.

I let my grin widen, but there's no humor behind it. "You won't, Kira." I walk to the desk chair. My cock is a rod of steel in my trousers as I think about what I'm going to do. Once I'm seated, I spread my legs.

"Come here." I hold out my hand to Kira. She appears unsure and afraid with each step she takes. When her small hand slips into mine, I pull her down.

"I'm going to spank you for lying to me."

She tries to pull away, but I clamp my fingers tightly, forcing her to stay in place. I tug her arm, and she falls forward, but not before I catch her and place her across my knee. I'm already anticipating her to fight, so I place a hand on the small of her back, keeping her in position. "Take your punishment and it's all over."

She glares up at me with red cheeks, and I'm sure my cock is prodding firmly into her stomach. I want to pull down her shorts so I can see her peachy ass, but she's barely containing her rage. My hand connects with her bottom, and I watch her face as her eyes widen. There's a moment of complete confusion before her face heats. She wriggles, trying to get away, causing my erection to grow.

My hand comes down heavy on her ass, and this time, she calls out in pain. I don't give her a second to recover as I bring my hand down heavier on her perfect ass. If the shorts were removed, I'm sure her skin would be red and scorched from my touch.

Her cry the next time is broken, and when she glares up at me, it's clear she's fighting tears that threaten to spill. I need to see her flesh. "Lift up your hips," I say.

She hesitates only a moment but arches her ass into the air, allowing me to pull down her black shorts. Her skin is pink, and her ass cheeks look delicious. She freezes when I run my hand along the plump skin.

"So perfect."

Her hands grip my thigh as I continue to caress her ass. My fingers dance further down until they slip between her thighs. As she stiffens, I pull away and run my hands along her marked ass. I want to bite the soft flesh. My hand dips between her thighs again. This time, she doesn't stiffen, and I do what I want to do. I push one finger inside her pussy. Which is wet. The walls tighten around my finger, and my cock turns solid in my trousers.

Extracting my finger slowly has Kira's grip on my thigh relaxing, until I push two fingers inside her. Her nails dig into my leg, and she moans. My fingers gleam with her wetness, and I trail it along her ass. My hand comes down heavily on the plump flesh, and Kira's screams aren't filled with pleasure like seconds ago. She tries to wriggle free, but I clamp a hand on the small of her back.

"You keep moving like that, Kira, and I won't be able to control myself." She falls still, and when she glances up at me, I see her fear, and that makes me want to stop, but behind the fear, there is lust and excitement, and that's exactly what makes me push two fingers back into her tight pussy. Her eyes widen, and she drops her head so she's no longer looking at me.

I spread my legs a little more, giving my other arm room to move under her, and she groans as my thumb finds her clit. The small bud is swollen, begging for release. I would love to hear her beg, but I don't think Kira is ready for that yet. I push a third finger into her tight pussy, forcing the walls to stretch while my thumb continues in a circular motion on her clit. Her hands sink into my thigh, and her body grows rigid, and that's when I pump harder and rub her clit quicker. Her release is so fucking sweet across my fingers, but it's even sweeter to hear her cry out in pleasure.

I continue to pump my finger inside her even when I know her orgasm is over. I release her clit and slowly drag my fingers out of her pussy. They're covered in her juices. Kira lifts her head, and she wears a look of bewilderment, and I wonder if anyone has ever pleased her before. I place a finger I used to fuck her into my mouth and suck. Fuck me. She tastes so sweet.

Kira scrambles off my knee and pulls up her shorts. She folds her arms across her chest, but she doesn't look away as I continue to lick my fingers.

Her chest rises and falls rapidly.

"Lie on the bed," she tells me.

I normally wouldn't take orders, but for Kira, I make an exception and let her think she's in charge. I rise, and she takes a quick step back from me. I'm not sure what flashes in her gaze, but I walk to the bed and sit on the edge.

She's watching me, and her face heats as I open my belt and push my trousers down. Her attention snaps to the bulge in my boxers. Kira's steps are small as she makes her way to me.

"Lie back." She tries to give me a suggestive smile, but she fails. Instead, she looks innocent, and that sends all the blood to my cock. I move up the bed and lie back, knowing it won't take much to make me come. The idea of her tight pussy around my cock has me gripping her waist the minute she climbs up on me. She squeals in surprise, and I want to fuck her so hard.

She pushes the long blonde strands behind her ears before bending down and placing a kiss on my lips. "Can you taste yourself?" I ask.

She freezes before her tongue flicks out and licks her lips. Her irises seem to grow, and I'm sure she's wet all over again.

She bends down and kisses me again. Her tongue enters my mouth, and that has me fighting not to fling her off me and take her. Her body wriggles against my cock as she stretches, and my control almost slips until she breaks the kiss.

I'm ready to fling her on her back when the cold blade of the letter opener presses against my throat.

CHAPTER FIFTEEN

KIRA

Tʜᴇ ᴍᴀɴ ʟʏɪɴɢ ᴜɴᴅᴇʀ me smiles like this is one big joke. I'm repulsed at how much I wanted his hands on me or how I wanted to explore his body. I've never had anyone touch me before. As I shift with discomfort, his hard shaft makes me go still. His grin widens, and he holds his hands up on either side of his head like he has nothing to fear from me. I have no idea what I'm trying to achieve. Right now, I'm overwhelmed. I'm overwhelmed that he punished me. I'm overwhelmed that I liked it. I have no idea what to do with all I'm feeling.

"Go ahead, Kira, stab me."

I flinch as he goads me. I shift again and curse myself when his green eyes darken.

"Don't keep doing that," he warns.

I find myself nodding in agreement.

"So either use the blade or..." He tilts his head.

He doesn't have to finish that sentence. His cock prods heavily into my backside. If I shift a centimeter back, I'll be sitting on it.

I wasn't going to use the blade. Violence isn't a trait I've ever possessed, but since meeting Jason, that's all I seem to be—violent.

He slowly brings his hand to the blade, and I wonder if he's afraid I might use it. He grips the letter opener, and in one swift motion, it's removed from between my fingers. Before I can get my bearings, I'm spinning as

Jason rotates us, and I find myself under him. The heat off his body is intoxicating.

He doesn't speak, and when I don't move a muscle, he climbs off me and off the bed. That's it?

"You look surprised," Jason says as he stands at the foot of the bed while he taps the letter opener into his open palm. I sit up and keep my words to myself. I had thought he would make me please him.

"You thought I would force myself on you?"

Is that a tone of disgust I hear?

He grins. "Don't worry. I don't need to force myself on women, Kira. There are plenty who would gladly suck my cock."

My core throbs at his words. Jason lifts his fingers and places them into his mouth. "But none have tasted as sweet as you."

The compliment shouldn't make my chest swell or send an invisible force to push my thighs closer together, but it does.

Jason puts the letter opener into his back pocket, and I don't move as he walks to the main door and leaves me alone.

My heart thumps, and I wonder if all that just happened. If I just let him touch me and spank me. I lie back on the bed and stare at the ceiling. Pressing my lids tightly together doesn't erase what I just did. And I hate how much I enjoyed his hands on me.

I roll onto my side, and all I smell is Jason. This is his bed, after all. I glance at the door. Will he come back? My core tightens at the thought of having him beside me.

I lie for a while, trying to rationalize what just happened. I had been under serious stress with Angel, and maybe her escaping had allowed me to let my guard down. I continue to think of reasons to explain why I didn't fight at all.

As I debate with myself into the night, sleep soon captures me and takes me to another dark place.

The memory of my dead mother's singing has every hair rising along my arms and legs. The white cotton nightshirt brushes the backs of my legs, sending electricity flowing across my flesh.

For a moment, I remember she's dead, rotting away in the ground of Kilmead's cemetery. How many times had I pictured the maggots eating away at the flesh on her face? How many times had I pictured worms and insects nestling in the hollow of her high cheekbones? How many times had I wept for the loss of my mother?

I climb out of my Grand Vividus bed and forget the truth that she is dead and follow her floating voice. I want to smile as she sings a song she made up for Nicco and me. She wouldn't be entering a singing contest anytime soon, but maybe that's what makes my stomach squirm and my heart jump. That slight off-key tone as she climbs the notes of her song.

"You're my eensy weensy spider, with your little tiny bum. You're Mama's goodie girly, and you know you are the one."

I round the corner with a pang of loss, and for just a moment, I remember all over again that she's dead. I see flashes of the white coffin, the stark red roses, and the crowds all in black, a sea of darkness and despair.

Her voice rises as she reaches the chorus.

"Mama loves you. Mama loves you."

I've passed more doors than we actually have along the sumptuous hallway. The darkened space that is normally bathed in light makes my footing slow. That, and my mother's fading voice, make me stop at a set of sliding doors that lead into my father's study. A line of light spills across the hall floor, cutting the darkness in two. I reach for the cream handles to push the doors aside.

My fingers curl around the cold marble, but I don't slide the doors open. Hairs rise along my neck, and I know. I don't know how; I just know my mother is behind me. I don't want to see her this time. Fear has me dipping my head, and my knees are ready to buckle.

"Mama loves you. Mama loves you," she sings, and I close my eyes against the wave of pain.

You're not real.

Since my mother died, my life has been one never-ending nightmare. So maybe this is real. Maybe it isn't. Either way, I can't face her. I'm too afraid. She continues to sing the short chorus on a loop, growing louder like she's demanding I look at her. Instead, I pull the study doors apart slightly. My mother's voice cuts off abruptly as if a conductor has sliced the air with his baton. The eerie silence hunches my shoulders, curling them closer to my face.

I can't look away from the scene that plays out before me. I can't look away from my brother, Nicco. His hair falls into his raged-filled blue eyes. The scar that tugs at his mouth is gnarled and twisted, making him appear as grotesque as he truly is on the inside.

I want to wake up.

I try to close my eyes as Nicco tugs on Father's tie, which he has wrapped around our father's neck. Yellow fish cover the tie, and they're the only light in this dark scene. I bought my father that tie. Nicco will ruin the birthday gift our father adored so much.

Close your eyes.

I want to, but something is keeping them open, or maybe I don't have eyelids. I can't look away as my brother strangles my father, who's clawing at the oak floor. His nails snap off, and red liquid flows from the tips of his abused nails. Blood vessels in his eyes burst, and he reminds me of a character from a zombie movie, at the peak of making his transition from man to monster.

But here my father stops fighting, and the real monster finally lets him go. My father's body hits the floor with a large thud.

Daddy! My mouth is open. My screams are that of a broken child. But my brother doesn't turn to me. He's lying over our father's dead body, weeping as saliva drools from his gaping mouth. Everything is wrong about this. I need to leave.

Wake up. Wake up. Wake up.

The room is dark, and a small pool of sweat sits on my breastbone. The therapist said it's the trauma of losing my mother that causes me to have night terrors. I nodded along at her explanation, which would also be given to my brother, as he wanted a full transcription of every single one of my personal therapy sessions. Nothing is private from my brother anymore. He controlled even the most minute aspects of my life.

The truth of my night terrors is the secret that's buried so deeply inside me, it's taken on a life of its own. A secret I can never breathe a word about if I want to survive Nicco. Not until I have proof, anyway. Now, I also have to fight Jason, but in an entirely different way than I thought. My attraction to him has me climbing out of bed. The morning light brings with it an odd sense of loss. I lost control yesterday in Jason's hands, and I can't let that happen again.

I have no clothes to get dressed in, and the shorts and tank top make me feel naked. I need my luggage. I need my clothes. I need my armor.

The handle of the door turns. I don't know why I thought I would be locked into the room, but I'm not a prisoner in Jason's home. I'm just a prisoner in my brother's world. The thought of Nicco sends shivers coursing along my body.

I step out onto the empty landing. In the light of the morning, the space has a warmth to it. The red Persian rug under my feet gives way to dark wood before I cross three more rugs and reach the top of the large and winding staircases. My footfalls make no sound as I step as lightly as possible down the stairs. I pause on the final step when a maid glances at me. Her small green eyes are kind, yet her thin lips make her appear strict, like a headmistress.

"Good morning." She offers a warm smile. I don't return the greeting but resume walking to the front door. Outside, the air is chilly, and I regret not grabbing a bathrobe or some shoes. But I'm outside now. The gravel pinches the soles of my feet. While two security men on the front lawn glance at me, I hold my head high. My teeth nip away at the inside of my jaw; it distracts me from the pain that's burning my soles as I continue to the door that will lead into the west wing.

I enter the main hallway and pause. My feet move in the direction of the room that Angel had been in. But I know she isn't there anymore. I hope she's far away. My chest tightens and I try not to let the suffocating feeling consume me, so I open one of my suitcases and pull out a pair of beige pants, along with a cream woolen jumper.

Once I dress, I search for socks and a pair of small black ankle boots. I'm not feeling as exposed. I grab the first suitcase and leave the west wing, making my journey back to the main house. The security pays me no attention, yet I'm sure they're aware of every movement I make. It takes effort getting the suitcase up the stairs and into Jason's room. I return to make the trip for my three other bags but stop on the landing as the two security men who were outside hold my bags. They place them at my feet.

"Thank you." My tone doesn't suggest I'm grateful, as them being here tells me they are very aware of every single move I make. There will be no freedom in Jason's home.

One of them walks away while the other gives me a curt nod of his head before departing. I place both suitcases in the room. Unpacking isn't something I'm going to do. I don't intend to stay long, or Nicco doesn't intend for me to stay long. The sense of foreboding returns when I think of the document I signed. I can't allow any of this to happen. And the only way out, I gave to Angel. I can't run. I can't leave when I know my father's killer is breathing and pretending he's looking for our father's murderer. His crime won't go unpunished. I'm pretty sure if the Bratva knew what Nicco did, it would be a death sentence, but I have no proof. It would be my word against Nicco's. That wouldn't be enough.

Our uncle is high-ranking, so going to him will be my only option when I have proof. I just have no idea how to get any. There was no murder weapon—only Nicco's hands.

My head pounds when I think of this scenario like I had a hundred times before. No matter how many times I revisit that night, I can't think of how to bring Nicco to justice. I'm clinging to the hope that one day I can, because that's my freedom. That's why I haven't run. I would be running for the rest of my life.

Always looking over my shoulder. I could never find happiness or bring children into this world while I ran from one place to the next.

I leave the bedroom, and the maid I saw earlier is in a large open kitchen with a chef and another servant. They all greet me warmly, but I can't find the friendliness they're seeking from me. Instead, I nod and walk to the counter, taking a green granny smith apple from a large crystal bowl that's overflowing with all different types of fruit.

The kitchen is hot, the air warm, and with so many curious eyes on me, I take my apple and walk to the large sliding door that leads out onto the gardens. Outside, I take my first bite, and my stomach accepts the food greedily. I haven't ingested anything since the glass of orange juice yesterday morning with Nicco. Why did it feel like a long time ago?

I try to take my mind off my worries, but they don't disappear, even as a gardener raises his head from weeding a flowerbed and gives me a wave with his trowel. His distance makes me braver, and I give a small wave back before turning away so he won't attempt to engage in conversation. I'm sure Jason's staff are curious about the girl who's arrived in his home. But I won't be the one telling them who I am. I won't be here long enough. The lawns stretch out, and when the hill dips, I continue down a slope and stop at a large man-made lake, where swans swim.

I walk to the edge, my apple nearly finished. My reflection shimmers back at me. I refocus on the swans as they swim peacefully. The apple feels heavy in my hand and stomach. I'm not sure how long I've been standing at the edge of the lake when a figure appears beside me. Jason's large stature has me gripping the apple. My mind reverts back to what he did to me only last night and how good it felt.

"Is that all you've eaten?" His voice rolls across my flesh, and as much as I want to look at him, I'm not ready. So I focus on his reflection in the water. It's easier to talk to him that way. He doesn't seem real or tangible.

"I like apples."

"That's not what I asked you." His tone is tight, like he's ready to snap at any second.

"Yes, that's all I've eaten." What does he care what I ate?

"Come back to the house." He turns away from the lake, but I don't want to go back.

"Why? Am I not allowed outside?" This time, I turn to Jason.

His gaze is guarded, and he doesn't speak straight away. "Yes, you are free to go outside, but first, you need to eat."

I want to ask why he cares so much.

"I don't need you passing out and your brother thinking I starved you," he says at my hesitation.

There's my answer: he's more worried about Nicco's opinion than my welfare. It shouldn't piss me off, but it does.

"And If I refuse?"

Jason's grin is slow and curls my toes in my boots.

"Then I will punish you, and you know how I hand out my punishment, Kira." The glint in his gaze has me wanting to tell him I'm not eating, but I won't allow him to touch me again. I walk past Jason and hear his low chuckle. He easily steps up beside me with long strides.

"We have a wedding to attend on Friday," he says as he opens the sliding door. I don't step back into the hot kitchen.

"I don't want to go."

Jason leans closer, and I smell his fresh minty breath as it brushes across my face. He's too close. "You are going." He stares at me, waiting for me to defy him.

What was the point? Only to provoke him into punishing me? That thought excites me, and I quickly enter the kitchen. The staff continues preparing food as if their boss isn't in the room. The tension is higher, but they don't speak.

"We will eat in the dining hall," Jason informs them while holding out an arm toward the double doors I hadn't noticed earlier. I step into the dining hall. The air is cooler, but that lasts for a few seconds until Jason passes me. He pulls out a chair close to the head of the table, and I'm tempted to object but slide onto the chair. He pushes me into his body, unnecessarily close. He also lingers longer than he needs to, the heat off his body pressing against my back.

I breathe when he sits down at the head of the table. A servant sets the cutlery as Jason watches me with a smile in his gaze.

"Marriott, I know you haven't met Kira, my fiancée." Jason introduces me like that's the truth.

Marriott smiles warmly, just as she had earlier when she met me at the foot of the stairs. "Welcome, Miss Kira, we are all so happy to have you here." She sounds sincere. She's a lot older than I first thought. She might be in her twenties.

"Thank you," I say to have her attention off me.

She leaves, and I glance at Jason, wondering why he told Marriott the lie about me being his fiancée when he signed the papers to send me back.

"I will have a dress arrive tomorrow for you."

"I have my own," I answer, knowing I have more dresses than I will ever need, and I'm sure some are in the suitcases.

"You will wear what I provide," Jason responds as Marriott returns with pastries, fruit, and orange juice. I instantly push the orange juice away. The sight and smell of it curls my stomach.

"You don't like orange juice?" Jason questions.

"No," I answer, not elaborating on why.

"Your brother will be at the wedding." Jason watches me carefully as he speaks.

I try to hide the fear I feel, and when Jason stiffens, I know I failed. My mind races, and a new fear starts to grow. What would Nicco do if he found out Jason had touched me?

CHAPTER SIXTEEN

KIRA

After Jason tells me Nicco will be at the wedding, I shut down and manage to eat two mouthfuls of a Danish.

"Kira, you are testing my patience," Jason remarks.

I stuff another piece into my mouth, but he doesn't look satisfied. Instead, his gaze hardens. "Why are you so afraid of your brother?"

The pastry lodges in my throat, and I pass the orange juice and pour out a glass of water. Jason waits while I wash down the lump in my mouth.

"You already know why," I answer before taking another sip of water.

He shakes his head. "You can't tell me that's the first time he's been violent." Jason cuts a scone, and with ease, he covers it with butter and jam before adding a dollop of cream. He takes a bite.

"It's the first time he's been violent toward my staff." The truth won't hurt.

Jason chews while observing me. "Has he ever been violent to you?"

What did Jason care? I don't think he cares. I think he's looking for something to use against Nicco. Does Nicco killing my cat count?

"No," I answer. Nicco has never put his hands on me. He never had to. The violence he exhibits to others is enough of a warning to me. And I don't think Nicco would ever harm me. I've never disobeyed him until recently, and Angel paid the price.

Jason places the scone onto his plate. "Why fear him?"

I take my hands off the table and place them on my lap. My father's eyes wide and panicked, his hands clawing at Nicco while he strangled him, play heavily in my mind now. "It's wise to fear my brother," I answer, and I can already see Jason isn't satisfied. "You know how this world works. Women are to obey."

Jason grins. "Obey?" he teases. "You clearly struggle with that." He pauses. "Maybe you need to fear me, too."

I stiffen, and my stomach squeezes. I don't know what Jason Murphy wants from me. Is this him flexing his control to make him feel more like a man? I should bend and play along. "I do fear you," I lie, and it's not until I say it that I hear the lie.

He exhales with a knowing smile and sits back in his chair. "We shall see, Kira."

I have no idea what that means. I don't like threats hanging over my head.

"The wedding we are going to"—he continues like us talking about fear and obeying didn't just happen—"is between Jack O'Reagan and his soon-to-be wife, Maeve."

I have heard of the O'Reagans. Women might have to obey, but we still are made aware of who the big players in this world are, and the O'Reagans are one of them. I've never met any of them.

"Sounds lovely," I answer too dryly.

Jason chuckles, and his laugh sends shivers racing down my spine.

"I'm not telling you this as a social introduction. I'm telling you to watch your tongue while around these people."

"I'll remain silent," I answer far too quickly.

"That might be so, but just be aware that the women are as dangerous as the men."

Jason continues to watch me, and I nod my head. He rises and leaves the room without a second glance. I would have slumped in the chair, but Marriott arrives to clear off the table.

"Would you like anything else, Miss Kira?"

I want a million euros and a fast car. Isn't that what I gave to Angel? "No, thank you." I leave the dining hall and return to Jason's room. Sitting on the bed, I think of how much I miss Angel. How I miss talking to her, how I miss her tall tales that kept me entertained. Right now, I could use a friend.

No friend materializes, and I get bored, so I sort through my bags. I do have three dresses with me, with matching shoes. I take out a long black gown with spaghetti straps and the matching high heels. If the dress Jason gives me isn't appropriate, I'll wear my own. I'm not going in something that might be short or overly revealing. The day melts together, and Marriott seeks me out for my meals. I go to the dining hall and eat alone. The fresh reminder of Jason's punishment has me going along with Marriott, but I don't eat much. When night finally comes, I retire to the room. I'm always on edge, waiting for Jason to make an appearance, but I haven't seen him since breakfast.

I change into fresh nightclothes. The cream silk nightgown falls to my knees, and it's far better than the small black shorts. I get into the bed, and at first, I stare at the ceiling, wondering how bad all of this will end for me. Will I go mad like my mother?

I roll onto my side to try to banish that thought. Reaching over, I flick the switch that plunges the room into darkness. And when I finally fall asleep, it's into another dream of Nicco.

"Another night terror." His voice makes me tremble.

I'm awake. It isn't unusual for me to wake up and find my brother in my room, yet his presence startles me every time and drives fear into my heart. I fear he knows the truth.

"Dreaming of Mother again?" he asks as he opens the heavy cream-colored drapes that keep my room in perpetual darkness.

I can still hear her voice. "She was singing," I say and sit up, pulling the white sheets closer to my overheated body. My head is fuzzy, and I wonder if I might still be dreaming.

Nicco walks back to my bed and tilts his head. The stark red necktie is striking against his pale complexion. The angry pink scar appears more prominent today. That scares me. It means my brother didn't sleep well, or he's worried about something.

He opens the button on his navy suit jacket before he sits on the side of my bed, and the distinct smell of citrus has my stomach curling. Every morning he cuts up twenty large oranges and squeezes them to make two large glasses of juice for us to drink on the large patio area.

It's a ritual he has ingrained into our morning routine since Father died.

His scar lifts along with the left side of his lip. "Mama loves you." His voice cracks as he sings her song.

I try to keep my breathing even, but I can't force the smile I know he expects, so I focus on his hand that squeezes my calf. The white sheet separates us. It wouldn't matter if it was the width of Ireland. I'd still feel too close to him.

I hate his touch.

I hate his smile.

I hate him.

"I wish she came to me in my dreams." His fingers tighten around my leg, forcing me to meet his gaze. His voice carries the undercurrent of jealousy, which he doesn't try to hide. As if I could tell her to leave my dream and go to his.

I hope she haunts him.

"It's never nice in mine," I admit. It isn't. I always know she's dead. I know everything about her is wrong. Sometimes I see her hollow cheeks or spiders crawling out of her mouth. I squeeze my eyes closed to stop the image that seems to be burned into the prefrontal cortex of my brain.

"I wouldn't mind. Just to see her would be nice." He pats my calf and gets up. He doesn't leave like I wish he would. Instead, he does what he has for the past one hundred and seventy-nine days. He holds out my pink silk robe. On autopilot, I slip out of my bed, pivot so my back is to my brother, and hold out my arms as he slides the robe on. The moment the silk fabric covers my arms and shoulders, he lays his hands close to my neck.

I freeze.

"You are very much shaken after your dream, my dear sister."

My heart skips a beat. I don't always dream of him killing Father, but he can tell when something is different from when I just dream of my mother.

"She frightened me," I admit as I tie the belt of the robe.

"Don't ever fear Mother. She was one of the good ones."

Yet she produced you.

I look over my shoulder and force a smile. He's too close, and I quickly face forward. His hands are still on the back of my neck.

"Shall I sing to you? Would that ease your pain?"

It's the last thing I want. But if I say no, he will grow agitated, and I can tell something is already bothering my brother. "Please, brother," I say.

He sings the song, and in my head, I turn down the volume. I don't focus on the heaviness of his hands on my neck or how his breath seems to brush against the back of my blonde hair.

I close my eyes and picture our father. He was a small man, especially in our family of men who sprung up well over six feet. His five-foot-two-inch frame made my father more endearing.

He didn't belong in the Bratva world. For our father, it wasn't a choice. He was born into the lifestyle. In my head, he's wearing one of his ridiculous ties. This one is decorated with dice, all showing number six. His small beady eyes made him appear as if he wore a permanent smile.

Nicco squeezes my neck as he finishes singing and drags me back to the here and now.

He releases me, and when I turn to him, he tilts his head. His blue eyes remind me of ice. I've never seen such coldness in a person. I'm so grateful I have my father's green eyes. I'd hate to look in the mirror and see Nicco's features staring back at me. I'm also grateful we look nothing alike.

"It's time, Kira."

My pulse pounds while peppering doubt into my next words: "Time for our orange juice?"

His tongue flicks out, and he licks the corner of his mouth, the corner of his ugly scar. "No, it's time for some truths."

He knows. He knows my secret, and now I will die because of it.

I wake up, and I'm shrouded in darkness. I scramble off the bed and hit the floor hard. My mind is frantic as I get to my feet and cross the unfamiliar room. I find the light switch, my eyes burn from the sudden burst of light, and it takes me a moment to try to find my bearings. I'm not at home. I'm not with Nicco. That should give me some relief, but it doesn't.

I might not be home, but I'm not alone.

Jason climbs out of the bed, wearing only a pair of boxers, and the sight of him with messy hair and sleepy eyes sends me back into a spin.

I hadn't heard him arrive last night, never mind felt him getting into the bed. "I had a bad dream," I say before he asks. His confused stare has me confessing the truth.

I can still smell Nicco, and I wrap my arms around my waist. I haven't moved from the light switch. I don't want to go back to sleep.

Jason sits back down on the edge of the bed. He's looking very much awake now, and I can't shake off the dream. That morning, I had been so sure he was going to kill me. That fear continues to swell, and I unfold my arms and take a step away from the light switch. I'm not ready to get back into bed, so I sit down in an armchair.

Jason watches me, and it's unnerving. I want him to say something, anything, but he just continues to stare.

"I have night terrors. It takes me a minute or two to come out of them," I say. They haven't been bad lately, but under stress, they often increase.

Jason gets up, and I get a full view of his damaged back. The skin screams of pain. He had said it was his father teaching him a lesson. What kind of man would inflict pain like that on his own son? Jason picks up a beaker of water from a small table and fills a glass. As he walks toward me, I'm becoming very aware of him. His room, the dream, is vanishing quickly. I take the glass and notice how my hand shakes. Taking a sip helps me, but I don't like how Jason stands over me.

"Thank you," I finally say.

He slowly descends until he's kneeling down at my feet. The position is intimate, and I'm aware of my bare legs and how my nightgown has ridden up. I want to pull it back down, but that would take standing up and readjusting the silk robe.

"Did something happen to you?" he asks.

"My mother died. That's when the night terrors started," I admit.

"How did she die?"

Pain surges hard and fast. "She was sick." I take another sip of water. "She was sick for a long time. It just got worse. Until she didn't want to live anymore." I swallow the saliva pooling in my mouth. "She overdosed." I finally speak the truth.

Jason stands. He doesn't walk away but glares down at me with hate in his eyes. I have no idea why he's so angry all of a sudden. Most people say they're sorry. That must have been tough.

He continues to glare at me before walking away. "I need my sleep." His words are clipped.

"I'm not ready to sleep," I answer and empty the glass of water. His sudden anger confuses me.

Jason doesn't get back into bed like I think he will. He's walking back to me. Each step is heavier than the last. Fear spikes in my system, and all of a sudden, I'm looking around me for a weapon.

"Are you lying to me?" he questions while reaching down and grabbing my wrist. I'm pulled from the chair. The glass flies from my hand and shatters on the floor. The sudden noise startles me.

"No."

Does he think I'm lying about my mother?

He's breathing heavily. His fingers are still tightening around my wrist. "You are a good liar, Kira."

I pull my arm away from him, but he tugs me forward until I'm against his chest. "I'm not lying." I half laugh. How I wish that wasn't the truth. But his anger is confusing me. "Why would I lie?" I ask while I try to pull away from him, but he won't let me go. I don't like the anger that tightens his features.

"You know about my father?"

"That he hurt you?" I ask, thinking of all the marks on his back. Jason lets me go as if I've burnt him. He runs his hand across his jaw.

"That he killed himself." His words come with no emotion. But that suggests his pain is deep.

"I'm sorry to hear that." I give the response and mean it. I understand that level of pain.

He's still looking at me like I'm the devil. "And my father never hurt me." He adds it as if it's an afterthought, which makes no sense since he said his father was teaching him life lessons.

"So you lied to me," I fire back.

He grins angrily. "A perfect match, we are. Two liars."

I'm tired, and his anger isn't fair. "My mother took her life. It's an easy thing to find out. I'm not lying."

Jason nods. "I'll find out."

I walk away from him and return to the bed. Not that I want to sleep, but I want to put distance between us.

I've never felt more alone than I do right now. Jason moves around the room, cleaning up the smashed glass, and when he disappears into the bathroom, I try to surpass my own anger. It didn't matter if he believes me or not. It shouldn't matter, but the idea of him thinking I would lie about something so close to me makes me feel unsettled.

I don't move even as he returns to the room. I don't look at him as he takes some items off the writing desk, and I don't react as he leaves the room, closing the door heavily behind him.

Leaving me with bleak memories and a horrible sense of hopelessness that I haven't felt in a long time.

CHAPTER SEVENTEEN

JASON

THIS WEDDING IS US paving the way for our future. The O'Reagans need to see my family and Frank united against the Bratva. The Bratva will be there too. The O'Reagans keep their friends close but their enemies closer, so I'm not surprised at the guest list.

The security at the wedding venue is overkill. We missed the church, as Kira refused to wear the dress I had picked for her. She had come down the stairs in a black dress that was stunning on her, but it wasn't the dress I told her to wear. With Kira, giving her an inch will encourage her to take a mile. She has demonstrated that several times already.

She's spent the drive staring out the window, but her silence doesn't bother me. She's wearing the green dress I picked. The back dips right down to her perfect ass, which I want to spank again. Later, I might punish her for her disobedience.

My phone rings again. Frank's name flashes on the screen. The car stops at the first checkpoint, and dogs circle the limo while a man bends low enough to place a mirror to check the underbelly of the car.

I answer the call while they check the limo. "Yes."

"Where are you?" Frank whispers.

"I'm here. I'm just going through security."

The line goes dead, and when I put the phone away into my jacket pocket, I notice Kira watching me with hate in her gaze.

The limo rolls forward after it passes inspection. When we stop for the second time, the door is opened for us, and Kira steps out. I'm right behind her and take her hand. She doesn't smile or hide her dislike for being here. Today, there are no paparazzi allowed, so there is no reason to force her to smile. As we climb the eight steps up to the old Victorian mansion, we pass through a set of metal detectors.

Jack wasn't leaving anything to chance. I had heard that his aunt was gunned down on her wedding day, so maybe this is the lesson they've learned.

We pass through, and I reach for Kira, who sidesteps my hand and picks up a glass of champagne. I don't like how quickly she gulps it down. I reach Kira and pull her to my side. "Steady yourself," I whisper before planting a kiss on the top of her head. Her scent rolls across me. When she glances up, I dip my head and press a gentle kiss to her mouth.

"My beautiful sister." Nicco's words have Kira quickly pulling away from me, and her brown eyes become guarded. This is my first time seeing them interact, and I'm expecting Kira to shrivel away from Nicco, but instead, she smiles and walks into his embrace; he places a kiss on both cheeks.

"You missed me," he teases.

"Of course, brother." Kira's still smiling, but she's not the Kira I've gotten to know over the past three days. This Kira is guarded, controlled, and very precise. Her movements are regal.

Nicco glances at me, and I don't like him. Not because he set all the terms of our arrangement, or not because he's part of the Bratva, and not because I think he's a complete asshole, but because he has the power to transform Kira in the worst possible way. She hasn't stepped away from her brother. Anyone else would think they doted on each other.

"I haven't received the paperwork I sent you."

I don't look at Kira. I told her I signed the paperwork that ends our marriage. I hadn't at the time. I wasn't sure why, but now I know. It's because I'm not giving her back. "I haven't gotten around to it yet," I answer and hold out my arm to Kira.

She's glaring at me.

"Shall we?" I hope she can see the warning in my gaze. She steps away from her brother and takes my arm.

He isn't pleased, not one little bit, but I don't give two fucks. "We better find the bride and groom." I depart and know he watches us.

"You told me you signed the papers. Was that a lie, or did you just lie to my brother?" We enter the main room of the event, and I decided not to answer her question. Doors at the end are open, and white tents cover the guests that pour out onto the transformed lawns. We're greeted immediately with glasses of champagne. Kira takes one but doesn't drink from the glass. I decline, knowing this isn't a social event. I'm looking for Frank or Alex. I pray Alex will come.

When I told him Frank's plan, he was enraged, but I just hoped he would see the sense in it. We need this meeting to work with the O'Reagans. Since the attack on myself and William at the Medical Examiner's office, we're no closer to finding out what happened. Forensics swiped the ME's office, and they found nothing. Just like the phone numbers I had taken from the Medical Examiner's phone and had Zach look into for me. They were old friends; nothing that lead us anywhere. I have a man tailing the ME's son, but so far nothing unusual has arisen.

The crowd shifts and parts unconsciously as we walk to the bride and groom, who sit together like a king and queen on large gold high-backed chairs. Security stands on either side of them, and Jack leans into his bride and whispers something that makes her smile. She gives a small laugh, and the love between them is clear.

"Congratulations." I break the happy couple apart. Jack's gaze grows wary, and I don't think he's aware of his actions, but he leans closer to his bride like he's protecting her from me.

"Thank you. This is my wife, Maeve. Maeve, meet Jason Murphy." Maeve is beautiful, and she smiles at me, making it clear that she doesn't know who I am. I wonder if she's from our world or an outsider. I'm already thinking she's an outsider by how friendly and open she is.

"Congratulations." I take her hand and place a kiss on the back.

"Thank you." She smiles shyly at Kira and me.

I hold out a hand to Kira. "This is my fiancée, Kira Tarasova."

Jack instantly glances at her. The second name would be interesting to him. Jack greets her before returning his attention to me. "We should talk later," he says.

I'm aware of the growing line behind us.

"Your dress is so beautiful," Kira compliments Maeve.

"I can give you the designer's name and number, or we could meet up and chat."

"That would be lovely." Kira smiles, and I think it's the first time I've seen her genuine.

I take Kira's free hand and move us along so others can congratulate the newly married couple. I spot Richard O'Reagan with Shay. Both of them are laughing. People around them watch the two Eastern Mafia leaders with interest, but they will never be welcome in their circle. The O'Reagans don't mix with anyone else, only the O'Reagans.

Frank is to my left, and he's talking to another O'Reagan I've heard of. Shane O'Reagan, even in his sixties, is a man who always commands respect. His serious nature and swift resolution of problems are things even I admire in the man. When I approach Frank, he gives me a look of relief. He's back to growing his mustache. It ages him. I take Shane's hand and shake it.

"Thank you for coming."

I'm surprised by his words. "I wouldn't miss the wedding of the century."

He snorts a laugh. "A little too lavish for my liking. But you know these young people." He glances in the direction of Jack and Maeve, and suddenly, he's not the loving uncle. If I had to guess, I'd say he hates them.

Shane has to know that Jack and I are the same age, so I offer a quick smile before I introduce Kira. That gets Shane's attention.

"Is your uncle Romero?" Shane asks while taking Kira's outstretched hand.

"Yes, he is. So you know my uncle?" Kira appears nervous now, and the name rings a bell, but I'm not familiar with Romero Tarasova.

"We go way back. He helped me out of trouble a time or two." Shane smiles with a quirked eyebrow. I can see why so many victims followed him freely. He has a certain kindness about his eyes. But I don't think that kindness goes any deeper.

"I'd love to hear about the troubles you found yourself in," I say and am glad when Shane lets Kira's hand go.

His gaze narrows for a split second before he smiles. "I'm sure we can tell war stories over a drink one night." The hollow invitation has Shane excusing himself seconds later.

"Where is Alex?" Frank snarls to my left, and I take Kira's hand, keeping her close to me.

"I asked him to come. I can't force him." I speak to Frank while glancing around the room.

"I gave you one job."

I face Frank with fire in my eyes. "I don't work for you."

If this meeting wasn't important to Frank, he wouldn't stand for my blatant disrespect, but he has no choice. We mingle for a while, and I don't let Kira's hand go. I'm glad to see she still grips the full glass of champagne. Seeing her brother seems to keep her on her toes.

We're seated three rows away from the bride and groom and with people who I don't know. Nicco is two tables away from us, but he may as well be breathing down Kira's neck with all the time he spends watching her. She keeps her head high, her back straight, but she's too controlled, too straight. She's aware of him watching her. I place my hand on the back of her chair. My thumb trails across her bare back. Her shoulder blades arch at my touch. I lean in and press a kiss to her shoulder.

Her gaze widens, and she gives me a questioning stare. While she's facing me, I seize the opportunity and take her chin in my hand before pressing a kiss to her lips.

Kira's eyes flutter closed, and she sinks into me. I don't deepen the kiss, but I let my lips linger longer than what would be considered proper table manners. I don't release her face after the kiss. Her gaze is troubled.

"Are you okay?" I ask.

Her inhale is sharp, and she exhales through her nose while nodding her head. She's not okay, and I wish she would trust me.

"Yes." She turns her face away, and I release her chin. The meal is over and the music starts. I'm not a dancer, so our table clears very quickly, leaving myself and Kira nearly the only occupants. I'm happy to have some time with her, but then Nicco arrives at our table. Slowly, I place my arm across the back of Kira's chair, something Nicco notices immediately.

"May I have this dance?" He holds out his hand to Kira.

I quickly remove my arm and take Kira's hand, guiding her to her feet. "We were just about to dance," I say.

The scar drags as he smiles. "Maybe the next one," he says.

"Maybe," I answer for Kira and pull her out onto the dance floor.

"You shouldn't do that," Kira says after I've tried not to stand on her toes.

"Do what?" I ask, focusing on our footing.

"Antagonize him."

I glance up at Kira. "You're to be my wife, Kira, and clearly you fear him."

She's shaking her head. "We're getting married?"

I don't answer as I accidentally step on her toe. Kira hisses, and I'm apologizing.

I'm ready to call it quits when Kira wraps her arm around my waist and takes my hand in hers. "Just follow my lead." She moves, counting out the steps. She's dedicated to teaching me how to dance, and I love the feel of her hands on me. I do step on her small feet a few times, but soon I get it. I lift her off the floor and twirl her slowly. Her squeal of surprise has me wanting to do it again. "I could just hold you off the ground so that way I won't stand on your toes," I say before stepping back and spinning her out with one hand. I twirl her back in, and her eyes smile up at me.

"You're a quick learner." She places a hand on my chest. My other hand touches the small of her back, bringing her closer to me. "I have a great teacher."

She smiles, and I press a kiss to her lips.

"We're ready to go now." Frank speaks from my left, and I reluctantly let Kira go.

"I won't be long," I promise her.

She gives me a weary smile before nodding. When I look around, Nicco is nowhere in sight. Maybe he got pissed and left.

Alex approaches us and gives me a nod, but he won't look at Frank. This should be fun.

The three of us leave, and I take one final look at Kira, who's watching me. She gives a small wave before we leave the large dining hall. We return to the hallway, and that's where Shay is. He holds up a crystal glass of brown liquid.

"This way, boys." He is one O'Reagan I really don't trust. We follow Shay into a room where Richard, Jack, and Cillian, who isn't an O'Reagan but married their sister, are. These are the four kings of the West Irish Mafia. And our lives are in their hands. This better work.

CHAPTER EIGHTEEN

JASON

JACK RISES AND TAKES the lead, greeting Alex first before he turns to Frank and then gives me a nod. Richard hands each of us a drink, and we all sit down around a circular table. The room is filled with art that hasn't been hung yet. Large paintings lean against the wall. A golden chandelier hangs above our heads. Cillian stands and leans across the table, shaking our hands. Richard doesn't, but he nods at us. He spent time in an asylum, so I'm wary of him. I'm wary of them all. Shay joins us with a smirk before he lights up a smoke. He holds out the box to everyone, and we all decline.

With the cigarette dangling between his lips, he rubs his hands together before removing it and blowing smoke into the air. "So, who clipped Warren?" He's looking from Frank to Alex and back to me. He raises both brows when no one answers. "Someone better talk."

"Word is, the Bratva did," Frank says.

Alex stiffens beside me at the sound of Frank's voice.

"We know the Bratva did it, and we will find out which one, but we want to know who gave the order." Jack says.

"I don't know," I answer as he eyeballs me.

"Warren was Finn's son. He was just a kid." Anger flares to life in Jack's gaze.

"I'm sorry for your loss."

"You weren't at the funeral." Jack holds my stare.

"Makes you look guilty," Shay says and blows smoke in my direction.

I wave my hand in the mass of smoke, breaking it up.

"Aidan went as a representation for us," I answer. It was the truth. One of us had to go to show respect. "Don't blow smoke at me again," I add. I wasn't going to bow to these fuckers, either.

"Speaking of Aidan, I thought he would be here." Richard joins his hands together on the table. I look at Cillian, who's just watching us. Shay is sitting back and blows his fucking smoke into the air. The tension in the room isn't what I had expected from this meeting. I had thought Frank would have at least smoothed all this bullshit out so we could talk about an alliance, not have a fucking interrogation.

"You boys don't like whiskey?" Richard asks, pointing at our three full glasses.

Frank picks up his glass and drinks it all. Alex and I don't touch our glasses. "I'm not much of a drinker," I say.

"We don't know who killed Warren, but we are willing to help." Alex cuts through all the tension and lays our cards on the table. "We have a problem with the Bratva, too, and need to sever their hold on us. We think we could manage that with your help."

"So we dig you out of the grave, and in return we get..." Shay gets up and walks to the sideboard, where a vase of roses sits. He pulls out the roses; water drips from the stems as he lies them on their sides before throwing his cigarette into the water.

"Our allegiance," Frank says.

"No," Alex answers, and I'm with Alex on this. That is exactly what got us into trouble the first time. Swearing allegiance to the Bratva. So, unless Frank has lost his hearing, he should be shaking right now. The O'Reagans don't just want the shooter; they want the person who ordered the kill on Warren, and if they follow the trail, it will lead right back to Frank.

"I've enough busboys," Shay sneers.

Alex rises. "You call me that again…"

Richard is standing. "Shay, stand down."

Shay holds his hands in the air.

"We have some inside information about the Bratva that could really help you." Frank continues to try to negotiate, but Alex still hasn't sat down.

"No. We can take them down ourselves," Alex declares.

Fuck.

"No, we can't," Frank snarls.

I'm watching Shay, who's enjoying this far too much.

"Let's go," I say to Alex, and I'm surprised when he listens to me.

"If you tell us what you know about the Bratva, we can consider it." Jack speaks up and his sincerity makes me pause. He stands up. "Look, we want to find who killed Warren. It's number one for us right now."

"Yes." Frank's gaze is filled with relief.

I, myself, am nodding.

"No, we don't need any busboys," Alex says before turning away from the table.

Shay snorts a laugh, and I'm staring after my brother.

"You can't make that call." Frank has risen, too, and Alex stops walking before glaring at Frank. "I should kill you right now."

"Alex," I warn.

"I only came here for my brother," Alex announces.

Frank smiles, and my gut tightens.

"You're not next in line to rule." Frank drops the bomb, and I don't think Alex fully understands what Frank is saying as he walks back to Frank.

"The Bratva gave me power to rule, thanks to fucking you. What I want to know is, what deal did you strike up with them?"

My heart beats faster as Frank squares up to Alex. "You need to learn your place, boy."

Alex smiles savagely. "No, you need to learn yours."

I take in the O'Reagans, who watch us. Shay, of course, is grinning. Jack looks pissed. Richard and Cillian are soaking it all in.

"Let's go Alex," I say again.

Frank points at me. "He's the next ruler. Not you."

Dread drenches every cell in my body, and I'm watching a car crash with no power of stopping it.

Alex frowns. "What are you talking about?" Alex looks from me to Frank.

I feel sick.

"Frank, don't."

Frank shrugs like a man with nothing to lose. He doesn't, but I have everything to lose. "He's my son. He's the next ruler. Not you."

Frank drops the bomb, and I watch Alex's gaze grow from confusion to pain to disbelief. He glances at me, and I don't have to speak. I want to apologize, but instead I'm walking out of the room even as Frank demands I come back. I spin and reach for the band where I would normally keep my gun.

"What, are you going to shoot me again?" His angry laughter has me walking back to him.

"You're dead to me." I nod. "You're dead."

His face pales, but he tries to recover. I glance at Alex, but I can see the hate in my brother's eyes. I take in the O'Reagans, who all look at me with a newfound respect. What Frank says is the truth. I should be the leader, and unlike the O'Reagans, we wouldn't have four kings, only one. That's how the hierarchy works for us. Before they get any ideas, I face them.

"Alex is the ruler. That doesn't change," I say before I leave the room.

Frank calls me back. I reenter the main dining area and look for Kira. I want to leave. I need to tell my brothers the truth before Alex does. Aidan will hate me. Matty and William won't take it too well either. I never thought Frank would reveal the truth. I never thought it would benefit him.

I've circled the room twice, and I can't find Kira. There is more security here than Fort Knox, so I'm not panicking, yet, and this place is huge.

A hand touches my arm, and I turn to Jack O'Reagan.

"I'm not in the mood," I say, and I'm ready to walk away.

"I've never liked Frank. But, if you and Alex ever want to talk to us..." Jack offers.

"I don't see the point, Jack. Shay doesn't make it easy."

"There are four of us for a reason. Shay can't make a decision without all of us consenting." Jack pauses and greets someone who passes us. "Maybe it could be a system you could implement with your brothers."

"Yeah, maybe." My brothers are going to hate me. "I have to go." This time, Jack doesn't stop me, as I'm haunted by my past. I had always thought I was Edward's. Frank was just the uncle who hurt me, telling me he was making me stronger. A few times when I had come home, Edward would fight with Frank, telling him things were done. But they never were. It wasn't until I was a lot older that I discovered who I really was.

Kira nearly walks right into me.

"We're going," I tell her.

She nods, her gaze distant. Her hands rest on her stomach. She walks far too slowly, and I need to get out of here.

"Faster, Kira," I hiss.

She does. The limo is waiting for us outside, and once we're in, we pull away from the wedding venue.

I dial Aidan's number. He answers straight away, and I wish now he hadn't. "I need to talk to you," I say.

"Do you?" Aidan sounds distant. Has Alex already gotten to him?

"Yes, something has happened."

"Save it. Alex rang me. I don't know what's annoying me more, the fact that you lied to us or the fact that we didn't see this. I mean, you knew things before everyone else because your *dad* was telling you." Angry words, I expect.

"Edward was my father. Can we do this face to face, Aidan?"

"No. Why aren't you angry at me?" Aidan's question confuses me. "I shot your brother." He clears up my confusion.

"I never considered Gilly my brother." I felt barely any loss when Aidan killed him. "He deserved what he got."

"Did you kill my father?" Aidan fires out, and he may as well have stabbed me.

"I loved our father," I whisper.

"My father—he wasn't yours." Aidan's anger grows, and he ends the call.

My fists collide with Edward's chest, and he lets me hit him. At thirteen, I can't control or comprehend my anger. "You don't want me!" I scream at Edward.

"I love you, son." His words have me stumbling away.

"But that's it. I'm not your son." I just found out that Frank is my biological father. My brain spins with all the whys, but I don't ask my questions. Instead, I want to hurt Edward, let him feel what I feel. "Is that why you let him hurt me?"

Edward's gaze softens, and he holds out a hand to me, tears glistening in his gaze. "Oh, son, I have so many regrets."

I smack his hand away. "Why are you so fucking weak?" I speak clearly, and he flinches at my words. "What man cries?" I ask him.

Edward shakes his head. "What has he done to you?"

"You lied to me, too." He has no right to think this is one-sided. "I hate you."

After that, I ran. Ran to the lost souls of the streets of Wexford, where heroin became my drug of choice and fighting became the outlet for my anger. That was until Alex found me and took me home. Everything in rehab was a blur, but it took me years to piece it all back together. I buried the truth. Edward acted like nothing had happened, and Frank kept his distance.

The house appears in front of us, and I can't go inside.

"You go ahead," I tell Kira.

She hasn't spoken. I'm sure she senses the anger pouring off me.

She's ready to climb out, but I reach over and take her wrist. She flinches at my touch. "Are you okay?" I ask.

She won't look at me. "I'm tired."

I release her wrist, and she climbs out of the car.

I haven't done heroin in nearly ten years, but the pull to leave the here and now has me taking out my phone and ringing an old friend.

CHAPTER NINETEEN

KIRA

Each step is painful. Each time I lift my leg, my stomach turns. What did Nicco do to me? My heart hammers, and my brain feels foggy. I reach Jason's room, and I cover my mouth with my hands. Nicco killed Lev. His anger was like something I've never seen before. He was livid over seeing Jason's affection toward me.

I squeeze my eyes tight as I try to piece everything together.

"He isn't signing the papers because of you." Nicco moves closer to me. "What did you say to him?"

I try to keep my shoulders relaxed, even as they want to rise like they can protect me. His hands curl around his cane, and I fear he might strike me. "Nothing, I swear."

"He had agreed to sign them," Nicco continues. He's watching me closely.

"I swear, Nicco, I have no idea." The door is closed, the sound of the wedding on the other side. It's the sound of people, the sound of safety. Nicco turned the lock in the door the moment he had pulled me in here with a friendly smile but a warning in his gaze.

I had considered going after Jason, but that would be silly behavior. "You were kissing him. Dancing with him."

My heart rate spikes. "It's all for show. We should get back to the wedding." I take a step toward the door. Nicco flicks out his cane, cutting off my path.

"Are you fucking him?" His mouth twists with uncontained rage.

"Of course not." I whisper the truth, yet my mind goes to Jason, pleasuring me.

"Why get rid of Lev? You didn't want him to report to me?" he quizzes, still holding the cane in place.

"Ask Lev yourself. I never dismissed him."

Nicco grins, and my skin crawls. "I know. I did ask him before I killed him."

Blood rushes to my feet. Lev is dead. Why?

"He was meant to stay with you, and he didn't," Nicco answers my unspoken question. "Where is Angel?" Nicco drops the cane, but I'm under no illusion that I can leave, so I stay rooted to the spot.

"I don't know."

He snorts. "Lies." Nicco eradicates the space between us. His free hand grips my shoulder. "I will find her and kill her too. I should have done it the first time."

I pull out of his hold. "You will not harm her."

"Oh, dear sister. You have forgotten your place." Nicco reaches out and touches my hair.

My bones grow heavier when my brother glances at my lips.

"Nicco," I plead, hoping he'll come to his senses.

My plea only angers him. "Did you sleep with him?"

I shake my head as my vision wavers. I'm thinking of Lev; I'm thinking of Angel. How could he be so callous?

I don't have time to react before Nicco shoves me. I'm sailing backward, not prepared, and I hit the ground hard. The back of my head takes the brunt, and the room falls into darkness. I get one final look at Nicco as he leans down beside me before everything disappears.

When I woke, I was alone in the room. My body felt like it'd been hammered on.

I swallow the bile that rises again. I know what happened without remembering. My body is screaming the pain at me. I'm walking to the bathroom, turning on the faucet, stripping out of my clothes. My hands tremble as I reach between my legs. Blood stains my underwear, and I grip the wall as what I believe happened to me is confirmed.

The water hits me. I see the stream pouring down, but I don't feel it on my flesh. With both hands braced against the shower wall, I take in three deep breaths before my breathing becomes erratic at the thought that Nicco raped me after he knocked me out.

I'm covering my mouth again like I can force the horrifying thought back down. He wouldn't. A sob tears from my lips. My core aches like I've been poked with a stick. Bile rises again, and I'm gagging, but nothing comes up, only air and horror.

No.

No.

No.

I sink to the floor of the shower and stay like that for a while as I keep replaying everything in my head, every detail, but once I was knocked out, I can't remember. I want to remember, but I also don't.

The stream of hot water continues to pound my back, and I know I need to focus on something else. Like finding Angel and warning her. Nicco will find her. You can't hide from him.

A dry sob has me standing. The weakness in my legs almost makes me buckle, but I manage to turn off the water and get a towel.

Terror keeps striking me with every thought I have. I'm back in Jason's room, and I wish he were here. I wish I could tell him. Would he care?

I get dressed into my nightgown robotically and wrap myself in a dressing gown also, before getting into the bed. I lie there for what feels like an eternity before the darkness transforms to a soft red hue of light.

All night, I have tried to remember what happened, but I can't. My mind has been spinning, and I'm pulling every scenario out of thin air. Maybe when I fell, he struck me again with the cane and it hit me between the legs. Maybe he kicked me while I was down. Maybe that's why I'm so sore.

I have never needed an answer so badly. I have never prayed to be wrong about something so much. The morning comes, and I'm grateful that Jason never arrived. I wouldn't have been able to stay strong last night.

I get dressed in a black pair of trousers and a white shirt. Glancing in the mirror, I look how I feel—like hell. My eyes are bloodshot, my skin white. I leave the room quickly, and all I can hope is that Jason isn't here.

Marriott greets me but frowns. "Are you okay, Miss Kira?"

"Too many drinks last night," I say automatically. My answer removes her frown. "I'm going shopping. Can you tell me where the car keys are?"

She frowns again. "I'm sure one of the drivers is free."

I shake my head. "I just need some time alone. A bit of retail therapy to clear my head."

"They are kept in the security hut. Do you know where it is?" She shuffles a stack of towels that she's carrying close to her chest.

"No, I don't."

"I'll show you."

I follow Marriott to the security hut. Only one security man is there. Marriott leaves, and the security man waits for me to tell him what I'm doing here.

"I'm looking for a set of car keys."

"Does Master Jason know?"

I fold my arms across my chest. "Of course."

He pushes his roller chair to the far wall, which has a row of keys on pegs. "Any preference on which one?"

"No." I unfold my arms and take a set of keys. "Thanks."

I remember seeing a garage beside the kitchen. I'm sure there's a door there. I ignore the cook when I enter the kitchen. The door to the right opens, and the lights power up into a large garage. Several cars are parked. I hit the buzzer, and the BMW lights flash. I don't waste a second before getting in. The minute I start the car, the garage doors start to rise automatically. Fear has me frozen as I wait for someone to either burst through the garage door and tell me to get out or to block my escape route, but that doesn't happen, and I roll out of the garage. Two security men on the lawn watch me drive past. Clearly, Jason isn't here, but no one stops me. At the gates, the guard takes a look at me before he waves me out.

My throat tightens. A part of me wants to be stopped so I can stop the madness of what I'm about to do.

I need to be strong. I need to know what happened to me. I drive to Columbia Hospital and sit in the car, staring at the large building. Getting out feels surreal. Walking to the doors has me trying to talk myself out of this. The double doors open, and I numbly walk to the reception area. It all starts to become a blur as I whisper that I need to see a doctor. I'm asked why, and I quietly say that I think I might have been raped.

That has me brought quickly into the back and into a private room.

The nurse is the first person I have to talk to. I try to stay detached, but when I say I think I was raped for the second time, my chest tightens, my head pounds, and I feel like I'm going to unfold.

The first few questions are easy. My name, date of birth, my address... I don't know why, but I give Jason's last name and not mine.

"Your phone number?"

"I don't have one," I say.

She doesn't look convinced. I'm sure there aren't many people my age who don't have a phone.

"Do you know who raped you?" the nurse encourages gently.

"No."

"Where did this happen?" Another question I won't answer.

"Could I please just be examined?" Tears trail down my cheeks, and I quickly wipe them away. Is this real? I'm considering leaving. I'm making this real. I could leave and let my mind believe that Nicco just hurt me, that this didn't happen. But the main reason I'm really here is that one question. If he did rape me, could I be pregnant?

"Sit on the bed. The doctor will be here soon."

I do as she asks and when she turns her back on me, my panic swells. "Please don't leave me," I beg.

She turns around. "Of course. I'll be right here." Her sympathetic smile has me lying back down.

The female doctor asks the same questions, but I refuse to answer.

"We need to take urine and blood samples. Is that okay?"

I nod, giving permission. Each time, I rethink, *What am I doing?* Yet I hand over the urine sample and let them take blood.

"I'm going to do a vaginal swab," the doctor says before I have to remove my trousers and panties. While she's examining me, the nurse stays the entire time.

I can't stop the tears. I can't stop the confusion that pulses before it turns to disbelief, then anger.

"Did you see who attacked you?" she asks.

I shake my head.

"Did you scratch him, fight him off?"

I shake my head again.

"If you did, we could get a sample from under your nails."

I'm overwhelmed and choking. "No."

She stops questioning me.

"All done." The doctor gently touches my knee. "You can get dressed now."

As I dress, the nurse explains I will be given a pill to help with any STDs or pregnancy. I take the tablet once I'm re-dressed.

"There is vaginal tearing and bruising, which suggest rape. But we will know more when the results come back from the lab."

I don't know how I'm standing upright.

"We can call the Gardaí."

I'm shaking my head through the mist. "No."

I'm ready to leave.

But the doctor stops me and hands me a referral and leaflets on what to do next. I take them and leave the hospital. The trash bin outside is where I deposit everything.

Nicco raped me.

My brother raped me.

CHAPTER TWENTY

KIRA

WHEN MY MOTHER DIED, I remember I put all my efforts into being there for my father. Every second, every breath I took, was for him. I never allowed myself to think about or cope with my mother taking her life. I suppose it *was* my way of coping.

Going back to Jason's makes that switch kick in, and I focus on Angel. I have to find her, but I have no idea where to start. My heart leaps as a phone starts to ring. I'm glancing down at the dashboard when I see a little icon of a phone ringing. I ignore it, and it continues to ring all the way to Jason's house. Once I stop at the gates, I press the icon, and Jason's voice booms in the car.

"Where are you?"

His tone should make me quiver, but I also get the urge to cry. *Think of Angel. Think of Angel.* I nod at the guard, and he opens the gates.

"I'm at the gates," I answer as I drive up to the house. The line dies, and my stomach tightens as Jason steps out of the house. I don't get to drive to the garage as he walks out in front of the car. His hair is messy, his green eyes tired. He looks like he had a long night, too.

My chest tightens, and I grip the steering wheel as he marches to the driver's side and opens the door. "Turn off the car, Kira," he orders.

I do. "I was shopping." I can't look at him.

He dips his head, looking into the car. "I don't see any bags."

I take the keys out of the ignition and hand them to him. "I'm back now."

He doesn't step away to allow me to get out. Instead, he touches the hood of the car and leans in.

"You can't just leave the property without telling me." His voice is calmer, and it almost sounds like he was worried.

"Okay." I take my first look at him.

"You didn't have breakfast," he declares.

I'm confused for a moment. Breakfast? The thought of food has my stomach turning.

"I'm not up to eating. Can I get out of the car now?" I ask, feeling trapped. Sweat beads along my neck.

Jason exhales before standing back, giving me room to get out.

"Go inside. Marriott has your breakfast ready. I'll join you in a minute."

I walk briskly to the house, and the engine purrs to life as Jason drives the car into the garage. The moment I'm standing in the hall, I want to run. But running to Jason's room will only have him following me and asking questions.

"How did the retail therapy go?" Marriott asks as I enter the dining hall.

"It was more like window-shopping," I answer as I sit down. Jason arrives, and he grumbles at Marriott before she scurries away.

"I've never heard of a woman window-shopping," he says once he's seated.

The glass of orange juice in front of me nearly undoes me.

"Kira," Jason says.

I look away from the glass and to him. "What?"

"I asked if you're okay."

Did he? How long was I staring at the orange juice? "Yes. I'm fine."

Marriott arrives with toast and places it on the table.

"You can take the orange juice away," I say, not touching the glass. I can't bear the smell of it.

She lifts the glass. "Would you like some apple juice instead?"

I shake my head. "Tea is fine."

Jason picks up the pot and pours me a cup. I have the urge to run. Run from my thoughts, my fears, Jason.

Angel.

"So, where did you go window-shopping?" Jason asks, and the disbelief in his voice has me picking up the milk and pouring a small amount into the cup of tea.

"I'm not sure. The main street. I was just looking."

"The main street?" His question is filled with irritation. When I don't respond, he continues. "I can find out where you went."

My heart jackhammers. "How?" I ask.

He grins. "So you did go somewhere specific."

My mind is frantic. "I was looking for my friend Angel. I need to find her."

Jason relaxes and butters some toast like he's giving some thought to my answer. "Why do you need to find her?"

"To make sure she's okay."

"And did you find her?" His question is calm, but it carries a lot of weight.

"No. I checked the hospital in case she went back there, but she didn't."

"I'll check the GPS on the car to confirm your story."

I nod. Thankfully, that's where I was. Just not for that reason. The real reason churns and swells inside me.

"Nicco threatened to kill her," I admit. "So I need to find her before he does."

Jason bites into his toast before answering. "Well then. Consider her dead."

The sip of tea I took sours in my stomach. I rise, unable to stay seated any longer.

"Sit down, Kira, and eat your breakfast."

"No." I get out of the dining hall and make it into the kitchen before Jason catches up with me.

"I'm only telling you the truth," Jason grinds out.

The chef had been chopping carrots and stops.

"Get out," Jason tells the staff. They all file out quickly. Marriott gives me a sympathetic glance as she passes me.

"You don't have to be so cold about it." My hands start to sweat as my temperature rises. I'm burning from the inside out. I'm burning with the knowledge of being raped. I'm burning with the truth that Angel may be dead. "She... she was all I had." I swallow down the emotion.

Some of the anger leaks out of Jason's features.

I hold on to the island and close my eyes before taking a calming breath. When I open my eyes, I keep my voice steady. "I won't give up on her," I answer. I can't just forget about Angel.

Jason runs his hand across his jaw, and I have this urge to walk toward him and rest myself against his chest. I want to hear the beat of his heart. I want to feel the warmth of his flesh. I need something stable. Something tangible that can hold me up for just a little while.

"I need some information about where she might be."

A spark is lit in my chest and I'm nodding. "At the hospital, I gave her an address to go to. I can give it to you. You think you could track her down from there?" Hope surges and strengthens me.

Jason steps closer and tilts his head. "I'll try, but you can't leave this property again. The staff are informed now. You may have tricked my security once, but mark my words, that won't happen again."

I glance down at the island. "I won't leave again," I say.

"That's not good enough."

I glance back up at Jason. "I promise."

He's observing me. "The address?"

I recite the address I gave to Angel, knowing it will raise questions.

"A storage unit?"

"I had a car and cash there."

Surprise lights up his eyes. "A getaway?"

"Yes," I admit. Would I have ever used it? Maybe only the things I know about Nicco kept me from running. If he hadn't killed my dad, maybe I would have run.

"Where would you go?" Jason folds his arms across his chest.

We're interrupted as the chef nervously hovers at the door. "Sorry, Master Jason. I need to turn off the stove."

Jason nods, and the sound of bubbling water has me looking at the stove with four pots. I hadn't even noticed. The chef powers the stove off from the wall, and Jason waits until he leaves.

"I don't know." I shrug. "I never got that far." Where would I go? A different country? But I wouldn't get to leave. Every airport would have been watched.

Jason comes closer, and there's only a foot that separates us. "I'm sorry about your mother."

My stomach jumps, and it's another uncomfortable topic. But since he's apologizing, he must have asked around about it and got his answer.

I nod.

"We have far more in common than I thought." His thoughts are far off, and his gaze grows weary. "I thought you lied to get close to me."

"I never lied about that," I admit.

He tilts his head. "But you did lie about Nicco having a son."

The mention of Nicco has me freezing. My hand automatically goes to my stomach and disgust has bile crawling up my throat. I want to scrub the skin from my body, but nothing will erase what he did to me.

Jason's phone rings, and he doesn't answer it straight away. He's watching me, and I wonder what he sees. Can he see the horror on my face?

He fishes the phone out of his pocket and answers. "Alex." Jason's voice is filled with surprise. "Okay." Jason turns his back on me, and I grip the island tighter to keep upright. My mind is on a loop.

"I have to go."

I blink, and Jason is in front of me again.

All I manage is a nod.

He frowns. "I'll do my best to find Angel."

"Thank you."

He gives me one more questioning look before he leaves me alone. A few seconds later, all the staff arrived back into the kitchen, and the noise of them moving around is soothing. I'm not alone. That is until Marriott speaks. "Can we get you anything, Miss Kira?"

"No, thank you." I turn and exit the kitchen. I need a shower. I need to try to wash some of the pain away. With each step, I try to reinforce that my focus should be on Angel, but as I clear the final step of the stairs and arrive on the landing, my vision is blurry as another wave of horror hits me.

And I have no idea how to stop the tidal wave that's dragging me into a dark, deep sea. My knees buckle with the weight of the truth, and I can't stop the sobs this time. They cut me open, and I grip the floorboards as sobs wreck my body.

"Kira." The voice splinters my hysteria, and I'm lifted off the ground and pressed against a warm chest. Jason's heart beats wildly against my ear, and we're moving. "Kira?"

I can't control the pain any longer, and I sob against his chest. I'm clinging to his wide shoulders as he carries me into the room. When Jason deposits me onto the bed and tries to see my face, I hold tighter and cry harder.

He pulls me back into his chest and allows me to break down. Somewhere in the back of my mind, I know I need to calm down, but calm is nowhere in sight. A scream bubbles from my lips, and I release it into Jason's shirt. It's not enough, and I scream my pain again until my breathing wavers and the air grows thin.

He pulls me away from him even as I claw. His large hands grip my face, but I close my eyes. This can't be real.

"Look at me," Jason demands.

I can't.

"Look at me, Kira." It's the softening in his command that has me looking at him.

"Breathe." He inhales a deep breath and releases it, and I copy him.

When we do this a few times, I think I'm calming down. I inhale again, and my lip wobbles. I can't keep the truth in. Everything is too much.

"He raped me," I say out loud to Jason, to a man I barely know.

CHAPTER TWENTY-ONE

JASON

THERE WAS SOMETHING ABOUT the way Kira looked at me in the kitchen that left me feeling troubled. So much so that I returned to the house, only to find her crying on the landing floor. Her gaze is filled with horror, and I've been taught how to control physical pain, but this is different.

"He raped me." She slaps her hand over her mouth like she can force her words back. I'm still holding her face, staring at her, and all I feel is a sense of cold. It numbs me so much.

"Who?" I ask.

She's shaking her head, still covering her mouth. I release her face, and as gently as I can, I peel her hand away from her mouth. Tears make a pathway between her parted lips. I'm watching her retreat, and the selfish part of me wants to allow her to so I don't have to hear this.

"Who, Kira?" I ask, dipping my head as she tries to look away from me. She's staring at the floor. Her tears have stopped, but when she looks at me, her brown eyes are so defeated. "I'm sorry." She licks tears off her lips and glances around the room. "I'm sorry," she repeats.

She tries to move away from me. The coldness that had kept me numb melts rapidly as fire surges through my body.

"Who raped you?"

Kira flinches as her troubled expression dances around the room.

I need her to look at me. I reach out and take her chin in my hand, tilting her head so she's facing me. I don't ask again with my words but hold her chin in place so she can't turn her head away from me.

"Nicco." His name is a whisper on her trembling lips.

Nicco.

Her brother.

I want to ask: When? How? How the fuck did something like this happen?

I don't ask any questions, as she seems ready to bolt, and I don't want to force the words from her lips. So I continue to hold her shaking chin between my fingers.

"At the wedding. He was so angry at seeing us together." More tears fall from her eyes.

That was yesterday.

Kira folds her hands in her lap, and I finally release her chin. Instantly, she stares at the floor, and her tears dry on her reddening cheeks. I want to leave and kill him.

The urge is almost overwhelming.

"What can I do?" I ask. Feeling weak and useless isn't something I'm accustomed to, but here with Kira, that's exactly how I feel.

She looks at me, and there's strength in her pain. I've seen it before with Kira, and I'm seeing it again.

"Find Angel." The two words are said with ferocity.

"I'll find her," I promise.

Kira's gaze glazes over, and she nods.

We sit in silence. She's not crying, but she wrings her hands together.

"Are you sore?" I ask.

She shakes her head, but that's got to be a lie.

He's a fucking savage. One I'm going to gut.

Is this how Aidan felt when he found out Gilly had put his hands on Raven? No wonder he pulled the trigger.

"You need to get checked."

She won't look at me. "I already did. I went to the hospital."

I run my hand along my jaw. That's why she was there. And on her own.

"What can I do for you now?" *Besides kill him.*

Kira finally looks at me with watery eyes. "I don't know." She sounds exhausted.

"Lie down." I take her hand and guide her back onto the bed. She follows me with hesitation. I lie down and pull her head onto my chest. We lie like that as she continues to wet my shirt with her pain. My phone rings. Kira tries to get up, but I stop her while getting the phone out of my pocket. It's Alex again. I turn the phone on silent before leaving it on the bed.

"It's okay," I say and rub her head. She relaxes again. William wanted to speak to me. Only seconds ago, it seemed like the most important thing in the world to get to William and hear what he wanted to say. I was hoping he would be the one to forgive me for lying. But being here with Kira is what I need to do.

I stay with her, and her breathing evens out. Even as she sleeps, I don't leave her. I think of finding Nicco and killing him. Each minute, my anger grows. Each time I glance down at Kira, the violence in me surges to hurt him. He must have gotten to her when I was with the O'Reagans. The idea of him hurting her never entered my mind. I thought he had left the wedding. All the while, he was waiting to get her alone, and I gave him the perfect opportunity.

A knock at the door has me slowly lifting Kira off my chest and laying her on the pillow. I take a final look before I answer the door.

Zach raises a brow. I hold a finger to my lips before I slip out the door and close it behind me.

"What?" I ask.

"Alex is ringing. He said he can't get through to you."

"I'll text him now," I say.

"Everything okay?" Zach asks. I'm ready to tell him it's fine, but I think of my promise to Kira.

"I need you to find the girl who was left at the hospital by Noah."

I give him the address. "She won't be there, but see if there are any cameras in the area that might have picked her up. Get the registration of the car that was parked in the storage unit and track her that way."

"No problem. I'm on it." Zach still lingers. "Rob called me." I wave off Zach's concern.

Last night I called Rob, one of my old dealers. But when I met up with him, I didn't take the heroin. I wanted to, but something made me walk away.

"A weak moment. I didn't take anything."

Zach nods. "I know. I just think going back down that road isn't wise."

"I didn't."

Zach holds up his hands in defeat. "Just looking out for you."

"I appreciate it. I'll text Alex now."

I slip back into the room, and I don't expect to see Kira awake, but she's standing close to the door. Listening.

I close the door. "One of my men is going to start looking for Angel."

She folds her arms across her chest. "Thank you."

"We will find her."

Kira bites her lip. "Thank you for everything."

I nod. I didn't do anything. Yet. "Are you tired?" She looks exhausted.

She shakes her head. "I don't want to sleep."

I'm sure she was plagued with flashbacks. "Your security guard sounded concerned," Kira says.

She had heard everything. Normally, I wouldn't tell anyone about my weakness. "He has no need to be concerned."

She's watching me with a less haunted stare.

"I used to be an addict. He was worried I had returned to my old habits." When Kira's eyes widen with concern, I wave a hand in the air. "I didn't."

She nods. "Good."

Stuffing my hands into my pockets, I track her as she sits down on the armchair while wrapping her arms around her waist. Her gaze glazes over, and I can assume she's thinking about Nicco again.

"I used to do heroin," I confess, getting her attention. "I lived on the streets of Wexford for two years, having fun. I don't know how I survived."

"How did you stop?"

"Alex found me and took me to rehab." That time in my life is a blur, and I'm happy for it to stay that way. The things I did for drugs were unthinkable. Thinking of Alex, I walk to the bed and text him.

I will ring you later. I hit send.

"I can't picture you living on the streets." Kira's looking at me differently. I don't think it's in a bad way. So I indulge her.

"I did. I slept in doorways, homeless shelters, and even the odd couch. Honestly, I don't remember much." It's not a lie. I did so many drugs. I wasn't lucid very often.

"You seem to have a good life here." Kira looks around the room. She wears the look of someone who just found out devastating news. She reminds me of Matty, the day we found out our father died. All you want to do is take their pain away.

I walk to the bed and sit down. I had never intended to share so much about myself, but I'm too weak right now to not answer.

"Remember, I told you my father taught me life lessons?"

She nods her head, and her brown eyes darken.

"Well, for most of my life, I had believed he was my uncle, until one day I found out he was my father. You can imagine my confusion. My actual uncle, who raised me as his son, knows about my former drug habit. So,

I ran and buried the knowledge of who my father was. When I got out of rehab, I never shared the truth."

Kira's eyes widen. "Your family members don't know?"

"They do now. They found out yesterday."

Pain floods her gaze. "I'm so sorry."

I smile at her show of compassion while she's suffering so gravely herself.

"We will be fine. My brothers and I are strong." I hope I'm right. I search for something to say, to keep her talking. Each time we fall silent, I can see her retreating back into her shell, back to the horror she endured.

"Tell me about Angel. You seem close."

Her face darkens before it lights up, and she starts talking about Angel, who sounds like a character. Kira doesn't just speak highly of her; she's smiling, and even the odd laugh leaves her swollen lips. Her laughter does die down, and her pain peeks out its ugly head. Each time, I think of how I'm going to kill him. Even as I smile at Kira when she smiles and laugh when she laughs, all the while I'm thinking about how painful I can make it.

Time moves in funny patterns while I stay with Kira. We talk, sleep, and she eats very little. My phone continues to ring, and as one day melts into the next, I enter a comfort zone with Kira where I'm comfortable talking to her. She tries to ask about exactly what my father did to me, but that's a dark place I'm not taking her. Each time I don't, she seems disappointed, but instead, I tell her about my brothers and me and all the stupid shit we did as kids. That makes her smile. Each day, her gaze grows less haunted, but my want for blood continues to grow.

They say all good things come to an end, and they do when Aidan arrives without notice.

CHAPTER TWENTY-TWO

JASON

I HAND KIRA THE bag of bread we've been using to feed the swans. She's looking at Aidan with s u s p i - cion.

"He's my brother. I won't be long."

She takes the bag and nods. Aidan waits a few meters away. I honestly wasn't expecting him to show. I had thought it would be Alex who would eventually arrive.

"You want to tell me what's going on?" Aidan asks once I reach him. He juts his chin out to Kira, who keeps taking peeks at us.

"It's complicated," I answer.

Aidan looks tired, and I know ignoring my family wasn't just about Kira. It was also about facing the shame of hiding something so huge from them. I want to explain, but I can't find the words.

"How long have you known?" Aidan asks. We're both facing Kira, watching her feed the swans while taking glances at us.

I know Aidan is referring to Frank being my father. "When I was thir-teen, he got into a fight with Edward." It's strange calling the man who I see as my father by his first name.

"Dad knew? Fuck. Of course he knew." Aidan kicks at the grass before looking at me. "Why didn't you say anything?"

I stuff my hands into my pockets. A part of me is grateful that Aidan is here. I've always been close to him, more so than Alex or William. Aidan and Matty have been the brothers I've always looked out for.

"I didn't want it to be real. I thought if I buried it, I wouldn't have to ever really face the truth."

Silence falls between us.

"Why?" Aidan asks the question I've always wondered. I've asked Frank before, but his answer was always short and didn't really explain why he would give up one son and not the other.

"Something to do with my mother. He said it was to protect me."

Aidan's features tighten. "And what now? He's back to claim you because you're the next to rule?"

I face Aidan. "That will never happen. I will never rule. Alex is our leader, and I swear to God, I would never fight that," I admit.

Aidan's watching me before he exhales. "I'm still trying to process all this, Jason. It's a fucking bomb. But we have more pressing issues right now."

I agree with him. I think Frank did this either in hopes it would dismantle our bond or that I would lead, and somehow that would give him protection.

"I know."

"You need to come and see William. He wants to talk to you."

I open my mouth to respond, but Aidan holds up his hand.

"Not about Frank. I'm sure he will eventually, but this is about the attack."

I take another look at Kira. "Okay. I'll just let Kira know."

"Okay. I can wait," Aidan offers, and it feels like more than just an offer to give me a lift. It feels like an olive branch. One I need right now. Nicco raping Kira can't go unpunished, but I'm not under any illusion I can take him down alone.

"Did you feel better after killing Gilly?"

Aidan startles for a moment before he grins viciously. "Yes. I only wish I could have made it more painful."

I nod. I get that. A bullet would be too good for Nicco. "Give me a minute." I walk away from Aidan, and Kira looks at me from over her shoulder.

"You have to go," she says while throwing another piece of bread into the lake.

"Yes." I don't want to leave her. "Will you be okay?"

She scrunches up the empty bag. "Thank you, Jason."

I don't want her gratitude. If I hadn't left her at the wedding, she wouldn't have gotten hurt. "I won't be long." My feet don't move, but I remind myself that she's safe here, and there is no way she can leave.

I step closer and press a kiss to the top of her head before I walk back to Aidan.

"I thought she was going back home," Aidan says while we make our way back to the house.

"I changed my mind," I answer, and he snorts a laugh. The sound is good.

Once we're in the car, I buckle up. "So, what did William say about the attack?" I ask. I'm hoping he knows something that clears my name. I saw the suspicion in Aidan's eyes at the hospital, but I don't see it anymore as he glances at me before driving off my property.

"He won't say. He just wants to talk to you. Alex and Matty are at the hospital."

I squash the nerves that bubble up. That's what we do, we face the music, and right now the band is in full swing.

***

The floor of the hospital where William is staying is quiet. We sign in at a desk before we're permitted into his private room. Security is outside his door.

The minute Aidan and I walk into the room, the boys fall silent. William is sitting up in the bed, looking bright. His head is still bandaged, a reminder of how he nearly died. Matty is slumped in one of the armchairs. His usual scowl would make anyone think he doesn't want to talk, but it's just Matty's normal look.

He juts out his chin in greeting, yet the weariness is there in his and William's eyes.

"I've been calling you," Alex says as he leans against the wall.

"I had a situation," I respond. Aidan closes the door, and I focus on William.

"How are you feeling?"

"I'm alive."

There's an awkwardness between all of us that I've never experienced with my brothers. "I know you are all pissed at me, but Edward was my father. He treated me like a son." I glance at each of my brothers. "You are my brothers. This changes nothing."

"It changes everything," Alex says, pushing off the wall.

I'm shaking my head. "I swear I have no intentions of ruling."

He smirks. "The only reason you would be next is if, somehow, Frank swindled his way into our father's shoes, and I intend to find out the truth."

I don't think Alex is really considering that Edward left everything to Frank. Maybe he had his reasons. Maybe he didn't see Alex as fit to lead. I'm not sure we will ever find out the truth.

"I'm just saying my piece. I won't ever try to take your throne," I say.

Alex turns away from me, addressing William. "Tell us what happened, since Jason is finally here."

"When I left you in the office, there was a guy in the alleyway. He had his hood up, but I was wary of him."

I step closer to William's bed.

"I got a good look at the bastard. He stopped me and asked where you were."

"Me?" I ask.

"Yeah, and when I told him to fuck off, he grabbed me, demanded to know, so I said you had left. He released me, and before I could think, I was hit on the back of the head. Someone else was with him, but I didn't see. I woke up here."

"The question is, why are the Bratva looking for you?"

His guess is as good as mine. "I have no idea."

Alex rubs his jaw. "Here is my theory. They know who you are. Maybe Frank blabbed to them that you are his son and next to rule. Maybe they wanted you dead."

I'm looking at all my brothers as they wait for me to give them an answer I don't have. "I mean, it's possible, but I don't know."

"You need to ask Frank." Matty speaks up from his slumped position. His deep voice always sounds like a growl.

"And what then?" I ask them all.

"Frank needs to die." Aidan speaks, and his callous tone isn't like him. But I think his revenge is based on what happened to Raven. He hates Frank.

"I've been thinking a lot about Frank over the past few days," I say.

"Yeah, when no one could reach you. So that's what you were doing, thinking about Frank?" Alex sneers.

He's getting on my last nerve, but I ignore him. Folding my arms across my chest, I continue like I wasn't just fucking interrupted. "The O'Reagans want blood for what happened to Warren."

"I know. You dragged me into that shit show of a meeting." Alex won't let up.

"What the fuck is your problem?" I snap and take a step toward him. "You knew the hell I went through. When I found out about Frank at thirteen, I ran, Alex. I couldn't cope with that knowledge. That's why I spent years on the streets, shooting up. I mean, you were the one who came to my fucking rescue."

"I'm sorry, did you mistake this meeting as a therapy session?" Alex teases.

"Lay off." Aidan steps up beside me. "Fighting one another won't resolve the problem."

Aidan's right, but Alex is being a bigger prick than usual.

"You think Frank clipped Warren?" William asks from his hospital bed.

I shake my head and take a narrowed look at Alex, warning him not to interrupt me again. "No. The guy who clipped Warren was a lower member in the Bratva, but the O'Reagans know that. They don't care about that. They want to know who gave the order." There is a lull in the room. "Frank gave the order. He wanted the O'Reagans wiped out so he could gain more power. He just had no idea what he was up against. The Bratva did, so that's why they picked off one of the weakest members." A decision I'm sure they're regretting. "If we give Frank to the O'Reagans, they might help us get out of this contract with the Bratva."

Alex shakes his head. "They won't. They'll just kill Frank."

"Maybe you're right. But it's worth a shot," Aidan says beside me. His hunger for Frank's death is driving his decision.

"I do think giving Frank to the O'Reagans will deal with our Frank issue and make peace with the O'Reagans, but we still have the problem of the Bratva," Alex says, and as much as I hate to admit it, my brother is right.

"So, we agree," William says. "Hand Frank to the O'Reagans."

We all nod, but my stomach sours. I know it's the price Frank has to pay for the choices he made. One way or another, the O'Reagans will find out. So it's better we do it now before they decide we're all guilty.

What a fucking mess.

"Did you hear Matty passed all his exams? He's now a fucking accountant." William smiles widely as he teases Matty, who sinks into the chair.

"Congratulations," I say.

He stuffs his hands into his hoodie pockets and grunts. He has brains to burn, but he's not much of a talker. I think that's why we all worry about him. Sometimes he seems almost void of emotion, like he's moving through the motions. I suppose after thinking our father took his life, we all panicked, thinking Matty could be next. But here he is, educating himself.

"The old man would be proud," Aidan says.

Another grunt from Matty.

I turn to Alex, who's watching me like I'm going to do something. I think of the photo of him with the ME. I've never had the chance to question him when I needed him on my side for the meeting with the O'Reagans, but right now wouldn't be a bad time to get the limelight off me.

"I found the ME's phone in his office the day William was attacked." Everyone is listening intently, but I keep watching Alex. I need to see if there's anything even subtle in his stance when I question him.

"I was able to power it up and found something... interesting," I drag it out.

Alex isn't giving anything away. He just looks impatient.

"There was a photo of you, Alex, with him. Why didn't you tell us you knew him?"

"I know all the men we work with. Rob liked to go fishing, so I went along a few times," Alex responds, and I can't hear any deceit in his voice.

"I just thought it odd that you never said that," I challenge him.

He smirks. "Not as odd as you lying about who you are."

I curse internally. I walked right into that one.

"I think we should focus on setting up a meeting with the O'Reagans," Aidan says.

I've always been the peacekeeper, but it's like Aidan has taken my role.

I nod in agreement. Bickering won't help.

"So we need to go for drinks to celebrate Matty being a good citizen," William teases from the bed.

Matty gives him the finger. "You are on the dry," Matty reminds William of his sobriety, which I'm also grateful for. Addictions in our line of work are a dime a dozen. Not many get through this life without relying on something.

"A drink would be great," Aidan chimes in.

William continues to tease Matty about being higher class than us uneducated fools. Aidan laughs along. Alex doesn't. He nods at the door. The boss wants a word in private.

I follow him out the door, and once it's closed, he crosses his arms.

"Not answering your phone or coming to a meeting isn't acceptable." Alex is throwing his weight around. He's right. I would never have dismissed Frank or Dad like that.

"I'm sorry, it won't happen again."

"You want to explain to me what happened?" Alex asks.

He's still hostile, but the weight of what happened to Kira feels heavier all of a sudden. "Kira..." I start. I know I'll eventually have to tell my brothers. Maybe my hesitation is in case they won't help me. "Her brother raped her at Jack O'Reagan's wedding."

Alex's hostile stare dissolves. "Fuck."

I nod. "Yeah, he's a piece of shit."

"I need to kill him, Alex." I lay it out on the table.

"Killing the Negotiator..." Alex starts.

I tilt my head, silently asking if he's fucking kidding me. "If she were yours, would you let it go?"

Alex shakes his head. "No. I wouldn't."

"Will you help me?" It's a huge ask.

Alex considers it for a moment. "You can't ghost me again, Jason."

"I know. I couldn't leave her."

"Then you tell me that." Alex grips my shoulder. "I'll help you, but we do this smartly. Maybe this can be our way out of the Bratva."

I flinch at the idea of using Kira's misfortune as an opportunity for us. Maybe Alex sees my resistance as his hand tightens on my shoulder.

"Remember what Dad used to say. When we're in a dark place…"

I finish that sentence. "And feel like we're being buried…"

Alex releases my shoulder. "We aren't. We just get the chance to grow again."

Dad loved plants, and this saying, I think, came from him planting them and watching them grow.

"So we have a seed. Let's make it fucking grow," Alex finishes.

I nod. "Okay."

CHAPTER TWENTY-THREE

KIRA

Hours have passed since Jason left, and the cold in the garden is the only reason I'm returning to the house. Lately, I've been having a sense of claustrophobia every time I go indoors. Even though Jason's house is huge, when I step into the kitchen, the house shrinks, and my   chest

t   i   g   h   t   -

ens.

I could go back outside, but I know if I don't keep pushing forward, I'll end up going backward. A quote I once heard from a famous actor sticks with me. *Don't fall back. Fall forward, because at least that way, you can see what's coming.*

As I pass through the quiet kitchen, a security man I often see around the house approaches me. I'm thinking he might have a message from Jason.

"If you need to get out, just say the word." He leans into me, keeping his voice low while he covers a small black mic pinned to his black suit jacket.

"Excuse me?" I'm a little thrown.

He looks me in the eye before he slips a set of keys out of his trouser pocket. He holds them up and jangles them. "I'll look the other way."

I'm a little more than stunned. I'm suspicious. The keys are a way out. Where would I go? I'm hit hard with the knowledge that I'm in the safest place right now. I'm about to tell the security man no, when another man approaches. I've seen the redhead around a lot, even talking to Jason. They seem close. He doesn't dress in a suit but wears jeans and a shirt. The minute he reaches us, he smacks the security man on the back of the head.

"What the fuck, Noah?" he barks.

Noah, who had offered me the keys, rubs his head as he tries to stash the keys away, but the redheaded guy pulls them out of his hand. "You're a fucking moron."

"Zach, I wasn't doing anything," Noah defends himself.

Zach growls. "Giving her the keys to a car."

All of a sudden, I feel very visible as both of them look at me. I was going to say no, but I don't voice that.

"What do you think Jason would have done?"

Noah shifts from one foot to the other. "It was for the best."

"No, it's not. He would spend all his time looking for her," Zach says.

I want to tell him how wrong he is, that Jason and I aren't really in a relationship, but I wisely stay quiet and leave him with his assumptions.

"I thought if she wasn't here, he could focus," Noah says.

"Go the fuck home, and don't pull shit like that again." Noah's face heats, and he gives me a cutting look as if this was somehow my fault.

I walk away after Noah leaves, but Zach stops me. "I hope you know what you are doing," he accuses.

"And what exactly am I doing?" Besides surviving.

Zach takes a cigarette from behind his ear and runs his fingers along it a few times.

The sound of footsteps has both of us looking up as Jason arrives. My stomach flutters as he approaches. He stops beside me and leans in as if he's about to kiss me, but at the last minute, he seems to think better of it. Or maybe that was wishful thinking on my part.

"Noah's gone home sick," Zach informs Jason. "I'm going for a smoke."

"Nothing serious?" Jason asks, and his concern is genuine.

"Yeah, a bit of a sniffle. He'll live." Zach walks away, and I'm wondering what he meant when he asked me if I knew what I was doing.

"Have you eaten?" Jason asks.

I'm exasperated by that question.

"Or have only the swans eaten?" Jason asks when I don't answer. "Come on, let's get you some food." He walks back into the kitchen, and like magic, the chef is there, when he wasn't moments ago.

Jason leads me into the dining hall, and we sit in the same seats as we do every day. Movements like this are making me comfortable, and getting comfortable isn't wise.

"I hope everything was okay with your brother."

Jason's gaze becomes guarded. "My other brother, William, is in the hospital, and he wanted to see me. He's made a great recovery."

"I'm happy to hear that." I truly am.

"The Bratva attacked him thinking it was me," Jason says.

A sense of exhaustion and disappointment cling to my shoulders, dragging me lower. "I don't know what happens in the Bratva, Jason."

I'm not sure if he hears the exhaustion in my voice, but he leans forward and places his elbows on the table.

"I managed to track down Angel."

My heart stalls before it thumps heavily in my chest.

"Is she alive?" is my first question.

Jason nods. "But she's with your brother."

Shivers break out along my arms, and a current runs across my body, once, twice—dread, that's what keeps assaulting my system.

I blink rapidly, trying to shake loose any other thought than dread. I'm floating in it.

A large warm hand encases mine. "I'm sorry, Kira."

I pull my hand away. "I need to get her out of there." I glance at Jason. "Can you get her out?" I frown, knowing what I'm asking isn't possible.

Jason shakes his head. "How?"

"I'll have to go. Make a deal with him."

Jason sits back. "That's not happening."

I grip the table to try to calm the hysteria that's biting into my flesh, looking for its pound of meat. "I shouldn't even be here. The three weeks are up. Why hasn't he come for me?" I stand up as Marriott enters the dining hall. She pauses.

"You want to go back to him?" Jason's angry words grow loud, and it's the first time he's raised his voice.

"I want to get Angel out of there. I can't do that from here."

I start to walk away and shoulder past Marriott, but Jason grips my arm and spins me. My hand splays across his chest as I try to push him away, but his grip is like iron.

"You aren't listening to me. You're never going back. You're staying here."

My pulse spikes, and I'm trying to clear the confusion. I want to say that's not the deal, that *we* aren't a deal.

"I never signed the papers," Jason reminds me.

Two things battle inside me. One is complete joy that he isn't sending me back, that he wants me here. The other is horror at the idea of Angel being left in my brother's hands.

I pull my arm out of Jason's hold, and he lets me step away. But the determination in his gaze tells me he won't give in. Not unless I give him a reason.

"If this were one of your brothers?" I ask calmly.

Jason exhales loudly and glances at Marriott, who's still standing with a tray filled with food. The moment Jason looks at her, she jumps slightly.

"I'll wait outside." She scurries away and closes the door behind her.

Jason's eyes are full of fire.

"If this were one of your brothers, what would you do?" I ask again.

"That's different."

"She's like a sister to me. How is this different?" I take a step closer.

"I can't walk into your brother's house and take a member of his staff, Kira. What you are asking isn't possible."

Frustration has me tightening my fists. "I'll sign the papers to end this marriage," I threaten.

He laughs humorlessly. "How long will that take? I'm sure she'll be dead by then."

The blood turns cold in my face. "How can you be so callous?"

"It's the truth." Jason doesn't seem to think his words are cruel.

"Why do you have to be so cruel?" All the frustration is pouring out, and when Jason laughs at me, it nearly undoes me.

"Cruel? You have no idea of cruelty." His green eyes are as dark as moss.

"Don't I?" I whisper. How many cruel acts have I witnessed? Countless. Watching my mother disintegrate until the woman she once was faded, and I was left with a madwoman.

"I'm sorry, Kira." Jason reaches out to touch my face, but I take a step back.

"What can I give you in return?" I beg as panic rises. A flash of Angel's damaged back has me stepping back to Jason. "I have to do something."

"There is nothing anyone can do," Jason grits out. "I promised you I would find her, and I did. My hands are tied."

Jason walks back to the table. "Now sit and eat."

How can he expect me to eat? "Fuck you." I walk away.

His laughter makes my steps faster. There is nothing funny about knowing your sister will die. The shattering of pottery makes me jump, and I turn to see all the contents of the table on the floor. The violence makes me pause.

"If I could do something, I would," Jason says, and maybe he believes what he's saying, but I still think if it were one of his brothers, Jason would save him. He owes me nothing. He barely knows me. Maybe he is right, but I can't form any words, so I leave him and find an empty drawing room where I can think.

I could ring Nicco and ask him to give me Angel back, and in exchange, I would come home. That thought has a sob clawing its way up my throat.

I can't.

I'm not strong enough.

I hold my stomach like I can stop the pain that's erupted in it, and pace. A phone on a small circular table has me pausing.

Ring him. My heart races as I take a step toward the phone. My vision grows blurry as I reach the phone. My life for hers. He would accept it; I know he would. I could save Angel. But I don't ring Nicco, because I want to live too. Tears fall down my cheeks.

I don't want to die.

I don't want to be raped.

I want to live.

After what Nicco did, will I ever really function again, or will I continue to feel like there's a fog over my head, clouding me? Each day carries with it a sense of strangeness, like a dream.

I wouldn't have survived the recent days without Jason. He never left my side, and at times, when he looked like he wanted to run from me, he didn't. He stayed and told me stories about his life. He didn't have it easy, either. Guilt starts to raise its ugly head but stops as I think of Angel.

I just need to get Nicco out of that house. If he weren't there, getting Angel would be so much easier. He leaves most mornings and doesn't return until late afternoon. But that's when I was there. I wipe my tears and go back to the dining room, but Jason isn't there. Marriott and another servant are bent over a pile of broken dishes, and both of them pause when they notice me.

"Do you know where Jason went?" I ask.

Marriott nods. "Outside."

"Thank you." I leave the house and find Jason at the lake, where we were this morning. "What if Nicco weren't at the house?"

"Stop it, Kira." Jason doesn't face me.

"Please, Jason, just consider it. If Nicco weren't there, would you help me get Angel then?"

I step up beside Jason, but he isn't looking at me, with his hands stuffed in his pockets. He seems so closed off. I close my eyes briefly before touching his forearm. Muscles bunch under my hand, but I don't withdraw my fingers. "If he weren't there, I could go in and get her. The staff all know me."

Jason's already shutting me down. "I said no."

I want to hit him. Bang his head so he listens to me. My hand tightens on his arm. "Please, Jason."

He spins, and I release his arm. He stops when he faces me. I've never seen him look so angry, and it's a stark reminder that I don't know this man that I'm pushing.

"What is the first thing that will happen when you arrive? His security will notify him. How long would it take for him to get back?"

"I could sneak in." My voice sounds as weak as this plan. He's right. One phone call and Nicco would be home. "What if they have no way of contacting him?"

Jason's eyes fill with pity, and that fuels my anger. "Kira... unless he was dead, I wouldn't let you walk into that house."

My lip trembles, but I hold my head high. The only way to get Angel back is for Nicco to be dead. If I could make that trade, I would. But I can't.

I nod and walk away from Jason again. My skin grows tight across my bones as I think of ways that Nicco could die. I just need him somewhere that he can't get home quickly enough. Maybe call him and ask him to meet me? That might work. I reentered the drawing room as I try to formulate a plan.

He would pick the meeting point, and honestly, I don't think I'm strong enough to face him. I sit down and let out a half scream of frustration. I've often heard the term 'a light bulb moment' happening to people. As my brain scrambles, I don't just have a light bulb moment; I have the whole chandelier light up.

I know how to get Nicco out of the house and to a place where no one can call him.

I stand with a new sense of urgency as I pick up the phone with a trembling hand and make the call.

CHAPTER TWENTY-FOUR

JASON

I'M TRYING TO THINK of a way to get Angel out for Kira, but I can't walk into the Negotiator's house and not start a war. The look of devastation in her gaze weighs heavily on my conscience. I should have never sent Angel away. I had no idea how much she meant to Kira. I had no idea how much Kira would end up meaning to me.

She's in one of the drawing rooms. I've checked on her twice to find her pacing. This time, I have no intention of leaving.

"You will wear a path on my good floors."

She pauses, and the fire lights up her brown eyes. She's so fucking strong. I want to kiss her so badly, but I'm sure if I touched her right now, she would hit me.

"If I got him out of the house and somewhere no one could call him, would you take me to Angel?"

"Stop it, Kira," I growl. I've never felt so fucking weak.

"Just answer me." She's half shouting. "Please, would you? If he were somewhere where no one could call him, if there were zero chance of him returning, would you help me?"

I entertain her question only because I want her to breathe. "That's why I said, if he were dead," I answer and smile at the thought of him dead.

Kira's shoulders tense with anger.

"Yes, Kira. If there were a zero percent chance." But that's not possible, as they all have phones.

"I thought of calling him and asking him to meet me."

I'm shaking my head. "Over my dead body."

Her brown gaze grows heavy. "I'm not strong enough to hear his voice." She sounds ashamed, and I'm crossing the room and grabbing her face. "I've never seen anyone so strong. You don't have to make that choice, Kira, because I'm taking it away from you. You will never see him again."

Her gaze widens, and she inhales sharply.

My gaze flickers to her lips, and I dip my head. A knock on the door has me releasing Kira. This better be fucking good.

Zach waves two fingers for me to come outside the room.

"Just say it," I bark. My frustration toward him is unjustified.

"There are two Gardaí at the front gates."

I frown. "What do they want?" Gardaí at my gates can only mean someone is dead.

"They want Kira."

Relief is engulfed with a need to protect her. "For what?" I ask.

Zach shrugs. "They didn't say."

"I called them," Kira says behind me, and I spin around to face her.

"What?" Is this her way to get out of here, saying she's a hostage or something?

Her gaze dances to Zach before it returns to me. She holds her head high, like she does when she's actually terrified but trying to fight the fear. "I'm pressing charges against Nicco."

I'm all for serving fucking justice, but I'm the one who's going to do it. "You don't have to. I'll take care of it," I promise her. Does she think I will let him live?

"If I press charges, they'll arrest him, and he can be held for up to twenty-four hours, giving us a window to get Angel out." Kira walks past me and toward Zach. "Let them in," she instructs.

When I glance at Zach, he raises a brow, asking for permission. Gardaí in my home? A Mafia member. I'm not sure what makes me nod, the idea of watching all this play out or the pleading look in Kira's gaze as she waits for me to give Zach approval.

She knew when she told Zach to let them in that he wouldn't without my permission. She's so aware of her limitations, yet she pushes them.

I don't want to let this happen, but she's right. It would give us an opportunity to get Angel, and that will make Kira happy.

I give Zach a nod, and he instantly speaks into the mic on his sleeve.

"Let the pigs in," he says.

"You can change your mind," I say to Kira.

She shakes her head. "I have to do this."

I get doing things that make us uncomfortable. It's only then that we can break through the barriers and really achieve things. My only hope is that Angel is still alive after this whole fucking fiasco.

***

Once the Gardaí leave, I send Zach to keep an eye on the Negotiator's house so he can inform me when he's gone.

"You're not going," I say to Kira for the tenth time. She's pale and shaking. Her adrenaline is crashing. "You need to stay here and eat." She's lost weight, and I just want to see her healthier.

"But if I go, we can walk straight in. It's easier." She's exasperated, repeating herself, and she's right. It would be easier. And I'm not sure how else to get in, but I've thought about the outcome too many times, and most likely, Angel is already dead. What would happen to Kira if she saw her best friend dead?

"No," I repeat as I peel off my shirt.

Kira glares at me. "You're being stubborn."

I laugh. "*I'm* stubborn?" I ask, while pulling on a black sweater.

Kira lowers her voice. "How about this? I go in, tell them you're going inside to get Angel, and I'll return to the car."

She's the Negotiator's sister. I don't voice that. She might take it as an insult.

I'm thinking... I don't like the idea of her not being here. She's safer behind my walls than out there. Anything could go wrong.

"Jason, you won't get in without making a mess, and the Bratva won't like that." She's staring up at me with defiance in her gaze.

She's the type of woman I want to spend the rest of my life with. She's the type of woman you bury yourself in and have a child with.

She's Mafia wife material. Strong and resilient.

"Okay."

Surprise lights up her gaze. "Really?"

"Do you want me to change my mind?" I ask.

She's already shaking her head. "No."

"You need to eat first."

She tuts.

"That's the condition. You eat or you stay here."

She looks ready to throw up, but it will make me feel better. I finish pulling on a suit jacket before arming myself.

"Fine." Kira doesn't sound happy as we leave the bedroom and make our way down to the dining area. Marriott prepares sandwiches and a pot of tea for Kira. I watch her nibble on the bread, and each swallow is followed by a wash of tea. But with each bite, I feel more satisfied.

My phone rings, and Kira's head snaps in my direction. My gut twists as Zach's number flashes on the screen. "Your woman is good. He's being taken out of the house and put into the back of the squad car."

"Okay. Stay there, keep watch. I'll be there shortly." I hang up.

Kira's watching me.

"He's been arrested," I say. She pales further. "You don't have to do this," I remind her, knowing it's pointless. Angel must mean a hell of a lot to her. I just hope Angel is as good to Kira as Kira is to her.

We leave the house, and each time I take a look at Kira, I want to place her back in the house. We get into the car. Two of my security team come with us, and the other two take a second SUV—just-in-case measures. It's not every day you get to go to the Negotiator's house.

Alex would be flipping his shit if he knew. I grin at the thought. The fact that Kira is with us changes things. We aren't breaking any rules. If I went alone, that's a whole different ball game.

"You can talk at the front gate to gain us entry."

Kira's wringing her hands. "Okay."

"I will pull the car close to the door so you can speak to security. You just let them know I'm here to pick up Angel. That's it."

She nods.

"Or I could just come with you."

My fear grows, and I grip the steering wheel. "Kira, don't test me. You stay in the car at all times."

Her small hand touches my arm, and I loosen my grip on the steering wheel. "Okay, I'll stay in the car."

"All they need is to see your face, and I can do the rest."

Kira is quiet and as we near her home, I take a peek at her. "Would you like me to get anything else for you?" I ask.

She frowns for a moment.

"This might be your only opportunity." I'll make sure of that. She can't ever return to this house. When Nicco gets released, he'll be on the warpath. I check my phone to make sure Zach hasn't messaged me. He hasn't.

As we near, I slow down and come to a stop at Zach's parked car. He nods, and I drive on to the gates. "Are you ready?" I ask Kira as I pull up to the security hut.

I already feel antsy just being here.

I roll down my window, and Kira leans across me and gives a wave. It takes the security man a moment to recognize her before the gates start to open.

We drive up to the house—one step closer to getting Angel and getting the fuck out of Dodge.

Two men stand on either side of the door. Kira reaches for the door handle, but I stop her. "You don't leave the car," I reinforce.

One of the security men breaks formation and clears the six steps before stopping at the car.

He bends and looks in at all four occupants.

"Jason is going inside to get Angel. He has my permission," Kira says.

The security man responds in Russian, and that leaves me uneasy.

Kira fires back something, and he nods.

"You can go in," she says.

CHAPTER TWENTY-FIVE

KIRA

JASON REACHES FOR THE door handle, and I grip his arm, stopping him from leaving. My fear of Nicco hurting him is unwarranted, since Nicco isn't here, but I can't stop the fear from raising its ugly head.

"I'll bring her to you," Jason says.

"I want you to be careful," I admit before releasing his arm. Jason gets out of the car, and I'm left with the two security guards as we wait. I think of following Jason inside, but the thought of breaking my promise is what keeps me seated. It should be the fear of what I find. It has entered my mind that Angel might not be alive, or maybe Nicco has hurt her even further.

I'm not expecting Angel to walk out the door I can't look away from. I roll down the window and let some fresh air in. Time ticks away, and I turn to look at the men in the back. "Maybe someone needs to go in and check."

"Master Jason said to wait in the car, so we wait in the car." The stiff-lipped security guard carries a level of disdain in his tone. I'm sure making Jason come to the Negotiator's house isn't high on their list of things to do. I'm sure I've pissed off most of his men.

I'm back to watching the door. *What is taking so long?*

The front door opens, and I blink as Jason walks out. He's alone and my heart plummets until he pauses and turns to allow Angel to leave the house. I'm out of the car. The security man behind me curses and gets out to try to stop me, but I run around the front of the car and pull Angel into my arms. I'm gentle with her back.

"You're okay," I say, more stunned than anything.

"We need to leave now." Jason's words break us apart, and Angel is ushered into the back of the car. I get in beside her, and the security man takes my seat up front. The minute Jason gets in, I meet his gaze in the rearview mirror. Thank you isn't enough for what he just did for me.

Angel grabs my hand, dragging my attention to her as Jason drives us away from the house. "Are you okay?" Angel asks me, her gaze flitting across my face.

The relief is all-consuming, and I hug her. "I am now," I admit. Having Angel safely out of Nicco's grasp has me feeling like anything is possible.

"The Gardaí took him away." Angel's voice is low as she chews on her lip.

I nod, knowing I'll have to explain everything. "We needed to get you out."

She's shaking her head. "I thought he was going to kill me," she admits, and all her terror is clear in her large blue eyes. Angel doesn't release my hand, like she thinks I might disappear, and I don't let her go either.

"Are you okay?" Angel asks again.

I think of all the damage Nicco has done, but I don't think it's fair to put all that on Angel right now. I'll tell her in time, but this isn't the right moment.

"Yes. Don't worry. You look tired." I want to know everything.

"He found me yesterday." Angel looks away from me.

"Did he hurt you?" I ask, while fearing the answer.

She shakes her head. "You didn't give him enough time." Angel grips my fingers nearly to the breaking point before she leans forward and touches Jason's shoulder. "Thank you."

He appears uncomfortable with the gratitude and just nods.

Angel sits back and closes her eyes. Her skin is pale, and I can only imagine what all the running did to her body.

"Once we get back, you can rest," I reassure her.

Jason's phone rings, but he doesn't answer it as we continue our short journey back to his house.

I keep trying to get Jason's attention, as the rearview mirror is pointed in my direction, but he focuses on the road. A muscle tics in his jaw like he's aware I'm watching him. What he just did for me speaks volumes, and I will be forever grateful.

We arrive at his home, and the moment we pull up, Angel dips her head to look up at the large mansion. I don't think she remembers being here the first time. "Is Lev here?" she asks, and the blood rushes to my feet before pouring back through my body.

"No," I say, and I can't look at Angel. I don't think she has any idea how he felt about her.

"What aren't you telling me?" Angel tugs at our joined hands, and Jason kills the engine outside the front door.

"In time." I give her an answer she doesn't want to hear, but she accepts it as I help her out of the car. Jason waits at the front door, and he seems uneasy but takes Angel's other arm. We don't go upstairs. Instead, he takes us to a spacious bedroom on the ground floor.

"I can walk unaided," Angel says, and it makes me smile. She's strong.

"I'll leave you to it," Jason says, and walks to the door. I'm on his heels, and he pauses at the door.

"Thank you." Words aren't enough, and I walk toward him and throw my arms around his neck. At first, he stays still and doesn't respond, but slowly, one of his arms wraps around me before the other does, and it's like he bends around me. When I pull away and look up into his green eyes, I see something there I haven't seen before. A fondness or admiration, I'm not sure which.

"Take all the time you want," he says before pressing a gentle kiss to my forehead. Once he leaves, I turn to find Angel watching me.

"He seems nice," she says with a smile.

I give a short laugh, and it eases some of the tension from my bones. Walking back to Angel, I direct her to the bed. "You need to lie down before you fall down. "She doesn't fight me. Angel winces as she lies on the bed, but she rolls onto her side.

"I can get a doctor." I can't bear to see her in pain.

"No, talk to me. I can't remember much after Nicco..." Angel trails off.

"Nearly killed you because of me?" I finish her sentence.

Angel frowns before shaking her head. She tucks her hands under her head. The strain is visible on her face. "I made the choice to help you, Kira, and I'd do it all over again."

I sink to the bed and rub her shoulder. "Jason tried to find you first, but Nicco's men got there before us."

"I didn't get far, to be honest. I passed out twice before I even got to the car, and then I had no idea where to go." She closes her eyes. "I'm not cut out for a life on the road."

She smiles up at me. "Thank you for coming for me. I was terrified." The terror she speaks about is visible on her face.

"Did he hurt you?" More than before.

She shakes her head. "No, he just threatened to kill me if I left."

Silence gives way to our own thoughts.

"What happened?" Angel asks, and she shifts slightly, trying to find a comfortable position. I remove my hand from her shoulder and place it onto my lap.

"Nicco wanted me to marry him and give him an heir."

Angel tries to get up, but I gently push her back down. "If you move, I won't tell you."

She doesn't look happy but stays still. When I'm happy she won't hurt herself, I continue. "After he hurt you, he had me sign a document. It was to petition to have the law changed so we could marry. I signed it without knowing."

"But that can't happen. No one in their right mind would pass such a law," Angel says with horror in her eyes.

"I don't know." I look at my hands in my lap. "I don't know what will happen."

Angel can't tell me it won't happen. No one can, because we don't know. And if the law is passed, what will that mean for me? Jason could hand me back at any minute, if he chooses to.

"Tell me about Jason." A softness enters Angel's voice, and I find myself happy to talk about him, even lighter.

"He's... He's nice," I settle on.

Angel smiles. "Nice? I mean, he seems more than nice to me."

I laugh. "He's great. He got you for me," I say.

"Stay with him, Kira." Angel's voice is serious.

And I realize I would if he let me. I could see a life here with Jason. He has shared so much of his past with me and has helped me through the worst of times. Strangers often become closer to us than family.

My stomach churns and I look at Angel, contemplating telling her about Nicco.

"I'm so happy you're safe," Angel says with a smile on her lips as she closes her eyes.

"Go to sleep," I say.

She opens one eye.

"You're safe," I say. I stand up and pull the throw from the base of the bed, dragging it across her small frame.

What could have happened? I stop that thinking and remind myself that it didn't. Angel is here and alive.

I close the curtains.

"I think you found a good one," Angel says, half-asleep.

I stop at the door. I think so too. "Good night," I say before closing the door behind me. I don't expect Jason to be standing outside the door.

"How is she?" he asks.

"Alive."

He nods.

"Thanks to you." I don't know how to show my gratitude. "When he finds out she's gone, he won't be happy."

"I want—" Jason starts.

I cut him off. "Don't mention food," I warn.

His lip tugs up. "I was going to say I want to talk to you."

"Okay." Nerves jangle as Jason walks down the hall, and I follow him.

As we walk through the ground floor, I want Jason to speak. "What do you want to talk about?" I ask.

He opens a door that leads into a large sitting room. A fire has been lit, and Jason holds the door until I enter. He closes it behind us.

"I want you to drop the charges against Nicco." That wasn't what I expected. Jason holds up his hand as I open my mouth, so I let him speak. "You will have to go to trial. Relive what he did to you."

My chest tightens.

"He might get seven years if we're lucky. Then he will be free."

Jason walks over to me and takes both my hands. "He would be protected in prison and live a decent life. I'm sure he won't even serve the full seven years. Two, if you're lucky."

My heart hammers at the truth of Jason's words. The system is so unfair. A heaviness settles around my shoulders at the injustice. "So, what, just let him get away with it?"

Jason releases my hands and holds my face. "He won't get away with it, Kira. I swear to God, I will kill him."

The violence in Jason's words makes me flinch. When he presses his lips against mine, I don't realize how hungry I was for his touch and kiss. How much it took me away from all this. I kiss him back and grip his shoulders, pulling him closer. Having Jason's lips on mine isn't enough. I want so much more. But fear only allows my fingers to trail up to his neck and along his pounding pulse.

I push my tongue into his mouth, and I have no idea what I'm doing, but I go with my gut and touch the collar of his shirt until I can feel the button under my fingers. I open three buttons before his hands leave my face and cover mine, moving my hands.

As he pulls away from me, confusion turns to embarrassment when I think of what Nicco did to me and what that would mean to a man like Jason. I never thought of it before, but to him, I'm soiled.

I will forever be soiled.

CHAPTER TWENTY-SIX

JASON

S HE'S SO FUCKING GORGEOUS and everything I want. I've never felt such pride as I did when I walked out of Nicco's house with Angel. The look of pure relief and joy in Kira's gaze made what I did worthwhile. My brothers, I'm sure, will disagree, and my actions will make them hate me even more, but for her, it was worth it.

My cock is begging to be buried inside her, and I want to so badly, but I need to know she's ready.

She blinks and drops her gaze, looking at the floor. I haven't released her hands, and she pulls them out of mine. I let her. I don't want to let her go, but I need to remember what she suffered.

"I get it." She frowns.

"Get what?" I quiz. But she won't look at me. What could she possibly get? That I'm falling so fucking hard for her that my judgment is screwed up?

She folds her arms across her chest, and when she looks up at me, pain radiates from her brown eyes. "We don't have to pretend, Jason. I'll be forever grateful for what you did for me. But we don't have to pretend."

"What are you talking about?" She looks away from me, and fuck this, I'm not keeping my distance. I grab her chin, making her look at me.

"I'm soiled." She fights angrily to get out of my hold, but I grip her chin, knowing the force will cause her pain, but nothing is worse than what she just said.

"You think that's why I broke the kiss?" I ask, astonished.

"Let me go." She jerks her head, and I release her chin, only to pull her into me.

I'm looking at the crown of her head. "I have never wanted to fuck anyone so badly." She freezes in my hold, and I should shut the fuck up, but I don't. "You're perfect to me."

She looks up, and she searches my face for deceit.

"What I did for you today, getting Angel, should tell you what I feel for you."

She swallows. "What do you feel for me?"

I want to growl at her. She must know. "I want you." I release one of her arms and tuck a strand of blonde hair behind her ear. "I just want to make sure you're ready."

She's breathing heavily, her chest rising and falling against mine, and my cock grows harder.

She nods. "I want you, too."

I smile victoriously. That's all I need to hear. I recapture her mouth with mine and taste her sweet lips. When her small tongue slips into my mouth, I get a visual of bending her over and spanking her perfect ass until she's begging me to stop. I move us back toward the couch and stop kissing her so I can unbutton her trousers. She freezes slightly, and it makes me pause.

"I want this," she repeats breathlessly.

Yet behind her words is fear. I won't take any more from her than I think she can give. I nod before unbuttoning her trousers and pushing them off her curvy hips. My fingers grip her thong, and I drag them down as they join her trousers at her knees. I recapture her mouth as I lower her until she's sitting on the couch. I keep going until I'm kneeling on the ground. She watches me with wide eyes as I undress her. When I remove her bottoms, she pulls her legs together.

"Keep them open," I say. Slowly, she opens her legs, her cheeks turning red. I gaze at her perfectly pink pussy, which looks good enough to eat. Gripping her thighs, I pull her ass closer to the edge of the couch and lean in, smelling her sweetness. Her breaths are harsh, and as she watches me go down, she groans as my mouth touches her lips. I use my tongue to part them and taste her wetness.

She tries to close her legs, but with both hands, I push them apart to give myself more access. My tongue trails along her clit, and she gasps. I suck the sensitive bud and go deeper as her hands sink into my hair. I devour and explore her warm pussy, letting my tongue sink inside her before pulling out. This is pure pleasure to me, but hearing her groaning and heavy breathing has my own arousal pushing against my trousers. I release her legs and use a finger, slipping it inside her while I work on her clit. She jerks, trying to pull away, but her hands force my head down on her. It's like she has no idea how to react to the sensations of being eaten out.

"Enjoy it," I say while pressing a kiss to her thigh. When she glances down at me, her gaze is overshadowed with lust. I don't wait for her answer but return to feasting on her pussy. It's wet, warm, and sweet. I could do this all day. My cock begs to be buried inside her, and as I eat her out, I think of pounding into her sweet pussy.

Her hands clamp harder on my head, and her groans are louder, her breathing more erratic. Pushing a second finger inside her, I increase the pace on her clit. But I want to feel her come on my tongue, so I remove my fingers and let my mouth work on her opening while my nose rubs against her, and I push her legs apart even more. I almost can't breathe, but who the fuck needs air when they have all this sweetness. She's jerking against me, moving with my movements, and I sense her coming before her juices trickle onto my waiting tongue, and I drink every drop of her. Her fingers tighten around my hair as she continues to come on my face, and it's so fucking perfect. I break away to breathe before I lick her soaking pussy, and she's begging me to stop, but I don't. I lick her pussy until all her sweetness is in my mouth and across my face. When I finally come up, she's staring at me in awe.

I smile at the look on her face. I want her to look at me like that every night when I eat her out. I lick my lips, and her gaze zeroes in on my mouth.

My cock is ready to burst at this stage, but as Kira comes down from her high, weariness starts to seep in, and it's not just about what happened to her. I know she's a virgin and most likely never experienced anything with a man. I grab a cushion off the couch and use it to clean my face before I help Kira pull up her clothes.

She seems conflicted, so I do what I think is right. "I have a meeting to go to. Do you think you'll be okay here with Angel?"

Relief and some disappointment enters her gaze. "Yes."

I don't want her thinking I'm running either, so I lean up and press a kiss to her lips. "You might return the favor tonight."

My cock pulses at the thought.

She nods and smiles at me. "I'd like that."

I get off the floor before I change my mind, and I hold out my hand to help her off the couch. She's almost shy after what happened, and that makes her even sexier.

I did have to go to the O'Reagans and let them know about Frank, make the deal, and see if they will help us with the Bratva. But I can't go anywhere with a raging hard-on.

"Go check on Angel," I say.

That's one way to keep Kira busy. She smiles, and as she walks out of the room, I call after her. "And don't forget to eat."

"I won't forget," she promises.

Once she leaves, I lock the door and sit on the couch where she had been. I open the belt of my trousers, push them down along with my boxers, and take my hard cock in my hand. The first stroke is almost painful. Beads of pre-cum gleam on the swollen head, and I run my fingers along it, using it as a lubricant as I stroke my cock while thinking about her sweet pink pussy. My cock jerks in my hand, and I pump harder and faster. I swallow saliva, and the taste of her sweetness has me pumping harder; the pressure has my hips rising as I push my cock heavily into my hand, each stroke faster than the last.

The cushion I used to clean my face is beside me, and I pick it up with my free hand and smell Kira. That's all I need to push me over the edge; my cream pours across my fingers. My ejaculation is messy and splashes onto my thighs, and I'm panting into the cushion. A few final jerks release the last of my cum, and I'm left with a sense of pure satisfaction before I grin. It's been a long time since I jerked off. I haven't had to. There was always someone there to do it for me. But thoughts of any other woman have my cock growing smaller by the second. I pull the cushion from my face as my phone rings.

Fuck's sake.

After wiping my hands on the cushion, I unzip the cover and use it to clean my cock and thighs before pulling up my trousers. Once I check the couch to make sure I haven't left a mess, I answer my phone.

"I'm leaving in a moment," I say to Alex as I roll up the cushion cover.

"I can pick you up," Alex says, and it sounds like he's driving.

"No, I'll meet you there," I say and hang up.

I leave the room and deposit the cover into the laundry room before going to my room and taking a quick shower. My cock grows hard again while I think of eating Kira out. I don't think I'll ever get enough of her. Maybe she'll please me tonight. I have to bury that thought as I turn off the water and get dressed in a fresh suit.

I need to get my head in the game. This meeting with the O'Reagans could help us break free of the Bratva. I leave the bedroom and am tempted to check on Kira, but seeing her will make it harder to leave. Zach is off trying to track down the ME for me, so I stop by the security hut where Noah is.

"I want you to keep a close watch on Kira. She's not allowed to leave, no matter what," I warn. I don't think she will try to leave, but I need to reinforce that with my men.

"No problem," Noah says, but he's staring at the feed from the cameras. The stiffness of his shoulders gives me pause.

"Are you feeling better?" I ask.

"Yeah, a few hours of rest is all I needed." He looks up at me this time.

There's something off about him. He's nervous around me. Or maybe I'm being paranoid.

"Okay, I won't be long." I leave the hut, and my suspicions that Noah is hiding something, behind as I go to meet Alex.

CHAPTER TWENTY-SEVEN

JASON

Brothers share a bond that, at one time, I thought would be unbreakable, but as I stare at Alex, I'm not sure. He's resting against the hood of his Mercedes, with his hands in his gray suit pockets. Alex has always been the odd one out. He's the oldest, the fastest, and the one who kept to himself. Not like Matty, but more in the way that he valued his p r i v a - cy.

I wonder if he still feels like the odd one out since he discovered who I am.

"They're already inside." He takes his hands out of his pockets and glances down at the heavy silver watch that's wrapped around his wrist.

"I had things to take care of." I think of eating Kira out.

"That was more important than this meeting?" Alex takes a step toward me.

"Yes," I say.

He looks toward the large warehouse where we're meeting the O'Reagans. Today, it will only be Jack and Shay. I would have preferred anyone but Shay, but Shay must know that, so he's making himself visible.

Alex pushes off the hood of his car, and I fall into step beside him as we make our way to the dilapidated building.

"You know, if you want me to do this, I will," Alex says as he holds the heavy metal door open for me to enter the warehouse. He isn't doing it out of manners. He's letting me walk into the unknown first, or maybe that's my pessimistic mind.

"I understand what we're about to do might not be fair to you," Alex continues, appearing uncomfortable with trying to let me off the hook.

"No. I want to do this."

The long paved corridor has been swept clean, but that's all the attention the hallway has received. No paint is on the cement walls. My mind jumps to Shay picking this place. I think Jack would be more accustomed to something luxurious.

A set of double doors at the end of the hallway is open. A makeshift meeting room has been set up with a table and a few chairs.

Jack rises from the table when Alex and I walk in. Like always, Shay shows the highest level of disrespect. He puffs away on a cigarette while wearing his signature grin.

I take Jack's hand, and when I sit down, Alex shakes Jack's hand, too.

"You better have something good this time." Shay sits forward, his grin gone, and I know not to piss him off. He's a fucking lunatic.

"Frank was the one who put the hit on Warren," I say quickly.

Jack's features tighten and he snarls. "Why?"

"That part, we aren't sure about," Alex says. His tone carries a level of boredom. It often does, but it's very evident right now.

"He's your father?" Shay leans across the table toward me, and I'm starting to think this is personal. That he doesn't like me.

"Your point?" I fire back.

He grins. "You must have known what he was up to."

His angry grin has me glancing at Jack, but he's staring at his hands. Fucking brilliant.

"Do you know everything your father is up to?" Before he can answer, I continue. "I wasn't raised by him, so we aren't exactly close." I knew he was starting a war with the O'Reagans. I told him it wasn't wise. Having

Edward's throne wasn't enough for my father; he wanted an empire. He may cause us to be left with nothing but rubble.

Shay sits back and taps the table a few times with his lighter.

"Where is he now?" Jack asks.

"I don't know."

Shay stands, and I track him around the room.

"I've tried calling him, but since our last meeting, I can't get through to him," I say.

"So you come here with one arm longer than the other?" Shay pipes up.

"We came here with information that you wanted," Alex says. Shay glares at him. "You need to show some respect," Alex adds. "We're respecting you, so you will respect us."

Shay continues to glare. He doesn't like being told what to do. He doesn't bend, but he doesn't say anything either.

"We will find Frank," Alex assures them.

My gut twists as I think of the reality of what I'm doing. They will kill him.

"What do you want in return?" Jack asks.

"The fact that we aren't coming after you for being accomplices with Frank..." Shay says while lighting up another cigarette.

"We had no idea," Alex says. He didn't. Aidan didn't. Matty didn't. William didn't. I did. And as Shay looks at me, I know he knows I was privy to every detail of what my father had planned. But admitting that would get me killed.

"Frank got us caught up with the Bratva, and we need to break free," I say to Shay. I want to talk to Jack, but that hasn't worked out well for me in the past.

"We have no dealings with them." Shay nods his head as he speaks before running his hand across his thick beard. "Even if we did, I don't know what we could do," he answers honestly.

"Aren't you marrying into the Bratva?" Jack says. His gaze is distant as he speaks.

"Yeah, it's complicated."

"Women are." Shay smiles while raising both brows.

"Something we can agree on," I fire back.

"So, we give you Frank, and we get diddly squat in return," Alex says.

"You did the right thing," Jack answers.

I tut. Like fuck we're here to do the right thing. "We want something in return, Jack."

Shay shifts forward and smirks. "We will call off the hit on your family."

That news makes me sit back. "What?"

Jack narrows his gaze at Shay.

Shay shrugs. "What did you expect? For us to sit on our hands as Frank picked us off one by one?"

They already knew it was Frank.

"Why are we here?" I glance over my shoulder, expecting to see someone with a gun pointed at me, but there isn't anyone.

"We were giving you an opportunity to come clean so we don't have to start a war. So, like Shay said, we will call off the hit on you, and you deliver Frank to us. This matter will be closed."

I'm so fucking confused.

"William?" Alex says beside me.

"They were Bratva that tried to kill William and me," I answer, looking from Shay to Jack.

"They are X members, low rankers that needed a few quid. Easy come, easy go," Shay says. "Fuck them. We weren't using the Irish." He grins before he leans across the table. "Remember when the British cunts sent all the Irish to the front line?"

Shay has ties to the Irish Republican Army. That was an area I would never get involved in.

"I'm not here for a history lesson," Alex says.

So, the O'Reagans tried to kill William and me. Now I wonder about Edward, but that was before Warren O'Reagan was clipped.

"What about Edward Murphy? Did you have a hand in his murder?" I can't breathe as I ask the question.

"No. I thought he took his life," Jack says.

I glance at Shay to see any deceit there.

"We would have no reason to touch Edward."

"Just William and me," I throw out there. Yes, I'm fucking pissed.

"The hit was on you, Jason. William just got caught up in it. And remember, you had Warren clipped. You should be fucking glad both of you survived, because of the sloppy cunts we sent," Shay barks.

When I kick back the chair and reach for him, he doesn't budge as I grip the collar of his jacket. "You're a piece of shit."

"Take your hands off him," Jack says to my right. He's standing, and I take a peek at him. I'm staring down the barrel of a gun.

He cocks the gun. "Don't make me repeat myself."

I take a look at Alex, who's also standing. We respected the code and didn't bring guns. I release Shay and stand back, but I don't sit down.

"You brought a gun." I nod my head. "That speaks volumes about your character."

"Never trust a criminal," Shay says like this is one big joke.

"So our family is safe," Alex reconfirms, trying to get this meeting back in line.

"Yes. Once our family is safe, too."

"Frank ordered the hit on Warren. Who ordered the hit on Jason?" Alex asks.

Jack smiles for the first time. "The four kings did. We don't make sole decisions."

"So, should we have all four of you strung up?" Alex asks. "You expect us to hand over Frank now?"

"If you don't, we won't stop," Shay threatens.

"Frank made the first move. Therefore, he should pay the price for this. Once we have him, all this ends."

I'm still a little shook that these men decided I was to die, yet Jack speaks to me like we could be friends. That's what makes us Mafia men, I suppose.

They've been in the game a long time.

"We will be in touch once we have him," I say, understanding that no help will come from the O'Reagan's with the Bratva. But at least this way, we'll secure our safety. There will be no more fear about having our family clipped. I get up, but I pause and look at Jack. "Matty was a target before Warren."

Jack frowns. "We would have no reason to hurt Matty."

"We had a good source."

"You need to check your source, because that cunt has been lying to you." We can't question the source because I sliced his throat. Aidan had questioned him.

I still don't trust the O'Reagans. Now I wonder if there is another outside force working against our family. In the Mafia world, you're never safe, but you don't expect the hits to keep coming from other Mafia families.

"What do you think?" Alex asks once we're out of the building.

"About what? Handing over Frank? That the fuckers tried to kill me?"

Alex stops at his car. "You think they had nothing to do with Matty?"

I shrug before fishing my keys out of my pocket. "It doesn't make sense for them to try to kill Matty. What could they gain?"

"Where is the man who told you the O'Reagan's were going to kill Matty?"

I shake my head. "He's dead."

"Are you sure?" Alex asks.

I'm already kicking myself. "I killed him myself."

"We need to look into his family, his movements, days before he delivered this news."

"I'll look into it," I say.

"I'll do it," Alex fires back before climbing into his car. I wonder if he doesn't trust me anymore.

The results aren't what I wanted, but at least our family is safe for now, and Frank will be out of our lives. I get into my car and watch Alex drive away just as my phone rings. I'm thinking of not answering it, but it's Zach.

"Everything okay?" I ask.

"Noah gave Frank access to your home."

I curse as I start the car. "Where is Frank now?"

"He's making himself a coffee." Humor fills Zach's voice.

"Okay, keep him there. I'm on my way."

I hang up and ring Alex. "Frank is at my house," I inform him.

"Why?" Suspicion fills Alex's voice.

"I don't know, Alex."

"Seems strange that he would have access to your home," Alex comments.

I grit my teeth. "One of my men let him in." Noah would have shown the same level of loyalty to Edward as he does Frank. He's also young, so I doubt it took much convincing on Frank's part.

"Did you ring Jack?"

"I rang you," I fire back and put on my windshield wipers as the rain starts to fall.

"I'll be there shortly. Can you manage to keep him in your home until I get there?"

"I'm not a fucking moron," I say and hang up.

I hate how Alex looks at me now, like I'm some kind of liability.

CHAPTER TWENTY-EIGHT

KIRA

I'VE CHECKED ON ANGEL several times, but thankfully she's still asleep. She needs her rest more than I need someone to talk to. I can't stop thinking about what Jason did. How good it felt, how much I wanted to touch him, but fear held me back. Fear of not knowing what to do and also the fear that if I touched him like that, this desire would flare to life, and I'm not sure I could douse the want. Already, the thoughts of never having him touch me causes panic to flutter to life.

Noah, the security man who offered me the keys, pauses in the hall when he sees me. He glances over his shoulder. "Get out of here." He half shouts at me, but he's also struggling to keep his voice low.

I have no idea why he's telling me to leave, but I don't, and another man walks around the corner. I know this man. I met him at Jack O'Reagan's wedding.

"Ah, Kira, how lovely to see you." Frank walks to me with an outstretched hand. "I was just about to make a coffee. Won't you join me?"

This is the man who beat Jason. "I'll have to pass," I tell him, and the look of relief on Noah's face gives me pause.

"I insist." Frank's voice carries no warmth. I know when a man is giving me a command and not a choice.

He doesn't wait for my response but turns and makes his way to the kitchen. I have no other choice but to follow.

He smiles at me the moment he turns. I wrap my arms around my waist. His smile is unsettling, and it reminds me of Nicco. Warning bells ring loudly in my mind, and I hover close to the door. He doesn't ask me to come in, so I stay exactly where I am.

He starts to work the coffee maker, and I become aware of someone behind me. Zach has the phone to his ear and takes a look at Frank before he walks away, talking too low for me to understand what he's saying.

"So, you're to marry my son," Frank says, taking two small cups down from the press.

"Yes." I keep my answer simple, and he glances at me over his shoulder, with a smile in his eyes that doesn't reach his lips.

"I'm going to be blunt with you, Kira." He pours out two small cups of coffee and carries them to the island. "A law was just passed that you and your brother requested."

My skin crawls. Frank pushes the coffee closer to the edge of the island and in my direction. I want to decline, but he doesn't touch his own and waits. I walk into the kitchen.

"Milk and sugar." He points at them on the center of the island.

"So, I assumed you were leaving," he finishes.

I pour a small amount of milk into the cup just to please him. I don't drink coffee, but I pick up the cup and take a sip. He seems satisfied. "I don't think so," I answer.

He smiles again, but anger flashes in his eyes. "It would be in your best interest to leave." He drinks from his cup and watches me over the rim.

What does any of this have to do with him?

"I don't want to get into politics, but your brother holds my son's life in his hands, and right now, your brother wants you back."

I have no idea if Jason wants me, but going back to Nicco is more than I can bear to think about.

Frank picks up the suit jacket he had discarded on one of the high-back chairs and takes out a rolled-up bunch of papers. He unrolls them and places them on the island. "This is for you to sign. I told Nicco I would get them to you."

So, he's doing Nicco's work for him. Frank pushes the papers toward me and slides over a pen. "You'll sign, then I'll have Jason sign when he gets back, and then you're free." He smiles at me like it's that simple.

I glance down at the contracts and already know they're the ones needed to leave this marriage, only to enter another with my brother.

"No," I answer. I can't do that.

He snorts a laugh. "No?" He exhales loudly. "Since when do women wield such power?"

He moves around the island, taking the papers and pen with him until he stops right in front of me. "Sign the papers. Don't make this harder on yourself."

My chest tightens, and I don't move.

Frank picks up the pen and holds it out toward me. I don't take it. Fear has me wanting to do whatever this man tells me to. I glance at the kitchen door, wanting someone to appear, even Zach, but no one is there.

"When did Nicco ask you to do this?" I find myself asking.

Frank's gaze narrows as he still holds out the pen for me to take.

"When did you get the right to question me?" he rebuts. "You do know who I am?"

I nod. "With all respect—"

"You are not showing me respect. Jason will gladly sign these papers, so you are better doing it now than later."

The pen is nearly in my face. "I can't," I whisper. I can't go back to Nicco. I can't subject myself to such a future. Jason might not want me here, but I can't stop fighting for my and Angel's safety.

He grabs my hand and I push away, knocking my coffee across the island. But he doesn't release me. Instead, I find the pen shoved between my fingers as Frank drags the contracts toward us.

"Fucking sign it!" He pushes the pen down on the page.

I try to pull away as his hand grows tighter around mine. The pain is crushing my fingers. "No!" My heart thumps when he starts to scrawl my name across the line.

"Let her go." The calmness in Jason's voice has both of us spinning, and just like that, I'm free of Frank's hold.

"She's being difficult," Frank says while dropping the pen. He runs his hand across his face, but the wariness in his gaze is evident.

Jason drops his keys and phone on a side counter and walks to the island. I want to run but stay still as he looks down at the contracts. "What is this?" He's angry—no, he's infuriated.

"Nicco wants her to sign the papers she promised to sign," Frank says, but he hasn't moved back to his coffee. He's staying right where he is.

Jason reads them, then takes a look at me. "Do you want to sign this?"

I take a look at Frank, who glares at me with murder in his eyes, but when I look back at Jason, I shake my head. Is that relief I see in Jason's gaze?

"There you have it, Frank. She said no." He turns to Frank and throws the papers at him. "So, you can tell Nicco just that."

"You don't say no to the Bratva," Frank grinds out.

Jason sneers. "I just did."

Frank walks back to his coffee and takes a drink as if there isn't any tension in the room. Tension that feels to me as if it were sucking oxygen out of the air. "Your mother was part of the Bratva," Frank says, and this surprises me.

Jason doesn't show any sign of surprise. He's only a ball of anger.

"She was part of one of the most powerful families. The Putins. Her brothers are very high up."

Shock rolls across me. They are the most powerful family. How did I not know this about Jason?

"Then go to them and beg to get us out of the mess you got us into." Jason glances down at the spilled coffee that's now dripping onto the floor. He frowns.

"They hate me. I already tried that before."

"Why do they hate you?" Jason barks. "Because their sister is dead?" He shakes his head.

Frank places the cup onto the counter. "I'm doing all this for you, son. I'm securing your future. Nicco will make you the head of this family, as you should be, and not Alex."

"I don't want to be the head of this family. This isn't about me. It never was. It's always about you." Jason walks over to Frank, picks up his suit jacket, and pushes it into his father's chest. "Leave now, before I do something I'll regret."

"What, like shoot me?" Frank snarls and grips his jacket. "If you marry her..." Frank points at me and Jason reacts. His fist connects with his father's face. I don't know who is more shocked, Frank or me. Blood trickles from his nose, and he wipes it away before staring at the red liquid that's coating his fingers. "She needs to go back."

I turn away as Jason hits Frank in the face again. The sound of flesh meeting flesh has me shivering.

"All this was Edward's, so it belongs to Alex. Not me." Jason's anger is growing and gathering darkness as he grabs Frank by the throat. "When will you understand that? I don't want it. I want none of it." Jason's roar has me moving away from the island.

"Don't be so fucking weak," Frank fires back, his own anger rising to the surface. He pushes Jason away, and it's the calm before the storm. I can see it in Jason's stance.

"I fucking hate you," he shouts before he launches himself at his father. The scuffle has Jason slamming Frank against the island. Frank's coffee spills, and the cup shatters on the floor. Jason's fists repeatedly slam into Frank's face until it's a bloody mess. I can't seem to react. I'm frozen, watching Jason lose himself in the violence.

"Jason, stop." My voice is low, but if he doesn't stop, he will seriously injure his father, and no matter how much he hates him, he'll regret it later. Jason doesn't stop, and I shout louder, taking a step toward the men.

"Jason." He pauses, and I feel a second of relief before Frank uses the moment and slams his forehead into Jason's face. I hear the crunch before blood pours from Jason's nose.

There is a lull in the room as I try to breathe. The savagery continues. They're going to kill each other. I dash from the room, and I don't have to go far before I see security.

"They're killing each other." I'm breathless, as if I've run a mile, but the two security men follow me back to the kitchen. I'm waiting for them to jump in and stop the madness, but they stand close by, as Jason has the upper hand and hits Frank in the face.

"Do something!" I scream at them, but they don't.

Frank stumbles back and his head hits the side of the marble island. I hear the crack. My stomach swells and bubbles as a wound opens along his skull and blood gushes out. Jason continues to beat him even as his father falls to the ground. He doesn't notice that Frank isn't fighting back.

"Jason, stop!" I cry and take two steps toward him. I find myself hitting the ground as someone knocks me aside and grabs Jason. Zach pulls Jason off Frank, but Jason continues to swing his fists. He's out of control with rage. Another person races into the room. I recognize Alex, Jason's brother, and between him and Zach, they manage to drag Jason away from his father, who's convulsing on the ground.

Horror opens up inside me as Frank struggles to breathe while blood comes from his mouth, nose, and head. I get a horrible flash of my father jerking as Nicco took his life, and I can't look away as Frank struggles to breathe. Alex leaves Jason and turns Frank onto his side to try to allow some air into his lungs.

The blood that pools on the floor has my terror growing, and when Jason looks over at me, the air halts in my lungs.

CHAPTER TWENTY-NINE

JASON

"H e's dead," Alex says.

I can't look away from Kira as she stares at me wide-eyed. She's so fucking pale. I push Zach off me, and he stands up, holding his hands in the air.

"He's dead," Alex repeats.

"I heard you the first time." I fix my tie and get up off the floor before walking over to Frank's dead body.

Fuck.

That hadn't been my intention, but I saw red when I walked into the room and saw the fear in Kira's eyes. He had spent his whole life bullying and terrorizing me, but I couldn't allow him to cast that net over Kira. Now, he would never hurt anyone again. But, I had promised Frank to the O'Reagans, in return of them calling off their men from killing us.

I reach down and look for a pulse in the bloody mess.

Alex stands and tilts his head. "We needed him." He shows no upset at having his uncle dead at his feet, but Alex never does. For him, killing is easy. I've never seen him show an ounce of remorse, and maybe that's why he was the better man to lead us. I've killed, but each time, it takes a bit from me.

I look down at Frank. "They never said what condition he had to be in," I say.

Alex nods a few times. I glance over at my security and Zach. "Have you tracked down Noah?" I ask Zach. Noah has been loyal to me, but to my father as well. Yet, I've never wanted to kill anyone so badly.

I see the uncertainty in Zach's eyes. He cares for Noah more than any of the rest of my men.

He shakes his head. "I'll find him," Zach says. I know he wants to ask that we don't kill him, but he sees now isn't the time. My answer right now would be that he has to die for allowing Frank into my home and to harass Kira.

I take another look at her, and she's still staring at Frank. I walk to her, and her gaze snaps to me as I kneel down.

"You're okay," I tell her.

She nods and tears fall from her eyes. Holding out my hand, I'm not sure if she'll take it. I pray she does, and my prayers are answered.

Her small hand fits mine, and I help her off the ground. I wipe the tears from her cheeks. She's looking over at Alex and Frank and back to the security, who still stands behind us.

"Are you okay?" I ask again. She's more aware of all my men watching us, but I need to make sure she's okay.

"Yes." Her voice is stronger than I expected. I smile even in the chaos. She's strong. "Why don't you check on Angel?"

She doesn't look ready to leave, but we need to move Frank's body, and I don't want her here for that. "Your friend needs you."

She nods, but her focus keeps returning to Frank's dead body. I look over her head at one of my men. "Walk her to Angel's room," I say.

"Go," I instruct, and finally Kira walks away, and one of my men goes with her.

"We can wrap him up and hand him over to Jack today," I say to Alex.

"Get me some plastic wrap," I order my other security man, and he leaves.

"Go hunt down Noah," I reinforce to Zach, who is still watching us.

He isn't happy, but he leaves me alone with Alex.

"You want to tell me how this happened?" Alex asks as he pats down Frank's dead body.

"He was hurting Kira, trying to force her to sign contracts. He was sent here by Nicco."

Alex meets my eye, stares at me, and nods like that's as good of an answer as any other.

When my security man arrives back with the plastic, Alex and I get to work wrapping Frank's body. We carry him through the house and out the front door, where a car is waiting with the trunk open.

"Do you want to get changed first?" Alex asks, and I take a look at the front of my blood-soaked shirt.

"Yeah, give me a moment."

He waits in the car while I change into a fresh suit. I enter the bathroom and wash the blood from my hands. I think of every time Frank beat me, broke my ribs, tortured me, burned my flesh—and all in the name of becoming a strong man.

I meet my gaze in the mirror, and I don't feel shame or regret. I wish I had done it sooner. I leave and get into the car with Jason and call Jack O'Reagan. He answers quickly.

"We have Frank. We can meet at Bective Forest to do the trade-off."

"Okay, I'll be there soon," Jack says.

I have no idea how this will work out, but like I said to Alex, they hadn't specified what condition Frank needed to be in.

"If this works out, at least our names are off the hit list with the O'Reagans."

"We still need to break free of the Bratva." Alex gives me the reminder I don't need.

"My mother was a Putin." I offer the small bit of information that Frank gave me.

Alex glances at me. "Really?"

I nod. "So Frank said. But he's a lying fucker, so who knows?"

"If it's true, they may help us."

I laugh. "They don't even know I exist. If my mother really came from that family." Now I wonder if that is why Frank gave me to Edward to raise as his own. Was it to keep me hidden from my mother's family? It feels like each time we take two steps forward, we take ten back.

We arrive at the forest, but no one else is here. "We still need to figure out who killed Dad," I say, looking around at the dense trees.

"We will," Alex reassures me.

I take a look at Alex, but there is no emotion on his face. "I don't think I ever thanked you," I say.

"For what?" Alex takes off his belt.

"For coming for me at that time and putting me in rehab." Once I got clean and left, I never spoke about what happened. I buried the knowledge that Frank was my father. I buried my memories of living on the street and using. I buried all the details, even Alex finding me. It's blurry, but I have some memories, just not all.

"I did it for Dad," Alex says and looks at me.

"Whatever your reason, thank you," I say.

He nods, and we both look at the approaching SUV. I'm glad to see that it's Richard who's with Jack and not Shay. I'm not sure I could take much more of his smart mouth.

We get out, and once the O'Reagans stop their vehicle, they get out. Jack looks behind me. "So where is he?"

Alex walks to the back of our vehicle and pops the trunk. Richard and Jack follow us, and we're all staring in at Frank's wrapped body.

"He's no use to us dead," Richard says.

"You never said." Alex looks up at Richard. "We promised you Frank and here he is."

But Jack looks at me, and I don't like how he addresses me all the time, like he sees me as the leader here and not Alex.

"When we left, he was at my home," I say. "He hurt my future wife, and things got out of hand."

Jack doesn't accept my explanation. He looks at Richard before glancing back at me. "It might seem that he's conveniently dead so he can't talk and tell us that he didn't order the hit on Warren, that maybe you did."

"Why would I do that?" I ask.

"Power, money, a trade-off with the Bratva. The list is pretty fucking endless," Jack says.

"We can stand here arguing over a dead body, or you can take Frank. We delivered like we promised. Now you deliver like you promised," Alex says, and his voice carries the same note of boredom as it often does. He grips the trunk lid. "Do you want him or not?"

Richard and Jack exchange another glance.

When no one moves, I feel like I've shot myself in the foot. "I didn't mean to kill him. It was an unlucky blow, and he hit his head," I say.

"You don't seem broken up over killing your own father." Richard narrows his eyes.

"He was a bastard," I answer.

I hold Richard's stare, and I have no idea what he sees, but he pats Jack on the back. "Let's take him. We never said he had to be alive."

Jack isn't happy, but relief has me reaching in for Frank's body, and I help Jack carry it to the back of his SUV. Frank is heavy and once he's out of my hands, I take a moment.

"So, that's it. Are we good?"

"Jack closes the back door. "Yes. You held up your end. So, we will hold up ours. But if another attack ever comes to our family, we won't ask questions."

The threat from Jack isn't necessary, and any other time, I wouldn't be happy, but I'll take it. I hold out my hand. There's something I like about him compared to the others.

"This will be the end." Jack hesitates but takes my hand and shakes it. "Good luck," he says, releasing my hand. Richard walks past me and gets into the passenger seat. I stand back as they reverse and watch the red taillights float into the distance.

I should feel more satisfaction that Frank is gone. We know who tried to kill me, and why, and we also know how William got hurt. It can allow us to focus on the Bratva, but I don't think they'll be easy to worm our way out of.

Nicco can't do anything about Kira. He might be pissed, but he can't react. If he does, we can retaliate. He will get his comeuppance soon.

As Alex and I get back into the car, my phone rings. It's Zach.

"Yes, I'm on my way back. Did you find him?" I ask as Alex starts the car.

"No, but I found someone else."

"Who?" I ask.

Alex glances at me.

"Rob, the Medical Examiner."

Hope surges hard and fast. I relay the information. "Zach found Rob, the ME."

Alex nods and focuses on the road. I thought he would show some emotion.

"He's being pulled from the river," Zach adds.

Fuck.

Another dead end.

CHAPTER THIRTY

KIRA

"H e's dead." That's all I can hear in my head. The door to Angel's room opens, and I'm standing at the foot of her bed. She pushes back her blankets. Her mouth moves, and shadows shift in the room.

"He's dead." The words repeat and Frank's face is replaced with my father's. I stood there and did nothing.

Angel touches my arms. She shakes me and I blink. Tears fall and I'm living it all over again. The sting of a hand against my cheek has blood rushing to my face and sound pounding in my ear.

"What happened?" Angel's voice is frantic.

She just hit me. I blink and let more tears spill so I clear my vision. "It's okay." I'm gripping her hands, trying to calm her. She's been through enough. "It's okay," I repeat.

Her blonde hair bounces with each shake of her head. "You look like you saw a ghost, Kira. What happened?"

"Jason just killed his dad." I'm half hunched, half whispering the words.

Angel clamps her hand over her mouth before she marches to the door and turns the lock. Like that would stop him. If Jason wanted to get in here, he could, but he would have no reason to hurt us. He has never hurt me.

You just witnessed a murder. A voice whispers in the back of my mind.

"Oh, fuck. Oh, fuck. Did you see him?" Angel asks while walking back to the bed. She slumps down, sweat beading along her forehead. She isn't able to do this.

"I want you to rest." I try to lift the blankets to get her under them, but she grabs my hand, stopping me. "Did he see you?"

I tilt my head, begging her with my eyes to just leave it.

"Kira, did he see you?"

I nod.

She exhales and closes her eyes. When she looks at me again, it's with purpose. "We need to leave."

I straighten and fold my arms across my chest. "He would never hurt me. He got you for me," I remind Angel. "And we can't leave. Nicco might come for us."

So many scenarios race through my mind.

"Are you kidding me? What's the first thing you learn about Mafia men? You witness a crime and you get clipped."

I know she's right, but I want to be the exception to the rule. I have to believe that Jason would never harm me. "Not Mafia wives." I try to defend us staying here.

"You're not his wife," Angel reminds me.

My stomach twists.

"I'm sorry, Kira." She tries to soothe me.

I hate how transparent I am. I want to be his wife. I want to stay with him. But I can't allow my heart to rule my head.

"You love him," Angel says as I slump down beside her.

I'm not sure what this is that I feel, but I know it's strong. Whatever my feelings are for Jason, they aren't the only reason I can't run.

I look at Angel before I speak. "Nicco killed my dad." I finally voice out loud the truth that's haunted me. I don't feel a weight lift. I only see that weight placed around my friend's shoulders as well.

"No, Kira." Horror floods her big blue eyes.

I nod. "I saw him do it." The guilt churns and sours as I think about how I did nothing. "I froze. I froze, watching him strangle my father to death in his own office."

Angel takes my hand. "I have to prove it somehow, Angel. Nicco needs to be punished." I squeeze her fingers.

"There are cameras in his office."

"No, there aren't," I say, wishing there were. But that's one room without cameras. Even the main bathroom has cameras.

"Yes, there are." Angel wriggles her fingers from mine. She won't look at me. "I know for sure." She glances at me from the corner of her eye.

"How?" The hairs rise along my arms from the look Angel gives me. I've never seen it on her face before. It's a look of defeat, a look of horror. "Angel." I'm ready to shake her.

"I stole from your father, and he caught me."

I stand up and try to process what she's saying. Angel would never steal. "What?"

"It was stupid. I know."

"He would have killed you." What she was saying couldn't be true. To steal from a man like my father would come with a death penalty.

Angel won't even look at me now. "Yes, he should have. But he knew we were close." She looks at me from under her lashes. "He spared me as long as I never left your side."

The ground shifts under my feet, and I move back, looking for the wall to hold on to.

"You stayed because you had to."

Angel rises. "Kira, I would have stayed anyway. You are my best friend."

"You lied to me," I whisper.

"I'm sorry."

I can't even answer her. I'm still trying to process what just happened in the kitchen to allow Angels's betrayal to register fully.

"You need to tell Jason about Nicco killing your dad. Maybe he could help us."

"Two seconds ago, you wanted to run."

Angel sits back down on the bed. "I'm trying to think of what's best for you, Kira."

I'd laugh if I had an ounce of energy. I don't. She's taken the last of it.

"Kira, please," she begs.

"Rest for now. We can talk more in the morning." I walk back to her even though I don't want to and make her lie down.

Tears run out of the corners of her eyes. "You're my best friend. I would have stayed."

I bite my lip to stop from crying and pull the blanket over Angel's frame. "Get some rest."

She blinks and more tears spill. I sit on one of the chairs and listen to Angel's gentle sobs, not ready to leave the room. Why did she steal from Dad? That's what I think as I look over at her frame.

Telling Jason about Nicco won't help us. He wouldn't care, and I can't expect him to do anything about it. If there are cameras in my dad's office, maybe the recordings are still there. That's all the evidence I need to get and take to Uncle Romero. Then I could finally be free of Nicco for good.

"Kira." Angel's gentle voice almost undoes me.

"We leave tonight," I say with conviction. The security guard, Noah, tried to let me leave before. If I can find him, maybe he'll let Angel and me slip out.

Angel pushes back the covers and slowly sits up. Each movement of hers is painful. "So, we leave here and go to Nicco's?"

Dread spreads fast throughout my system. We need to get into the house, but the thought of seeing my brother has me wanting to curl up in a ball and stay here where we're safe. Where I *thought* we were safe, but how safe am I? After witnessing Jason kill Frank in front of his men, that won't play out well for me.

"Yes." I run my palms along my thighs.

Angel nods, but she already wears a look of defeat. "And if he catches us?" she asks.

"We can't let that happen."

"He was taken away by the Gardaí. Maybe he won't be back."

He will be. Because I'm not pressing charges. "I rang the Gardaí to get him out of the house so we could get you."

Astonishment widens Angel's eyes. "Oh, Kira. What did you tell them? Did you tell them about your dad?"

A shiver races along my shoulders. "No. Nicco hurt me, and I reported it."

Angel freezes, gripping the bedsheets. She's looking at my face, my hands, any piece of skin as if she's looking for wounds. But she won't find any.

"When? What did he do?"

I shake my head. "We just need to get into the house without his knowing."

I still can't look Angel in the eyes after her deceit. "Why did you steal?" I finally ask.

Her cheeks redden. "I don't have any family, and Nicco terrified me. I wanted to get out."

She was always paid a very good wage, but I also get it. To break free from the Bratva, no matter who you are, you need to run and hide and take a lot of money. "The money and car I gave you?"

"I parked it close to a beach. It should still be there."

"When we get the tapes showing Nicco killing my dad, you can leave. Start over."

She's shaking her head. "I'm sorry I tried to leave."

Waves of guilt roll over my flesh. "No, Angel, you were right to try to get out. Just stealing from my dad…" I don't finish that sentence. It was stupid. She was one of the lucky ones. My father never showed any signs that he didn't trust Angel. He spared her for me.

"I know. I can make it right. I can go back and get the tapes." Angel chews on her lip. I want to agree, but it wouldn't be right.

"We go together. Get some rest." I pull my legs up to my chest to cut off the conversation. I do get why Angel stole, but it didn't change how it made me feel. Like she was only there with me because she feared for her life, and if she'd had a choice, she would have left.

Time ticks away, and Angel soon falls into a light sleep. I shower and get back into the same clothes. I don't attempt to leave the room. I'm not ready to face what just happened. Flashes of Frank's dead body keep assaulting my mind, along with my father's limp frame. I want it to stop.

A soft knock on the door hours later has me sitting upright. Angel stirs from her light slumber as the door opens.

Everything in me clashes: the joy at seeing Jason, the pain at seeing Jason, the fear at seeing Jason.

He closes the door behind him and Angel sits up, clutching the blanket to her chest. I remain seated.

"How are you feeling, Angel?" he asks before stuffing his hands into his trouser pockets. He's in a fresh navy suit. The last time I saw him, he was covered in blood.

"I'm okay." Angel glances at me with fear in her eyes.

"I thought you ladies might be hungry. I had the chef prepare a meal for us."

"That sounds great," I say too quickly, and Jason's gaze narrows. He's always trying to get me to eat, but the thought of being in a more open space and out of this room has me agreeing. "I'm hungry," I finally say as he continues to watch me.

"Whenever you're ready." He gives Angel a curt nod before leaving. Once the door closes, I'm off the chair.

"You need to hide how you're feeling," I say to Angel as I help her up from the bed.

"You just told me he killed his father. That's a bit hard to hide." Angel's hands shake.

"We need him to relax and trust us so we can leave tonight."

Angel swallows, nods, and gets up. "Okay."

We leave the bedroom, and I link my arm with Angel's, helping her walk. She's stiff, but she's a lot better than she was.

An obscene amount of food trays cover the large dining table. Marriott greets me and Angel like we're regular guests here. I wonder if she helped clean up all the blood in the kitchen we just passed. There isn't a drop to be seen.

Jason stands and pulls out a chair beside him for either Angel or me. I sit closer to him to give Angel some distance. Once we're seated, Jason sits back down.

A large roast steams in the center of the table. The vegetables are separated into several silver dishes. Marriott stands behind us, and when Jason nods, she leaves.

I nudge Angel gently to stop staring at Jason and to get some food. She does, and I do the same.

"Nicco has been released," Jason says. I wasn't expecting him to talk about Nicco in front of Angel. Maybe he assumes I told her, considering how close I told him we were.

"So, he's back home?" Angel asks.

Jason's jaw clenches. "For now," he grinds out. His gaze softens when he looks at me. "Are you okay?" he asks, like all the pretense of this moment dissolves, and it's just us.

How easy it would be to stay here with Jason, but I can't erase what he did, and he can't erase what I just witnessed. It hits me so hard that I couldn't tell him about seeing Nicco kill my dad. He might think one day I would go forward to say I witnessed him killing his own father.

"I will be fine." I focus on my plate, not wanting to keep looking at Jason. Having dinner with him is harder than I could have imagined. The idea of leaving slams into me, and I reach for a glass of water.

"Where are you from, Angel?" Jason diverts his attention to my friend. I just hope she can hold it together.

"Originally, Poland. But I've been in Ireland since I was ten."

"What made your family come here?" Jason continues to quiz Angel, and some part of me thinks he's doing it for my benefit, to make us relax.

"I was a refugee. I didn't come with my family."

I take a peek at Angel. For all I know about her, she never spoke about her past, and now I wonder what she survived.

"Are you Irish?" Angel asks.

Jason smiles. "Yes, true and true. But my mother was Russian."

The uneasy conversation continues, and I zone out as I think of what we have to do. The loss each time I think of leaving Jason has me consider staying. Bury my head and hope that Nicco never gets his hands on me, but then my father's killing will never be brought to justice.

The main course is cleared away, and Angel and I decline dessert.

"Would you mind if I have a moment with Kira?" Jason asks Angel.

She glances at me, and I nod. "I'll go for a shower," she says and rises. Her footfalls on the floor sound heavy, and Jason doesn't speak until she's out of the room.

"I'm sorry for what happened with Frank."

I place my hands in my lap.

"He shouldn't have touched you," Jason adds.

I look at him now. I'm picturing Jason losing himself in the violence. I want to point out that he killed him, but I keep my mouth closed.

"He didn't hurt me," I settle on.

"He had no right to touch you," Jason bites out. "But I'm sorry you had to witness that."

That? Him murdering his father?

"What are you thinking?" Jason asks me when I don't speak.

I'm looking at his handsome face, and I think about what a shame this is. Why Nicco, even from far away, continues to destroy my life.

"Do you regret it?" I blurt out. "You don't have to answer that," I say quickly.

Jason wipes his mouth on a napkin. "It's a fair question. I regret you being there."

My heart hammers. "But you don't regret killing him?" I need to shut my mouth, but I've never wanted to understand someone so much.

"He tortured me my entire life. He kept my mother's identity hidden from me. He allowed me to carry a huge lie about who I was. He has done so much wrong to my brothers, and I fear he may have had a hand in his own brother's death. So no, Kira. I don't regret it."

I nod. That list does justify his death, especially in our world. But the rules can be bent when it suits men in power.

Just like with Nicco. He won't be punished for raping me, but I can hope to have him punished for killing my father. I'm tempted to tell Jason everything, to ask for his help, but fear keeps the words buried inside me. Jason stands and walks to me, holds out his hand, and I take it. My body sighs at his touch. His hand is warm and familiar, and I know how it feels on my body. He helps me rise, and when I'm standing in front of him, he gently pulls me into his arms.

Tears brim my eyes, but I refuse to lose the small amount of strength I've gathered. "Things will settle down now, and you can spend your time with Angel," he says before pressing a kiss to my forehead.

I look up into his eyes and my stomach quivers. His smell wafts around me. One second he's looking at me with a softness, and the next, his gaze pools with what I can identify as lust. His lips consume mine, and I want to hold on tight to my strength, but it bends and snaps, and I'm leaning into Jason, kissing him back like a starving woman.

I'm clinging to him like a drowning victim, and I want to get lost in him. In his touch. His hand slips from my face and along my neck, leaving a path of goose bumps in its wake.

He breaks the kiss, and he's looking at me, and I'm looking at him. I'm thinking about his getting Angel for me. No one has ever done anything like that for me before. I'm bound to the truth that he has stayed by my side all through my hardships with Nicco.

I reach up and grip the back of his neck and kiss him with everything I have. I won't hold back this time.

CHAPTER THIRTY-ONE

JASON

SHE'S PERFECT. I NEED her right now. What she asked about my father eats away at me. I don't regret that he's dead, but it doesn't stop the blood from pounding in my system. Every life I take weighs heavier on my heart and soul, and I think Kira can calm the frenzy in my system. Her mouth is perfect on mine, and when she slips her tongue between my lips, the blood goes to my cock. I want her.

When I break the kiss, I don't think as I take her hand and lead her out of the dining hall. She glances at the spot in the kitchen where Frank bled out. I tighten my fingers around hers as we walk into the hall, and she doesn't hesitate as we walk up the stairs. When we reach the bedroom, I close the door and release her hand.

I turn to her, and a pulse pounds in her neck, but she doesn't look afraid. She wears the same expression that I'm sure I wear. Maybe we both need this release. Thinking about her sweet pussy has me pulling her back into me. I don't kiss her but stare down at Kira. Her gaze grows nervous as she bites her lip, and I feel amused watching her.

"What do you want?" I ask. I know what I want to hear.

"What do you mean?" Her tone is low.

I touch her neck, and her lids flutter closed. "What do you want right now?" I press a kiss to her cheek before trailing down her neck. "Do you want this?" I ask, kissing her collarbone.

"Yes." She sounds breathless. I take my time pressing kisses along her neck before I return to her mouth. Her lips are wet and parted for me. My tongue slides in, and I love the taste of her. I prefer the sweetness between her legs. Her hands reach up and push my suit jacket down as far as it will go. I shrug it off the rest of the way.

She touches the top button of my shirt. I smile into the kiss as I unbutton my shirt. I break the kiss to take it off, and Kira's gaze travels across my chest. When her gaze drops lower, my cock throbs. She doesn't reach for the belt of my trousers, so I don't remove them. Instead, I take her face in my hands and kiss her again before leading us to the bed. The hem of her top rises as I pull it over her head. The black bra is full, and I reach around and unclip it. Her breasts bounce free. Her pink nipples are hard, and I do what I want and take one in my mouth. Kira's head rolls back, and she groans as I suck the hard nipple before moving to the other.

"You want a repeat of earlier?" I ask. Thinking of how perfect her pussy tasted. She nods, her gaze like someone who's drugged. Opening the button of her trousers, I don't take them off but dip my hand below the waistband and find my way inside her. She's so fucking wet. She's gazing up at me, and I've never wanted to devour someone so badly.

I want to bury my cock between her legs. When her hand touches my belt, I don't need any more encouragement. I remove my wet fingers from between her legs and bring the two fingers to my mouth and taste her before taking off my trousers. When I push my boxers down, my erection is there for her to stare at, and she does stare. Her chest rises and falls, her nipples harden, and I already know she's ready for me. She doesn't try to touch me, and I'm sure it wouldn't take much for me to come right now. She's perfect, but I want her trousers off.

I start to reach for them, but with shaky hands, she unzips them before shimmying out of them. All she's wearing is a black pair of soaking wet panties. Stepping close to her, I press a kiss to her lips before gripping her hips and lifting her onto the bed.

I leave her there as I open the bedside table and take out a condom. Before I can roll it onto my aching cock, Kira stops me.

"Wait."

I groan, knowing if she doesn't want to have sex, then we won't, but I want her so badly.

"I want to touch it." She holds out her hand and I walk to her.

My cock is in her face, and I can imagine her small mouth wrapping around me. She runs her index finger along my shaft, and it jumps at her touch. I close my eyes, and when she wraps her hand around my cock, I bend over, pressing both hands onto her shoulders.

"That feels so fucking good," I tell her.

She strokes once, twice, but I don't want to come like this. I want to bury myself inside Kira. I pull my cock away, and this time, Kira doesn't stop me when I roll the condom down my shaft.

Once it's on, Kira lies back, and I climb up on the bed and settle in between her thighs. The small piece of black fabric is all that separates us. I want to thrust into her and fuck her hard, but I restrain, and instead, push her panties aside and slip a finger into her pussy.

She groans loudly and her pussy tightens around my finger. I push a second finger inside her. My cock aches for its turn, and I can't hold back. Gripping her hips, I pull her closer to me. Her eyes are closed and I want her to look at me.

"Open your eyes."

Her lids flutter open, and I push the head of my cock inside her. Instantly, she reaches up and grabs my shoulders as I slowly let my cock slide inside her. Bending my neck, I suck on her perky nipple and she arches, giving me more access to her. I push a bit deeper. It takes all my concentration not to fuck her how I want. In time, I will, and that's what gives me control as I push a bit deeper inside her. I don't stop until I fill Kira, and she takes all of me.

She grips my shoulders tightly, and I release her nipple from in between my teeth before I press my mouth to hers. Her kisses are breathless as I withdraw and push in again. When she groans into my mouth, I push inside her again. Each stroke gets easier as her juices continue to lubricate my cock, allowing it to slide in and out of her. I go faster but still keep some amount of control, aware I need to be gentle with her. When my tongue enters her mouth, her own dances with mine, and I move faster and deeper inside her. Her core clenches around my cock, and I know I'm going to come. I open my eyes and fight the oncoming orgasm as I continue to slide in and out of her pussy. I leave her mouth again and tease her nipples with my teeth. She's panting and groaning, and I want her to come all over my cock.

Her nails dig into my shoulders, and I feel them down to my soul. Everywhere our bodies touch, I feel it fully, and I'm moving faster, pushing her legs further apart, wanting more, needing to moan louder.

She's wiggling under me, panting heavily, and I know she's going to come. I move quicker but still hold back, not wanting to hurt her. I keep focus on her face as she comes so sweetly on my cock. My own release follows her, the release I've been holding back, and I enter her as deeply as I can as I cum in her sweet pussy. I jerk a few more times, emptying myself completely before I stop and bury my head in Kira's neck. She smells so sweet, and I kiss along the soft skin before pressing a final kiss to her mouth. Her eyes are open, and she stares up at me.

No words are exchanged, but I sense something has shifted between us. She trusted me enough to give herself to me, and I want to tell her I won't let her down. I'll make her happy. I press a kiss to her lips before I slowly extract myself from her. I check the condom that's filled with my cum and slowly take it off. She's still sprawled out on my bed when I enter the bathroom and deposit the condom into the bin.

When I return, she's sitting up with her knees pulled up to her chin. She's a picture. "Are you okay?" I ask, picking my boxers up off the floor and putting them back on. I climb back onto the bed and kiss one knee at a time.

She smiles at me. "Yes." She bites her lip, and I smile back at her.

"I didn't hurt you?"

She shakes her head, blonde hair falling into her eyes. I push the hair behind her ear. "Good." I kiss her forehead.

I want to pull her into the bed and stay like that for the night, but Kira gets up, and I watch her as she gets dressed.

"I'm going to stay with Angel tonight. I don't think she should be alone." She isn't looking at me as she speaks.

I'm trying to catch her gaze. "Are you sure I didn't hurt you?"

She finally looks at me. "It was perfect, Jason."

She says it so softly, and I detect sadness in her tone. I don't understand and hate the loss I feel as she finishes getting dressed. I want her to stay, but I also understand she wants to be with her friend. Kira gives me one final look filled with regret. I want to ask if she regrets sleeping with me, but I'm a coward and let her leave.

I'm sure it's my mind playing tricks on me. The minute I'm alone, I think of Frank's face, covered in blood, and the satisfaction I felt with each hit. Each time he beat me, I had dreamed about hurting him, but I was never strong enough, physically or mentally. It took him touching Kira to unleash the anger that burned through my fear faster than anything imaginable.

I get dressed, not wanting to be alone, and ring Zach. "Any sign of Noah?" I ask.

"None," Zach answers me quickly. I'm not sure how hard he's looking. Zach won't make this easy.

"Okay, I want you to look into something else for me. An old member. Do you remember Mark?"

"Yeah, the guy who sold out Matty?"

"Yeah, well, he lied. So I want you to find out everything about him. Get his phone, and check the GPS on his car. I want the works."

"And what about Noah?" Zach sounds hopeful. Hope is a dangerous thing in our line of work.

"I'll deal with him myself."

"He thinks the fucking world of you, Jason." Zach jumps to his defense.

"Just do your fucking job." I hang up on Zach, not needing a guilt trip. He has to understand if he betrayed me, he would die too.

I go downstairs and take out a bottle of whiskey. With each swallow, I hope I'll drown out some of the noise that's started to roar in my head. When I'm with Kira, she silences the noise, but now that I'm alone, all of my demons have come back, and they want blood.

CHAPTER THIRTY-TWO

KIRA

Each step I take away from Jason's room is heavy, filled with fear and regret. I move straight away to put my plan into action before I back out. When I arrive at the security hut, I ask for Noah, but I'm told he isn't here, and that he won't be back.

My mind reels. That was my plan: to get him to help us. I stay outside Angel's room for a while, trying to convince myself that what I'm about to do is the right thing. I close my eyes and lean my head against the wall. If I stayed here and did nothing about Nicco killing my father, it would make me as bad as Nicco.

The dread of facing my brother has me still leaning against the wall. The fear of never having Jason touch me again is unbearable. If I can right just one wrong, I need to take the chance. I push off the wall and open Angel's door. She stops midstride.

"What happened?" she asks, alarm widening her eyes.

I close the door behind me and try to stop my blush from reaching its full fruition. But I can't stop the memory of Jason on top of me. Inside me.

"We need to do this now."

Angel shakes her head. "I don't think this is a good idea." She chews her lip.

"I've been thinking about it, and you can't come."

Angel releases her lip from between her teeth. "You aren't going alone."

"Both of us leaving won't go unnoticed. I can't get past the front gates. While I was feeding the swans, I noticed a wall that has some water features against it. That's how I'm getting out."

Angel's brows drag down. "So I can go with you."

"There are too many cameras. I need you to go to the security hut and distract them while I scale the wall." I hate asking her to do this, but realistically, there's no other way off this property. I can't take a car, and even if I did, Jason said there would be GPS on them. Walking out the front gate won't happen either.

"What happens if Nicco finds you?" Angel clears the space, taking both my hands in hers.

"I can't think about that right now," I admit. If I do, I know I won't go.

"What did you tell the guards the last time? Can you do it again?"

I shake my head and remove my hands from Angel's. I received the report from the hospital to confirm I was raped, and semen was found inside me. That semen belongs to my brother. I could prosecute, but I've already told the Gardaí I won't be pressing charges. Jason is right, he would serve a very short amount of time, and I think justice for my father is more important right now.

"No. Angel. Are you going to help me or not?" I hate standing here debating this with her as time slips away.

"I just want you to make sure you know what you're doing." Angel's voice is low.

"I need those tapes."

Angel nods in agreement.

"I'm ready." There's nothing holding me back.

"What happens when you get the tapes?" Angel asks.

"I haven't thought that far, but I'll turn them into the Gardaí."

"Are you going to come back here? Do I wait? What about Jason? He'll be pissed." So many questions are fired at me, and I have no answers. All I know is I need those tapes.

"Are you going to help me?" I ask again.

"Yes."

I don't wait any longer before making my way to the door. "I need you to go now. I'll wait by the swan lake for thirty seconds, and then I'll walk to the wall."

I'm holding the door handle. "I don't want you to do this," Angel admits.

I close my eyes. How easy would it be to turn around and tell Angel I'll stay here with her?

"He killed my dad, Angel," I say, while looking at her over my shoulder.

She takes in a large lungful of air and exhales while nodding.

I take that as agreeance. When I leave the room, I try to relax as I pass the security. My heart thumps wildly as I think of Jason standing around a corner, ready to grab me. But that doesn't happen. I make it to the kitchen, which is almost in darkness except for the small pin lights that shine down on the marble counters. I touch the sliding door that leads outside, and I'm tempted to look back, but instead, I go to the bread bin and take two slices of bread with me.

Sensor lights come on as I leave the house, lighting up portions of the garden. Large outdoor lights are already shining on the lake. The swans are nowhere in sight, but for the cameras, I hold out the bread like I'm calling them. Shivers break along my neck as I close my eyes and count to thirty. Each second feels long. My legs grow heavy, and I shift into a different stance to try to get some life back into them. Opening my eyes, I drop the bread on the ground and walk to the wall. The only sound I hear is the thumping of my heart. Scaling walls isn't something I've done. I have to believe that Angel is now distracting the security. I told her once I left the pond to distract them, so my time is limited.

I stand up on the water feature and grip the top of the wall. Kicking at the wall, I try to push my body to the top. My fingers take abuse as small stones on the top of the wall dig into my palms. I keep kicking, half climbing until my torso clears the top of the wall.

With all my energy, I throw one leg over, and then I'm falling back down. A scream is pulled from my lips as arms tighten around my waist, and the water feature is clear as I'm brought back into the garden.

My breathing is erratic but nothing like my heart, which has taken on a heavy beat I've never felt before. The smell of drink off Jason's breath washes across my face.

"I'm so sorry." My head snaps up in the direction of Angel, who has her arms folded across her chest. "I couldn't let you."

The pain in my stomach swells and rolls all the way to my chest. She told Jason, who's standing in front of me, and I don't need to look into his eyes to know how angry he is. His tight fists are enough.

"You were going to leave?" he finally asks, and the cold of night slowly sinks in through my light blouse.

Angel is my sole focus. How could she do this to me? "I got you out of that house?" I remind her, but it's stupid.

Her blue eyes grow small as guilt tightens them.

Warm fingers touch my chin, and I hate when Jason does this, forces me to look at him, but my gaze travels up as he tilts my chin back, and I'm looking into angry dark-green eyes.

I swallow.

"You were going to leave me?" he says quieter.

Is that pain I see in his eyes? I feel so much for him in such a short amount of time, but could he also feel the same?

"I had to go back," I answer.

My voice is like the call to a captain to release the anchor of a ship. That's the transformation I see on Jason's face as he lets my chin go and shakes his head.

"Go back to someone who fucking raped you? Why?" His raised voice has me folding my arms across my chest.

"He raped you?" Angel's voice carries the horror I still feel. Angel doesn't seem aware of Jason anymore. She's grabbing me, pulling me into her arms. "Oh God, Kira. I'm so sorry."

She's catching on her words, and I look up at Jason, who's not done.

"I want a fucking explanation. *Now*!"

I push Angel back, unable to deal with all of this right now.

"I needed to get something." I take Angel's hand and attempt to go back into the house. I know it's a silly thing to think I can do, but I take the chance that he might let us go.

His footfalls are fast, and I'm pulled back away from Angel and into his chest. "What was so important that you lied to me?" He sounds so hurt.

Angel is standing where I left her, looking at me and Jason, and I see all the pain in my friend's eyes. So much has been done to her. She looks ready to fall down.

"He killed my father. I watched Nicco strangle my dad. And I recently found out there are video tapes in my father's study. That's what I need to get."

Jason's hold on me lessens, and I wait for him to say something, but it's just silence. I turn in his arms. "My father was a good man who didn't deserve that death. I did nothing, Jason. It's a way to prove what Nicco did."

Jason's gaze still holds a lot of anger. "He won't let you walk out with the tapes," Jason says.

I nod. "I know. I hadn't thought that far ahead." I was hoping that, somehow, I could get away from him and go to the Gardaí with the tapes.

I lean my forehead against Jason's chest and let the weight of not getting justice for my father or my rape fill me up. "It's not fair," I whisper through the onslaught of pain that rides high.

Jason's arms slowly come around me, and I'm so close to breaking in his arms. "Nothing, and I mean nothing, is worth your life, Kira."

The first tear falls.

"Not your father's life, not my life…"

I push away so I can look up at Jason.

"Not Angel's life. You should have told me." So much regret flashes in his eyes. "I wish you had trusted me enough."

Guilt swells and tightens my throat. Jason looks over my head and nods. I turn to see two of his security men there. "Go and rest," Jason tells me without meeting my eye.

"I don't want to rest." My stomach roils. What is he doing?

"I'm not asking you, Kira." Jason meets my eye.

I glance at Angel, who's already being guided back into the house.

"Am I a prisoner now?" I ask as the other security man approaches.

"I'm protecting you from yourself as I try to figure out what to do," Jason says and gives a final nod to the security guard behind me.

I knew if I was caught, the price would be high. Either way, the price of staying or going is high. Now, a new fear consumes me. What will Jason do with me and Angel and also with the knowledge I just gave him?

CHAPTER THIRTY-THREE

JASON

A HALF A BOTTLE of whiskey pumps through my system—that, and a lifetime worth of anger pours through my veins.

She was going to leave. That thought spins so fucking fast in my head that I'm close to being dizzy. I glanced at the wall she had nearly scaled. If the water feature hadn't been there, she wouldn't have reached the top. I make my way to the shed that the gardener uses to store his tools in. I haven't been in here much, but I do recall seeing a sledgehammer.

Flicking on the lights, I spot the hammer in the back. After picking it up, I make my way back to the water feature. She stood on the side and climbed onto the feature that was meant to look like large rocks. I don't stay on the side but climb into the small pool of water. Each stroke of my legs sends water splashing against the side. The small pin lights send light jumping as I make my way to the back wall.

Each time the hammer hits the concrete feature and removes a lump, my energy grows, until I'm hitting the feature with strength I didn't know I possessed. I keep going until the feature dwindles down to almost nothing. Rubble and debris have fallen into the pool, but I'm not satisfied. Not even close.

I drop the sledgehammer and fish out my phone to call Alex. He needs to know that Nicco killed his own father. We could use this against him, and if we managed to get the tapes, we could nail the bastard.

Alex's phone rings out, and I curse him as I climb out of the small pool of water. Water soaks my trousers from the knee down. I still don't feel the cold of the night. I should, but the whiskey and Kira's actions have warmed my blood to boiling.

Through my anger, I have admiration for Kira. She was going to risk his wrath just to get the tapes to prove he killed his father. What did it feel like to watch her brother commit that act? And she just watched me kill Frank?

Fuck.

Does she see me as a monster like her brother? I throw my head back and glare into the starless night. My feelings for Kira are like nothing I've felt before. Is this love?

I have no idea, but it's deeper. I try Alex again, but he still doesn't answer. Returning to the house, I stop by the security hut. Two of my security men are situated outside Angel's bedroom, where Kira is too.

"If either of them even opens the door, I want to be informed," I announce. "If Kira gets out, I will hold you both responsible."

Nervous gazes flicker between me and the cameras; that's exactly what I want. I want them to understand their lives are on the line. What if Angel hadn't come to me? Would she have successfully distracted my men like Kira had told her to do?

Fuck's sake.

I change my trousers before going to my office and picking up the contracts that Nicco had faxed over to me the day that Kira had arrived here. That felt like a lifetime ago. I hadn't signed them then, not really understanding why.

I leave the house and try Alex one more time. No answer. The drive to Nicco's residence doesn't take long. She could have walked here in forty minutes. Each time I picture her here with her brother, my anger rises until I'm squeezing the steering wheel.

He would have raped her again, the fucking bastard. This will be my first time facing him, and in order to go forward, I must first go back. Back to my past, back to memories of Frank torturing me, and each time I fought not to cry or call out. Eventually, it worked, and that's what I seek right now—the ability not to feel.

I pull up at Nicco's home, and the guards stop me at the gates.

"Do you have an appointment?"

"No. Tell him Jason Murphy is here," I say.

The guard scratches his neck before he turns his back on me, closes the window, and picks up the phone. If he doesn't grant me access, I'll have to get out and kill him. I don't want to hurt anyone unnecessarily, but I won't go back empty-handed. I can't allow Kira to even have a second of thinking she has to return here. The only way to take that thought from her head is to get the tapes for her.

The window slides open at the same time the gates start to open. "Mr. Tarasova is looking forward to seeing you."

That doesn't sound good. I nod and focus on the house I was at earlier. Driving up to the door, the two security men don't react to my presence. Bringing in my gun would be foolish, so I leave it in the car and grab the contracts.

I turn off the engine and climb the steps to the front door. I'm waiting for it to open, but that doesn't happen, so I knock.

I'm left waiting for over a minute before Nicco opens the door.

The sight of him has my control wobbling.

"Jason Murphy on my doorstep? To what do I owe the honor?"

The only thing that's real right now is the paper in my hand. That's what I tell myself as I step into Nicco's home. *Kira's home*, a voice whispers.

"Frank sent me," I manage to say as I glance around the hall like I'm taking in the interior, while I'm trying to convince myself not to kill him.

He has no idea that Frank is dead. "He came by my house with contracts for Kira to sign."

I look at Nicco.

He leans heavily on his cane. "What about Kira's?"

"She signed them."

He doesn't look convinced. "How is Angel?" he asks, taking the contracts from my hand.

"Settling in great." I can't look away from him. He's so fucking slimy, and he doesn't deserve to breathe any more oxygen.

"You haven't signed these?" He narrows his gaze at me.

I grin. "Do you have a pen?"

He fishes one out of his suit jacket. A silver one that I'm sure cost a few euros. I take the contracts back and walk to a small table. I lean over and sign on the dotted line.

"You came all this way to give me the contracts?" he quizzes.

"Frank was adamant that I came," I say as I hand him back the contracts.

"Hmm," he says before clicking his cane three times on the floor. "Unless you can speak to the dead, I think you're lying."

Fuck.

How did he know that Frank was dead? Noah—it could have only been Noah.

He pulls the contracts from my hand. "Did Kira send you here to defend her honor?" He sneers.

I take a step toward him, gripping the pen in my hand. He glances at the pen that could easily become a weapon.

"Get out of my home. I got what I wanted." He holds up the contracts.

"I know you killed your father." The minute I say it, it's so clear on the fucker's face.

His scar wobbles as he tries to control his features. "What?"

I grin, gaining the upper hand. "Strangulation isn't a nice way to die. I'm sure your father suffered. Did you look him in the eyes as you took his life?"

His features grow tight with anger, and he slams the cane down onto the floor.

Hands grab me from all angles, and I don't struggle. I glance over my shoulder at the large men to gauge my situation.

I didn't break into his home. He has no right to hurt me.

"Did it feel good as he fought for you to stop?"

"Shut your fucking mouth. He had it coming." He's in front of me, holding his cane to my throat. "He wouldn't agree to me marrying Kira." His eyes widen with madness as the cane touches my throat.

"You touch me, and you will have all the Murphys at your doorstep." He has to know this.

He removes the cane. "You have no proof."

"Tell your men to let me go, and I'll tell you what proof I have."

He shakes his head and grins. "Sorry, but I'm not stupid enough to release you. Why don't you drop the pen?"

I release the pen and it rolls across the floor, but his men still don't let me go.

"So, tell me about this proof." He's grinning. "I can assume you have none. But I am curious how Kira knew."

Her name coming out of his mouth has my anger swelling and pushing against the wall I built in order to remain calm.

"I'll tell you, but I want something in return."

I have his attention. He narrows his gaze before clicking his fingers, and his men let me go. I fix my suit jacket, but they don't step away.

"I'm listening." He smiles.

"I'll tell you where the evidence is if you let my family break free from the Bratva since Frank is dead." That's my deal. I'll hand over the evidence that Kira said is here, and that way my family is free. Her dad's death will never be resolved legally, but when I take Nicco's life for raping her, I hope it's enough for her.

"Break free from the Bratva?" Nicco says. "You *are* Bratva, Jason. Your mother was part of the most powerful family. Why do you think Gilly was made a leader?"

That makes no sense. When Aidan killed Gilly for putting his hands on Raven, the Bratva replaced him with Alex. If they really considered him as their own, they wouldn't have let it go. Aidan would have had to die.

"You didn't give two fucks about Gilly during our negotiation at Aidan's."

"It was discovered that he had a different mother. Blood tests are very important to us. Especially when you're crossing the line into Bratva royalty."

"So…" I grin. "Since I'm Bratva royalty, according to you, I want my family to be free of the ties that Frank made."

"You would have to prove you're Bratva royalty. Since we only have Frank's word, and he's dead." Nicco leans in with a smirk. "We have something in common."

I snap and lunge for him. My hands wrap around his neck, and everything around me ceases to exist. The sound is gone. My fingers tighten around his neck, and he's gasping for air. Hands grab my arms, but I don't let him go. *I need him to stop breathing*—that's all that filters through my mind. He has to die.

He can't be allowed to live.

His face turns a shade of purple, his wide eyes and frantic slaps give me satisfaction.

The hit to the back of my head sends me to the ground, and I land on top of Nicco. I still keep my hands around his throat, even as my vision completely goes and the energy I'm hanging on to starts to slip faster than I can pull it back.

Warmth runs down the back of my skull and onto my neck before the darkness pulls me under.

CHAPTER THIRTY-FOUR

KIRA

TWO DAYS HAVE PASSED since I tried to escape. There's a constant flurry of activity around the house. More men continue to pour in, and no matter how many times I search their faces, I don't find the one I'm looking for.

"You can't go out there again." Angel grabs my arm.

"Something bad has happened." I'm gripping the door handle, knowing I need to try to get someone to talk to me. I haven't seen any of the staff or Zach. The security won't answer my questions, and our meals are served in our room. We can leave, but our movements are monitored to the point of being uncomfortable.

I open the door and step out into the hall. I've been staying with Angel on the ground floor. I pass through the halls, and just like the past two days, the security has doubled. The kitchen is empty, messy countertops from this morning's breakfast are all that I'm faced with. I turn as heavy footfalls sound rushed. I follow them into the hallway, and Zach and Alex pause but continue into a room on their left, their voices hushed. Both of them look through me like I'm a ghost. The door closes to the room they entered, and I walk to it and pause outside. I can't hear anything. I'm not sure if that's because they aren't speaking or if the room is soundproof.

I turn the door handle and pause when it clicks open, and I hear them.

"We need to move in now." Zach's angry tone has me pausing.

"That's what he wants," Alex says.

I don't linger but push the door open. There are several other men in the room, and I want to curl up and hide. I search each of their faces, but none of them are Jason. My heart deflates.

"I want to speak to Jason," I say.

This is the first time I've gotten to speak to someone with authority. The security just kept blanking me.

"He's not available right now." Alex speaks with his back to me.

Another man rises from the couch. "You must be Kira?" He holds out his hand. "I'm Aidan, Jason's brother."

I take his hand with hesitation. "Do you know when Jason will return?" I ask Aidan, as right now he's the most approachable.

Aidan releases my hand and frowns at Alex's back. "No one has told her?"

"I had more important things to do." Alex continues to keep his back to me. He's looking over a set of plans.

My heart thumps. "Told me what?" Dread has me moving my legs, and I stop beside Alex. It's a map of a house, the layout of which, I recognize. Without anyone uttering a word, I get this horrible sense.

"No." I touch the room that was my bedroom.

"Maybe you could help us," Aidan says, and I spin and look at him before I take in all the men who have hostility in their gazes toward me.

"She's done enough. Escort her back to her room," Alex says.

"Where is Jason?" I plead with Aidan. I think I know, but I want someone to tell me I'm wrong.

Aidan's gaze fills with sympathy as he looks at his brother's back, and he doesn't answer me.

"Alex, please. Where is Jason?" I'm looking up into Alex's profile.

"Nicco has him."

He went there to get the tapes; that's why I haven't seen him. Horror of what Nicco must be doing to him has me wanting to run from the room.

I'm overheating, freezing cold. My heart thumps too painfully before it almost stops.

"Is he alive?" I whisper. Two days. Two days.

For the first time, Alex looks at me. "We don't know." I see the raw pain in Alex's eyes.

"She could help," Aidan says.

Alex laughs, and it sends shivers down my spine. "Help. He's there because of her." Alex doesn't point at me or even look at me, but it's clear he's speaking about me.

"You don't know that." Aidan tries to defend me.

"I do." This time, Alex glares at me. "You signed a petition to bring back the law to marry in the family," Alex says.

Aidan's gaze fills with disgust.

"It's not what you think," I defend.

"Jason wasn't willing to give you up, so your brother took him, and in exchange, he wants you back."

"I was forced to sign that paper." I try to stop the sickening feeling that's consuming me.

"Did Nicco make contact?" Aidan sounds astonished.

"No, but I'm sure that's why he has Jason." Alex defends his theory, and he may be right. "So if you want to help, let's get you packed and back to your brother."

I already know I can't do that. Pain scorches my flesh and spreads across my chest, restricting my airway. My vision blurs, and I shake my head as tears fall. "I'm sorry. I can't."

Alex turns to Aidan. "Get her out of here before I do something I regret."

And like that, I'm being escorted from the room by Aidan. "I could help in a different way," I plead with Alex, but he's done talking to me.

Once we're outside the room, Aidan lets my arm go and closes the door over behind him. "What other way could you help?"

I'm surprised he's willing to listen to me, but he has a look of desperation in his eyes. He runs his hands through his hair.

"Two days ago, I attempted to leave, and Jason caught me."

Aidan closes his eyes briefly. "So Alex is right. You are trying to get back to your brother."

"No. I was trying to get back to the house to get tapes. I told this to Jason, and I think he went to get them."

Aidan folds his arms, but he still looks intimidating as he towers over me. "What's on the tapes?"

"Something that could get Nicco killed," I answer.

Aidan shakes his head, and I see a strike of Alex there as he grins. "What's on the tapes?" he asks again.

"Nicco killing my father." I straighten my spine as I say the words so I don't bend and break.

Aidan's gaze widens. "He killed your father."

I nod. "Yes. I saw it."

"So Jason goes to your brother's to get the tapes, and Nicco catches him in the act? Maybe that's why we haven't heard any demands." Aidan's hope dwindles to despair. "He would have no need to keep him alive."

Tears blur my vision. I won't be able to stay here without Jason. I will be handed back to Nicco. I cry for my future and the loss of Jason.

"Go back to your room, Kira." Aidan's voice is low and devoid of any emotion.

The door opens, and I blink Alex into vision. He's towering over us both.

"Come in." He points a finger at me and beckons me into the room.

I follow him and he walks back to the table where the plans are. He presses his fingers onto the large wooden table.

"If he were to keep Jason locked up, where would he keep him?" Another man joins us at the table. He's staring at me, and I feel like he wants to say something, but he doesn't.

I look over the plans, but I already know. "You won't find it on the plans. There's a basement. That's where he would keep Jason." Even as I say it, my legs grow weak at the thought of what Jason could be going through. If he's alive, he could be wishing for death.

"I'll go," I whisper.

"Tell them what you told me," Aidan says, joining me, Alex, and the other man, who won't look away from me.

"I tried to leave two days ago to get some tapes from my home." I can sense all eyes on me. "Jason caught me." I'm picturing the moment I was pulled from the wall. Yesterday, I had gone back to see that the feature had been destroyed. "I think he went to get the tapes for me."

"They show Nicco killing his father." Aidan sounds gleeful, and for a moment, the focus is on how they can break free of the Bratva. They think of how they can get their hands on the tapes. There's almost a buzz of excitement, but I'm thinking of the basement and what might be happening to Jason.

"Nicco won't keep Jason alive for long." I end their brief excitement. "My brother is cruel."

"If she goes and gets Jason out, what then?" Aidan asks. "What about the tapes?"

Alex runs his hands down his face before turning to me. "Can I have a word in private?"

I nod. I'd prefer to stay around Aidan, as he seems nicer, but the man who's staring at me is making me uncomfortable. I leave the room with Alex.

"Who is the other man at the table with us?" I ask.

Alex walks slowly down the hallway. "Matty, my brother."

Matty has their dark eyes, only his are black, creepy. He makes me uncomfortable.

"We can't do everything at once. But the main priority is to get Jason out," Alex says before stopping. He's looking at me for the first time like he's really seeing me.

"I need you to convince me on how you will get my brother out."

"I... I would... I would talk to Nicco," I stutter as my heart hammers. I can't do this. "Nicco raped me." My throat and nose burn. I'm pleading for someone to take this burden off me. I'm looking up at Alex. "He nearly killed Angel." A tear runs into my mouth.

"You aren't convincing me," Alex says.

And I'm pleading with him with my eyes. "It's my life for Jason's." I blink and more tears fall.

"I know," Alex says softly, and for the first time, I see a human peeking out behind his hardened gaze.

"He told me my life was worth more than his." I wipe the tears away from around my mouth and sniffle.

"I don't agree," Alex says honestly.

I nod. Of course he wouldn't agree. It's his brother.

I can't keep eye contact, as every ounce of hope is hijacked and ripped from my body. Tears continue to pour into my mouth. "Okay. I'll get him out."

My life for Jason's. If I say no and stay here, I'd only be buying time I can't afford. If I run, I won't get far. Eventually, I'd be returned to sender. Returned to Nicco.

Pain feasts on my misery as I take a final look at Alex.

"We will get ready to leave in ten minutes," Alex says before he walks away with my life in his hands. I crumble inside. I'm the sailor walking the plank. I'm the hanging man waiting for the floor to disappear under his feet.

It's the most terrifying feeling I've ever had, and I'm sinking to the floor. My breaths are harsh, but no more tears come as the onslaught of hopelessness consumes me.

CHAPTER THIRTY-FIVE

JASON

*"**Y**ou will never know what it's like to tear into flesh. This is the best way to learn." Frank stuffs a knife into my hands. I'm staring down at the cat. He's dead, thankfully, but the idea of cutting his belly open is making me sick.*

"One day, this will be a screaming man. Now cut it open." Frank doesn't raise his voice. He doesn't have to. My knife sinks into the cat's belly, and I swallow my queasiness several times.

"You feel the hardness of the skin? A man is tougher. It takes more force, but the feel of the inside is the same."

Cutting the cat's belly open takes some sawing, but I finally manage it.

"Now take everything out," Frank orders.

I stare up at him, hoping he's joking. But his eyes tell me he isn't.

I remove all the cat's organs before I throw up.

I turn my head as my stomach muscles clench, and bile runs from the side of my mouth. The room is dark, damp, but the smell of burning skin has my stomach churning.

"I love picking at a scab," Nicco says before he sticks a hot poker to my back. He holds it longer than the last, and I bite down on the piece of wood that's been placed for me to scream my pain into. At first, I didn't use it, and Nicco almost seemed impressed. But time blurs, and I think days have passed since I woke up chained to the bed.

Nicco stands back with a smile on his face, but my skin still sizzles and burns.

"I've never seen anyone tortured so much and not give in."

He keeps asking me where the proof is of him killing his father. If I tell him, he'll kill me. But I'm not sure how much longer I can stay alive.

"So, what's the proof?"

My teeth are still clamped down on the stick. Drool pours from my mouth as my back screams for this to stop.

"Oh, come on. Tell me to fuck off again."

I'm breathless from the pain, but I manage to mumble "Fuck off." I'm waiting for the torture to start up again, but Nicco exhales loudly.

"You are starting to bore me. At first, this was fun. Now, not so much."

Tears burn my eyes, but he doesn't see them as I close my eyes and fight through the pain that's dug itself into my flesh. Every part of me aches, but I remember my training with Frank. He had me once go three days with no sleep. A week with no food.

I've suffered worse, so I can keep fighting.

"Alex made contact," Nicco says.

About fucking time.

I don't show any relief. I don't look at Nicco but keep my eyes closed and fight through the pain. Why does it feel so much worse than before?

"He's offered Kira, if I give you back."

Now he has my attention. I don't speak, but I'm looking at him now.

"It's tempting. It really is. But what's more important to me is finding the proof you spoke about. And it got me thinking that Kira must have told you. So, I have agreed to your brother's terms. I will give you back, and Kira will take your place." He's smiling.

I swallow. "No."

Nicco moves closer. "Sorry, I didn't hear you."

"Leave her out of this."

He laughs. "Or what? What can you do?"

"I'm going to kill you," I promise him.

He laughs and walks away. "I won't even ask Kira any questions. I think I'll bring her down here and let new blood grow inside her."

I rattle against my chains. I want to kill Nicco, but I can't believe that Alex would allow Kira to walk into this trap.

She doesn't deserve this fate. Pain roars to life as I continue to rattle the restraints around my wrists. I need to stop this from happening. I can't just lie here. But no matter how much I pull against the restraints, they don't loosen.

Minutes have passed since Nicco left, when the lights overhead go out, and I'm plunged into darkness. The only sound I hear at first is my heavy breathing. Shots are fired somewhere in the house. Three more are fired. I'm turning, staring at the ceiling, trying to track the gunshots. Louder ones ring out. A machine gun has been fired. It's a war zone. I rattle my restraints again. Fuck.

The shooting continues for a frightening ten minutes before it stops. Light filters in as the top door opens, and pounding feet reach me before several men enter the space. The red laser lights on their guns cover my body. As they approach, I try to shield my eyes. Everyone is masked, and one of them walks closer and pulls off his face covering.

Alex's gaze travels the full length of me. "Can you stand?" he asks as he opens my restraints.

"I'm going to kill you," I say.

He laughs. "You aren't exactly in a fit state to kill anyone. And why would you want to kill me?" he asks while walking around and opening the other restraint.

The minute I'm free, I grab his arm. "You traded her for me."

"I pretended to trade her for you to get entry."

Surprise filters through me. "She's safe?"

"She's outside the gates." Alex unlocks my legs, and I push myself off the bed. The rest of the men spread out before moving back upstairs.

"Is he alive?" I ask.

Alex wraps his arm around me and helps me stand. "He's restrained upstairs. But we need him alive."

I nod as Alex helps me to the foot of the stairs.

"Did you find the tapes?" he asks me.

"No."

We take the first step. "Aidan is searching for them now."

Each step takes me closer to safety, closer to Kira, closer to Nicco. Each step is fueled with pain. When we arrive in the kitchen, the light is sharp on my eyes, but as soon as they adjust, I take in all my men, who one by one, pull off their masks, and the look of horror in their eyes has me guessing I look pretty fucking bad. I nod at them.

"I want to see him," I say to Alex.

"That's not happening." Alex grabs a blanket and places it across my back like he can cover up Frank and Nicco's work.

"What can I do, Alex? I have no weapon. I'm barely fit to stand," I say as he directs me out into the hall. I stumble as the blood loss took more of my energy than I expected. Falling to my knees, I hold up one hand to tell Alex I'm fine as I scoop up the pen that rolled to the side of the room after my and Nicco's scuffle. I stand up and stay still. "Just give me a minute."

"Jason," Alex says. "You need a doctor."

I look at my brother. "I do. But first, I just want him to see that I'm alive."

Alex glances at a door to our left and runs his hand along his jaw. "We need him. You understand. We will never break free from the Bratva unless we hand him over with the tapes. This is our ticket to freedom." Alex's eyes light up.

"I know, brother," I say.

He nods and leads me to the door. When he opens it, Nicco looks up. He's not smiling, but he doesn't look afraid.

"I see my brother is treating you far better than you treated me," I say, stepping into the room.

Nicco is sitting on a couch, not a mark on him. Alex is playing his cards the right way. He'll hand Nicco over to the Bratva, along with the tapes, and we'll have our freedom. But what will happen to Nicco? Will he still terrorize Kira? Will he be moved to another area to rule over?

"I have more worth." He grins.

I manage to grin back. "Clearly."

I walk toward him, and two of my own men look behind me at Alex. That annoys the fuck out of me, but I keep going, pulling the blanket around my shoulders. Being in Nicco's presence sends adrenaline pumping throughout my body, and I think that's what's keeping me upright in this moment.

"You look nervous," I say to Nicco. He doesn't at all.

He laughs. "I'm terrified." He glares at me. "I'm also impressed at how much you withstood."

"And he will continue to live on," Alex says, getting close. "We better go. Kira is looking for you, Jason."

Nicco's features tighten at that. Alex's desired effect, I'm sure.

All I want is to destroy him. The blanket falls to the ground. The cold air ignites every single burn, and I use it like fuel to jump on Nicco. At first, no one reacts. I raise the pen, clutched tightly in my hand, and Nicco tries to block my fist, but the pen plunges into his neck.

I'm thrown back to the memory of cutting my first cat. The sense of the hardened skin being penetrated with pure force. Blood squirts. I've hit an artery. I get to remove and sink the pen back into his neck before I'm pulled off Nicco. All the strength is gone, and I allow my men and brother to take me to the ground. Alex is roaring, but I'm giving in to the agony of my wounds. I glance up at Nicco. His wide eyes stare up at the ceiling as blood continues to pour from his neck.

"Why?" Alex roars as I lie on the ground.

"He had to die." My explanation is simple, but I've never seen such a look of devastation on a man's face before.

"He was our way out. You could have gotten your revenge at another time." He knows that's pure bullshit. If I didn't kill Nicco now, I would never have gotten the chance.

Alex looks like he wants to throttle me. "You have ruined everything for this family. You and your..." *Father*. But he doesn't finish his sentence.

The pain is almost as unbearable as the pain inflicted on my flesh. "If Nadia had been raped...."

Alex's face turns blank before he steps up to me. "I would never have allowed that to happen." Alex's words hit me so fucking hard. But he's right. Nadia is watched twenty-four seven. Alex has loved her since he was a boy, but she doesn't know that. She has no idea how much my brother obsesses over her.

"If she had, Alex, you wouldn't think twice about killing the man who did it. No matter what the cost is."

Alex doesn't answer. Instead, I'm escorted out of the room. Aidan pauses in the hallway. His gaze roams my entire body, which is covered with the blanket.

"I'm alive," I say.

He nods, and a slow smile covers his lips. "Good. But on the flip side, we don't have any tapes. There was a camera in the study, but there was no backup. It seems to record the last seventy-two hours. That's it."

The tapes don't matter now. Alex tells Aidan as much.

"Jason killed Nicco, so the tapes won't matter. We will have to answer to the Bratva for killing one of their men."

I see the disappointment in Aidan's eyes, but it disappears. I wonder if he's thinking about how he killed Gilly for touching Raven. He nods, jumping to my defense. "He captured and tortured our brother."

"Let's hope they believe us," Alex says, and we step outside.

A car pulls up, and the back door opens. Kira pauses, her exit interrupted as her gaze wavers, her lip gnawed with worry.

Everything in me sighs. It's odd how my whole body relaxes because she's safe. She's here. She takes a few rushed steps toward me.

"You're alive." It's like she can't believe I'm standing here in front of her. I'm ready to fall down, but I can't allow her to see how badly I'm hurt.

I walk to her and keep the blanket tightly around me. "I'm alive," I whisper. She's looking over my shoulder.

"Nicco's dead, Kira."

Her gaze snaps to mine. Tears fall and she nods. Relief swims in the depths of her brown eyes. She reaches up on the tips of her toes and presses a kiss to my lips. "Thank you."

"You need to be seen by a doctor," Alex says behind me.

Kira's trying to peek under the blanket, her worry evident. I walk to the car and let Kira get in first. "I will, once Kira is back safely in my home. Where she should have been kept."

Alex snarls. "No harm came to her. We kept her outside the walls. All she had to do was let Nicco see she was here."

I get into the car. The pain roars to life, but I clamp down on my cheek. The metallic taste of my blood floods my mouth. The door closes and the world dissolves, until a small body warms my side. I lean my head back and take comfort that Kira is beside me.

She's safe.

She's alive.

She's mine.

CHAPTER THIRTY-SIX

JASON

WHEN AIDAN KILLED GILLY for touching Raven, we had to wait three weeks to hear what the Bratva's verdict was. I had thought those three weeks were torture, but nothing compared to my own wait. It's been five days of waiting for the phone call I've just received.

I end the call and meet Alex's gaze. "They're ready for me." Kira is with Angel back at my home, with all the security we could spare.

Three days ago, a package arrived at my home. It was signed with "Jack." The only Jack I know is Jack O'Reagan, and when I took out the small storage device and uploaded it to my laptop, I knew it was Jack. The scene on it will haunt me forever. It's Nicco raping Kira while she's unconscious.

This is the proof I'm bringing to the Bratva jury. This is why I've admitted to killing Nicco. They wanted Kira to come forth and say her part, but I forbid it. She's suffered enough.

"You could run," Alex says as he starts the car.

I grin at my brother. "Where would I go?"

"You have enough money now." Is that bitterness I detect in his tone?

After Frank died, I found out I inherited our billion-euro empire. I'm the sole owner. None of this is right, and I can't blame Alex.

"Kira deserves to settle down. I won't allow her to spend the rest of her life looking over her shoulder."

I also want to tell Alex I don't intend to keep our fortune to myself. It should be equally distributed among us. One person shouldn't possess so much money, so much power.

We stop at the hotel where the jury is being held. When Alex doesn't get out straight away, I look at my brother. "It will be okay," I say. Reassuring Alex isn't something I would normally have to do, but he looks so doubtful.

"Frank said my mother was a Putin. That makes me like Bratva Royalty." I grin to add humor to this situation.

"What if Frank lied?" Alex asks.

He's right. I've given blood to be tested, and the results will no doubt be revealed here today. I'm hoping Frank told me the truth for once; otherwise, I'm a dead man.

"Keep the faith." I tap Alex's shoulder, but I can no longer look at my brother.

"I searched for you for over a year," Alex tells the windshield. "I walked past you several times on different occasions. You had disintegrated to nothing." He glances at me now from the corner of his eye. "I thought we had lost you, Jason. I can't go through that again."

I can't promise him anything, and he knows it. "If this doesn't go right, promise me you'll make sure Kira is taken care of."

"She inherited her family's wealth. She won't need anything."

He's right. She inherited everything after Nicco died, as she was the last member of her family.

"I'm not talking about money. I want her to always be protected."

Alex unbuckles his belt. "Well, you'd better get this meeting over with so you can protect your woman."

I grin before tapping Alex on the shoulder one final time. We get out, and the parking attendant takes the keys from Alex's outstretched hand as we enter the hotel.

The hotel is busy, and people are checking in and out. The lobby has several bellhops with trolleys. The manager has been watching our arrival and quickly approaches us.

"Jason and Alex Murphy?" he asks with a raised black brow.

I nod.

"Follow me."

We follow him through the lobby, into a more private part of the hotel that's often used for meetings like these. The deeper we go down the corridor, the more distant the noise grows. Is Alex right? Should I have run?

He opens a set of double doors, and three people are talking, laughing, and I'd almost think I had stepped into the wrong room. The woman is wearing a tweed suit, her blonde hair pinned on top of her head. Red lips stretch into a smile. The other two are older men, maybe in their sixties. They both nod in greeting. It's in their eyes. No matter how much Botox they inject into their faces, or how much hair dye covers their heads, you can see all the cruelty in their eyes. The doors close behind us.

We have the right room.

"Jason and Alex Murphy. Please, take a seat."

No one else is in the room, and the two men and one woman take a seat behind one long desk. Two black chairs are sitting in the middle of the room. Alex and I sit down as we've been instructed.

I take in each face, trying to figure out how this may go. But the men's hardened gazes give nothing away, and the woman continues to smile.

Seeing a woman on the panel isn't something I expected of the Bratva. They're often stuck in their old ways, but I suppose the times are moving faster than us, and we need to keep up. Having women rule is an idea I could get behind. Kira would make a fair ruler.

But I'm not here to debate what genders rule.

"My name is Anya, and I represent the Putins," the woman begins, and she looks directly at me. She could be my aunt. "Jason Murphy, you are being judged for killing Nicolai Tarasova. How do you plead?"

Alex glances at me, but I hold Anya's gaze. She wears her smile in place. "Guilty," I admit.

"We received the tapes." The man to the left of Anya speaks up. Three gold teeth catch the light as he does. Tattoos run along his neck and disappear into his hairline. "But Kira's words would have been more important to us."

What utter bullshit. "She wasn't awake while he raped her. The tapes make that clear." I try to keep the anger out of my voice as my mind replays Nicco thrusting violently into his sister's still form.

"What Mr. Vassiliev is saying is that any information from Kira would have helped your case."

"As his leader, what do you have to say?" Anya fires at Alex, and that, I hadn't expected.

"He acted in self-defense. Nicolai had raped his soon-to-be wife and held him hostage. In any case, he had every right to take Nicolai's life." Alex defends me, but it doesn't mean shit right now. It's all down to this panel of Bratva leaders. We're the Irish Mafia; they hate us. They aren't going to side with me because what I did was justified.

The only hope I have is that Frank didn't lie to me and that I am a Putin; otherwise, I'm fucked.

"We have deliberated already, and we have come to a verdict." Mr. Vassiliev speaks up.

My heart races. That was quick. I want to ask about my blood results. Have they taken that into account? I brace myself.

"We find you, Jason Murphy, guilty of the murder of the Negotiator, who was a valuable member of the Bratva."

"Your sentencing will be decided by the most powerful family." Mr. Vassiliev holds out his hand toward Anya. "Mrs. Putin."

She hasn't taken her eyes off me. Power with Bratva isn't decided by killing or force; it's decided by money.

"We did your DNA test, and you are a Putin." Anya doesn't sound pleased. Mr. Vassiliev and the other man seem surprised by this fact. They obviously weren't privy to the information that I may be one of them.

Anya looks down at Mr. Vassiliev. "You just ordered the death penalty on one of my family members."

I want to rise and protest the death penalty. No one fucking mentioned that, but Mr. Vassiliev jumps so quickly that his chair tumbles to the ground. He staples his fingers into the desk.

"How dare you withhold information like this from us!"

Anya reaches under her desk, and I glance at Alex. Is she reaching for a weapon? We weren't patted down, but I didn't risk bringing a gun. I wonder if Alex did. He doesn't move, so I have no idea. Anya places a tiny bag on the table and opens it before removing a silver container.

"The information was there. You just didn't see it." She opens the container and removes a white cigarette. Once she lights it, she looks back to me, not fazed at all by Mr. Vassiliev, who's still standing. If he could breathe fire, the room would be engulfed.

"You are one of us, Jason." She glances at Alex. "You are not like them." She might hold my life in her hands, but she's taking the piss.

"He's my brother."

Disgust curls her lips around her cigarette. "Killing Nicolai was justified. You are higher ranking, and no charges will be laid against you."

She could have started off with that, but something tells me this was more about her and the Vassiliev family than it was about me.

His threatening to kill me seemed to outrage her, and she called him out on it.

"Here are the terms." She moves pages in front of her that I hadn't noticed.

"You will give up your title of South Irish Mafia Leader back to Murphys."

I want to tell her I'm a Murphy and that Alex holds that title, not me, but I keep my mouth shut.

"You will assume the title of Negotiator and will be sworn in as a Bratva member."

I'm already shaking my head. I'm not going to negotiate people's lives. "No."

Mr. Vassiliev sits down, but he's angrily staring at the desk. The other man doesn't seem as fazed as his gaze bounces between Anya and me.

She withdraws the cigarette from her mouth. A red ring of lipstick is left around the top. "No is not the answer, Jason. You will learn that soon enough."

I glance at Alex, but he doesn't look at me. I know I should be grateful that I'm alive, but working for the Bratva is the last thing I want to do.

"What about my family? Frank made a deal with the Bratva that should no longer stand," I say.

"It passes down to you as your responsibility," Mr. Vassiliev says with a smirk. He leans on the desk and looks at Anya like he just won a round.

She nods. "He is correct. But since Jason is a Putin, that contract is void."

Alex exhales loudly, and I want to thank her. Being part of her family is really coming up roses. Before I open my mouth, she holds up her hand. "Nothing is free, Jason. The contract is void, but in its place, you will work as the Negotiator. You will transition from the Irish Mafia to the Bratva. That is our terms."

"And if I don't?"

"Then you will face the death penalty," Mr. Vassiliev says this while smiling.

This time when I look at Alex, he's staring at me. I want him to tell me that I can't work for the Bratva. But he doesn't. I know this means freedom for him, Aidan, William, and Matty. It's not the outcome I wanted, but it's better than what I thought I might be getting.

"Where do I sign?" I ask Anya.

She puts out her cigarette in a small gold ashtray. She beckons me with her finger before turning her attention to her bag, where she extracts a small silver pen knife.

She pushes a set of contracts that have been turned to the final page. "Maybe I need to have my solicitor look these over," I say as she holds the knife out to me.

"Take my advice, Jason. Sign them."

Do I really have a choice?

"With blood." She still holds out the knife.

I stare at it for far too long.

"Kira will be under our full protection for the remainder of her life," Anya says.

I flick the knife, and the blade shoots out. I slice the top of my finger and press it on the white piece of paper.

Anya smiles. "Welcome, nephew. You are now a Putin."

My blood bleeds into the page, but her words sink into my soul. I'm no longer a Murphy but a Putin.

When I look back at Alex, I see the unease in my brother's gaze.

At least with this kind of power, I can protect my brothers and Kira. That's all that should matter right now.

The meeting ends, and Alex doesn't speak as we leave the hotel. I'm waiting for him to say something, but he doesn't. Once we're in the car, I speak.

"Your father's fortune will be returned to you. Split it between Aidan, Matty, and William."

Alex nods as he grips the steering wheel. He nods like that's how it should be, that it's his birthright, but it pisses me off.

"Aren't you going to say anything?"

"I'm glad you're alive," he settles on before starting the car.

"What the fuck, Alex?" I bark.

"What?" His gaze bounces from me to the road. "I thought Frank was lying. I'm letting the knowledge that you're a Putin sink in." His stunned expression makes sense. "I'm also trying to accept that we no longer owe the Bratva anything. That we're free to rule once again."

I sink into my seat. "It's a lot, but it's a good outcome."

"Not the outcome I expected," Alex admits. "How are you feeling?"

"My family is safe. Kira is safe, and I am alive." I look out the window. "I'd say that's a good outcome."

"Yeah." Alex doesn't sound so sure, but to me, it's the best we could have asked for.

Finding our father's killer still hasn't been resolved. Every time we dig a bit deeper, we hit a brick wall, and with the ME turning up dead, we have no line of questioning. I glance at Alex. I still don't believe him about the image of him with the ME.

"You won't stop looking for Dad's killer," I say.

"We'll find out who did it." Alex glances at me. "You will be here to help us too, Jason. Don't act like you're about to disappear."

I grin. "You never know where I will be placed."

"It's a good outcome," Alex says, as if he's trying to convince himself.

But it is. Once we find our father's killer, we can all rest and rule like we were supposed to. It's the last loose end we need to tie up. We're free of the Bratva—well, my brothers are, and that's the most important thing.

I smile when I think of Kira waiting for me at my home. I can't wait to hold her and tell her it's over.

She can have her peace.

EPILOGUE

KIRA (THREE MONTHS LATER)

T HE CHARITY EVENT IS in full swing. And I can't stop looking up at Jason. He looks so handsome in his black suit. The black-tie event is to raise money for cats and dogs.

I confided in Jason about Nicco killing my cat, and I know that's why we're here and why he donated one hundred thousand to the charity.

"A kitten would have worked just as well," I whisper, linking his arm.

"I wanted to show you off." He smiles down at me. So much has happened since Nicco died. Jason is now the Negotiator with the Bratva, and it's caused a huge wedge between him and his brothers. Time heals most wounds, and I hope it helps bring them back together.

Jason invited Alex to the event, but so far, he hasn't arrived.

Jason takes a glass of champagne off a silver tray and hands it to me. He doesn't get one for himself. He only seems to relax when we're at home. Otherwise, he's on guard. It's part of the job, and as long as I get the real Jason, that's all that matters to me.

"I thought Angel would come," I admit, and I take a sip of champagne as we navigate our way through the crowd to our table.

"Why didn't she?" Jason asks while he pulls out my seat.

"She said she was tired."

Jason grins. "I think she and Zach are enjoying each other's company." Jason misses nothing.

Angel told me she liked Zach, and they have been chatting lately, but I can't believe that's why she blew me off.

I smile happily for my friend. We sit down, and Jason keeps looking at the two empty spaces beside us that have been reserved for Alex and a friend.

"I hope he will be good to her," I say.

Jason places his arm along the back of my chair. "I'm sure he will." Jason places a kiss on my forehead, and no matter how many times he touches me, it's never enough. I always want more. He moves to sit back when I touch his cheek; it's all it takes for him to hold still for me. My gaze drops to his mouth, and I lick mine.

His lip rises, and my heart jumps before I lean in and press my lips against his. His warm mouth was made for mine. That's how I feel about every part of Jason. That he was made for me.

I love every single part of him, and right now, I want to taste every single part of him.

"Maybe we can leave the check and go home early."

Jason laughs into my mouth. "That's an idea I can get behind."

"Sorry I'm late." I immediately sit back in my chair as Alex joins us.

I'm so happy he came for Jason. I try to rise. "I'll swap seats."

Both men protest. "No."

I find myself slowly sitting back down. Okay.

"No date?" Jason asks, glaring at the empty seat beside Alex.

Alex's jaw is tense, and he shakes his head. "She declined."

I can't imagine anyone declining Alex. Although he's extremely handsome, he isn't very warm. He wears a scowl most of the time, and his sharp words always make him seem grumpy. Maybe his negative personality overrides his good looks.

Jason laughs, and his eyes sparkle with genuine humor. "Nadia, I can assume."

Alex doesn't answer but fixes his bow tie. "She had martial arts practice."

Jason laughs harder, and I want to know why that's funny. I'm watching Alex as he touches his cutlery.

"Nadia is one of my maids," Alex informs me.

Jason sneers. "Alex doesn't think martial arts are appropriate for women."

"It isn't." Alex doesn't hide his disgust. "I can protect her."

"Maybe she has a reason for wanting to be able to protect herself," I say.

Alex's body reacts to my words in the most defensive way. He leans toward me. "Like what?"

He's intense, and I nervously look at Jason.

"She doesn't know, Alex," Jason defends me. "Kira is just saying that maybe she has her reasons."

Alex doesn't unwind; instead, he looks more troubled by the second. "If anyone were bothering her, she knows I would take care of it," Alex says.

I nod. I'm not saying anything else about Nadia, who obviously means a lot to Alex.

"You seriously think any of your staff, especially Nadia, would come to you for help?" Jason says.

Alex's jaw clenches. "What did you bring me here for? To let me know how much she hates me?"

I'm looking from one brother to the other, wondering what this is all about. It sounds like he likes Nadia, and she doesn't return the sentiment. I want to meet her.

The room is hushed as the host takes center stage. The two brothers drop their private matters, and we half-listen.

Dinner is nice, but we don't even make it through the main course when Alex says his goodbyes, leaves a check on the table, and disappears.

I glance at Jason. "At least he came." I touch his hand.

He nods. "Yeah, it's something. I'm sure he's gone to check on Nadia." Amusement still lingers in Jason's tone.

"Are they a thing?" I ask.

"No. He's been in love with her for years. She doesn't know and seems to dislike him, anyway. It's funny to see Alex getting pushed back by a woman."

I can see how that would be amusing but also sad if he's loved her for years.

It makes me think of Lev and Angel. I wonder if he told her how he felt. Would they have left, and would Lev still be alive?

Jason's hand covers mine. "Are you okay?"

I lean into his shoulder. "When I'm with you, everything is perfect."

He kisses the crown of my head.

We end the night at the charity with dancing, and as Jason swirls me under the overhead lights, I smile. I smile because I'm where I want to be.

Where I need to be.

Here with Jason.

***

Do you want to know when Jason and Nadia's story is available? Sign up to my newsletter and never miss a new release. HERE

Want to read about Jason and Raven? Grab your copy now with Kindle Unlimited HERE

ABOUT THE AUTHOR

When Vi Carter isn't writing contemporary & dark romance books, that feature the mafia, are filled with suspense, and take you on a fast paced ride, you can find her reading her favorite authors, baking, taking photos or watching Netflix.

Married with three children, Vi divides her time between motherhood and all the other hats she wears as an Author.

She has declared herself a coffee & chocolate addict! Do not judge

Social Media Links for Vi Carter

Website

Facebook Reading Group

Facebook Author Page